Praise for *Fashionistas*

"*Fashionistas* is quietly hysterical, a stealth satire of magazine and celebrity culture."
—*New Jersey Star-Ledger*

"Wickedly entertaining.... Messina's prose is witty and assured (she's read her Austen, her Wharton, her Noel Coward), and her novel is an irresistible frolic."
—*Publishers Weekly*

"*Fashionistas* has genuine style, plus wit and wisdom. Messina is an acute observer.... The premise—indeed, much of the book's affectionate satire of the magazine industry—is frighteningly believable.... Displaying a light touch, Messina has written a book that captures the idiocy and humor of the fashion-magazine world."
—*Time Out New York*

"Messina's tale is a hip and funny parody of trendy magazines and the people who toil at them."
—*Booklist*

"Well-written, funny and sharp."
—*Pittsburgh Post-Gazette*

"Get the inside scoop on the scandalous world of fashion magazines..."
—*Elle*

"Delightfully witty."
—*New York Daily News*

lynn messina

fashionistas

**RED
DRESS
I N K**
™

First North American edition March 2003

FASHIONISTAS

A Red Dress Ink novel

ISBN 0-373-89544-5

© 2003 by Lynn Messina.

Author photograph by Chris Catanese.

www.RedDressInk.com

Printed in U.S.A.

For Mom

ACKNOWLEDGMENTS

Thanks to: my father, my brothers, the Linwoods, Roell Schmidt, Elena Ro Yang, Jennifer Lewis

And: Susan Ramer, Farrin Jacobs, Margaret Marbury

Also: Chris Catanese—peace, love and lightbulb

My First Day of Work

"Vig, what does your roommate look like?"

"She's tall and blond and has green eyes."

"Does she have a boyish figure like yours?"

"Uh..."

"Is she a stick, a lollipop, a drainpipe with no dents?"

"Uh..."

"We're talking completely flat. Not a curve to be found, even with surveying equipment and six of the Royal Cartographers Association's best men."

"Uh..."

"Because if she has any shape at all, it won't do. We need flatter than the salt plains of Utah. We'd use you, but company policy prevents us from employing our own employees. I could fire you, but then I'd have to go through the hassle of finding another assistant, which is twenty minutes I just don't have. Listen up, go down to the Ford Agency in Soho and tell them that we need a girl just like you for our story on bridesmaids with awful figures. Stress the fact that we need a model who looks real, like one of our readers but not as dumpy. And tell them we need a large girl, too. But only a plus-size model with a pretty face. Make sure her face is pretty. We are not in the magazine business to give airtime to ugly women. Go on, what are you waiting for? Shoo. Be back in thirty minutes and don't forget to pick up my lunch. I want tuna on toasted rye bread with one lettuce leaf on the bottom. Make sure they put it on the bottom. I can't eat a sandwich with lettuce on the top. Order it from Mangia. Their number is in your Rolodex. All right, stop staring and go do something. This isn't one of those jobs where you stand around the water cooler talking about must-see television. And don't forget my coffee. I like it black."

My 1,233rd Day

The offices of *Fashionista* are like the streets of San Francisco, only with microscent zones instead of microclimates. Every editor in every office is always burning some kind of candle—lilacs, vanilla, cinnamon, multifragranted concoctions called Grandmother's Kitchen—and if you don't like the smell, all you have to do is walk a few feet to the left and breathe different air.

But things are different today. Someone is burning incense. Its scent is heavy and powerful and floats down the hallway like a thick-soled phantom, seeping under doorways. Even the bathroom's ordinarily antiseptic aroma is undermined.

We aren't prepared to deal with incense. It is the heavy artillery, the big guns, and we have no place to take cover. We are exposed in the center, a shantytown of cubicles, and our only recourse is to breathe the cigarette-infused air outside the revolving door on the ground floor.

"It's frankincense and myrrh," says Christine, popping her head over the cubicle wall.

"What?" I'm trying to write an article about celebrity-owned restaurants, but I can't concentrate. The smell is too distracting.

"The incense. It's frankincense and myrrh," she explains.

I'm surprised by her revelation and not quite sure I believe her. This is the twenty-first century, and we have all forgotten what frankincense and myrrh smell like.

"Myrrh has a bitter, pungent taste," says Christine.

"It's not myrrh," I say, my eyes focused on my computer screen. "Myrrh doesn't exist anymore."

Christine leans against the wall and it gives slightly under her weight. "Vig, you can't deny the existence of myrrh."

I look at her. "I can. I deny the existence of myrrh."

"That's ridiculous. The wise men brought it to baby Jesus as a birthday present."

"So?" I say with a shrug before making some comment about dodo birds. My point is only that dodo birds used to exist and now they don't, but somehow I've managed to suggest that dodo birds were another gift of the magi.

Christine's eyes widen as she misunderstands me. "The wise men didn't bring dodo birds to Bethlehem. What a ridiculous thing to imply," she huffs.

"How do you know?" I ask, because the vehemence in her tone is too strong. You should never be that sure about anything. "I mean, how do you know for a fact that they didn't also bring dodo birds?"

"Because it's not in the bible," she says with more insistence than the topic calls for. I'm only teasing. "There's no mention of dodo birds anywhere."

I don't have Christine's religious bent—in fact, I don't have a religion at all—and I'm amused by her vehemence. It's not my intention to upset her. The last thing I want is for her to clutch the thin thumbtack wall with clenched fists, but I don't apologize. It's my belief that myrrh no longer exists and even though I don't believe in much, I have the right to these thin convictions. I have no problem accepting the existence of frankincense, with its ugly *f* and traffic-stopping *k,* but not myrrh, something so light and airy that it is only a soft breeze on your lips.

"Besides," she says, "I know for a fact that myrrh still exists. We had some in my cooking class."

Christine is trying to get out of *Fashionista* and the route she has taken is aspiring food critic. She harbors dreams of being a food writer. She wants to be one of those people who is paid to detect the impertinent flavor of cumin in a spring roll. She wants to go to James Beard foundation dinners and sit next to Julia Child. She wants to work at a magazine that has a little more substance than seeping incense.

Fashionista

Fashionista is a magazine about nothing. It's aggressively hip and overwhelmingly current and every glossy page drips with beauty, but the nuggets of wisdom it dispenses are gold for fools. Despite what they say, you can't steal Gwyneth's arched brow or Nicole's flowing tresses.

But stealing things from the rich and famous is central to *Fashionista*'s raison d'être. The magazine devotes itself completely to the tireless pursuit of all things celebrity, especially those aspects most basic for survival—food, clothing, shelter. Fame is the planet around which everything orbits. This is Jennifer Aniston's plunger. This is where you can get it.

It's not a new concept—ever since Mary Pickford stepped onto the red carpet batting her Max Factor eyelashes, the press has been foisting these images of glamour onto the public. But this is the magazine I work for and it makes me cringe. I cringe because insider's tidbits that have been spoon-fed to us by self-aggrandizing prophets are presented as news. *Fashionista* is a shrine to celebrity, and publicists carefully place their idols in the center of the altar for maximum exposure.

In the five years that I've been working here, we've never run a story that doesn't name-drop at least one celebrity. The closest we came was an article I wrote three months ago about the preservation and presentation of teeth (the new braces, the new bleaches, the new bonds). For the most part, it was a full-service piece, the sort you'd find in any other women's magazine, the useful kind that actually lists names of dentists that ordinary people go to. However, this much-needed information ran alongside a list of the top five sets of teeth in Hollywood. The practical sidebar on gum disease—what to look for, how to prevent it—was quickly axed. At *Fashionista,* we don't mention a disease unless a celebrity is trying to cure it.

I spend most of my time on the phone, charting trends and inventing cultural drifts. It's exhausting business finding out who's going where and who's using what and who's wearing who, and I impatiently wait for spa directors and salon owners and store managers to return my calls. The information always trickles in and it's never as pat as it should be. A trend needs three examples to be declared—two might be a coincidence—and I frequently have to dig deep to find the third. This is why you often see the picture of an unknown actress with a humiliating ID tag under her name next to a silhouette of Julia Roberts.

Despite *Fashionista*'s huge readership and record-breaking ad revenues, it's a magazine about nothing. Regardless of what our press releases say, we aren't the epicenter of hip. This empty stillness you feel is not the calm at the eye of a hurricane.

Marguerite Tourneau Holland Beckett Velazquez Constantine Thomas

The Monday afternoon meeting is an extremely dull affair. Fifty people gather around a large conference table with coffee cups in hand to talk about prints and photographers and shoots and stylists and schedules and all the other mind-numbing minutiae that go into a successful layout. Only seven or eight people are actually needed for these conversations, but we all have to go and suffer. We all have to drag our overworked carcasses to the conference room and listen to the photo department argue over which photo of Cate Blanchett best represents her curly phase.

We rarely discuss anything copy-related and when we do, it's just to establish if an article is in and, if it's not in, when it can be expected. One Monday a month—usually the second, but sometimes the third—there is extended debate about who's going to appear as a contributor. The contributor's page is that page after the editor's note that you skip over on your way to the letters. Readers barely glance at it if they even look at it at all. Still, finding the right balance of people is a delicate science and we discuss the ingredients of the contributor's page as if preparing a soufflé (a soupçon less stylist, a dash of writer). When Jane isn't at meetings, I'm usually hard-pressed to keep my eyes open.

I'm trying to keep my eyes open now when the conference room door opens. A striking woman in a classic black dress enters carrying a Chanel bag. She has an Audrey Hepburn thing going, with her long cigarette holder, her string of pearls and her tall, thin frame, and she's standing inside the doorway, as though she hasn't decided if she wants to stay, as though she might just flag down a cab and leave. There are no cabs in the conference room.

The managing editor stops berating the staff for not filling out green sheets and looks up. She sees the smoke swirling around the conference room and starts coughing pointedly. Smoking is allowed but only in one's office with the door closed.

"Am I late?" the woman says, having decided she might as well stay.

Lydia coughs again and then shakes her head. "No, of course not." She smiles in the obsequious way we all do when Jane is present. But this is not Jane, so the smile seems out of place and toadyish. "We were just going over some preliminary information while waiting for you."

The woman smiles and puffs on the cigarette through six inches of plastic before sitting down to the right of Lydia. "Excellent."

Christine leans in. "That's the woman who was burning incense this morning," she whispers in my ear.

"How do you know?" I ask.

"I followed the scent. I think she's the new editorial director."

This is news. "What happened to Eleanor?"

"She was fired in Paris last week. I don't know the details."

"Eleanor was sitting in Jane's seat during the Anna Sui show," says Delia, the editorial assistant for the events pages. She's sitting behind us, on a bench that lines the conference room's east wall, and she leans forward to speak quietly in our ears. "Jane was forced to sit in the last row and, as soon as the show was over, she fired Eleanor right then and there. Eleanor insisted that it was all a misunderstanding—someone showed her to that seat—but Jane didn't believe a word of it. As it turns out, the publisher was at the show sitting next to an old acquaintance who just happened to be perfect for the job. He hired her on the spot."

I stare at Delia, amazed by the details she's managed to track down in a few hours. "How do you know all this?"

Delia shrugs and rests her head against the wall. "I hear things."

Before I respond to Delia, Lydia coughs again. The new editorial director shifts the cigarette from her right hand to her left. She will let no cough pass unavenged.

"I'd like to introduce a new member of our staff," Lydia says with little enthusiasm. "She comes to us from Sydney, where she served as editor in chief for Australian *Vogue* for six years. Say hello to Marguerite Tourneau Holland Beckett Velazquez Constantine Thomas."

There is a quiet murmur of people mumbling and saying hello.

"No," I say very quietly in Christine's ear.

She smiles. "Yes."

"No," I say again, more insistent. She can't be for real. Nobody drags a laundry list of names behind them.

"I think she's on her fifth husband."

"But still...."

"She loved them all."

"Can you see that on the masthead? It'll take up three lines. She's an editor, for God's sake. She must know how to cut for fit."

Christine smiles but doesn't say a thing. She's watching the drama unfold with unprecedented interest. Everyone around the table is now alert, not just the photography department.

"Thank you, Linda, for that—" she pauses here to find an

adjective but after a long search abandons the endeavor "—introduction. So kind of you. Well," she says, blowing smoke once more in Lydia's face before turning her attention to the people around the table, "I'm very happy to be here. I've long been an admirer of *Fashionista* and look forward to working with the team that puts together such a fine magazine."

We are not used to being told by editorial directors that we put together a fine magazine and some of us actually titter at the novelty.

"Now, I want to get to know everyone around this table," she assures us with a convincing amount of sincerity, "but since time is of the essence, why don't we start with each of you telling me your name and what you do at *Fashionista.*"

Despite the fact that we perform this sort of ritual with alarming regularity—every time someone new starts or a person from Human Resources comes down to "say hi"—it's still one of my least favorite activities. I hate having to say, "Vig Morgan, associate editor," and I hate hearing everyone else say it as well. There is something vaguely embarrassing about identifying yourself like you're a Von Trapp child stepping out of line at the sound of a dog whistle.

David Rodrigues from the art department goes first, and instead of just nodding vaguely like the people from Human Resources do, Marguerite asks him a question. She asks him about the shirt he is wearing, a brown cotton tee with a curious logo. David tells her that it's his own design. Our new editorial director says something about him being the next William Morris and orders one for herself. She continues around the table in the same vein, getting a feel for each staff member and paying at least one compliment. She asks Christine about her cooking classes. She tells me that she's thinking of getting her teeth whitened thanks to my article.

Marguerite Tourneau Holland Beckett Velazquez Constantine Thomas is winning and it works. We are won.

The afternoon meeting lasts until three-thirty, but nobody minds except Lydia. Lydia has watched the proceedings get away from her like a little girl who's lost her kite to a strong gust of wind. There is an odd, helpless look on her face. She tries several times to regain control—she still has the string and is holding on tight—but Marguerite, with her seemingly endless cigarette, just blows smoke at her with indifference.

In the end, there is little talk of photo shoots. Lydia has no idea where matters stand for most of November's layouts and she now has to do things the hard way. She now has to visit each editor with her mock-up and her map and talk one-on-one in order to sort it all out.

But nobody cares. Lydia is a nice enough managing editor and she gets the job done, but she never goes to bat for you. She's not one of those managers who goes to the boss and stands up for "her people." She's a kowtowing minion. She's a yes gal with a limited vocabulary. When you work three nights straight until two in the morning because Jane decides at six o'clock that she hates the whole issue, don't expect anything. Don't expect a raise. Don't expect comp time. Don't expect a dashed-off, handwritten note saying thank you. Don't expect Lydia to remind your editor in chief that six o'clock isn't the time to start tearing up layouts. Just don't expect a thing.

The Beginnings of a Plot

Allison is a series of loosely connected stories that travel through the thin thumbtack wall that separates my cubicle from hers. Her tales are so disjointed that sometimes she seems less a person than a device, like the Illustrated Man in the Ray Bradbury book whose only function is to provide a narrative arc.

Because we work for the same magazine, Allison and I see each other regularly, across the conference table, outside the bathroom, but we never get beyond polite nods and blank, meaningless smiles. I know so much about her life—the men who don't call the next morning, the awful women whom her father dates, the vacations that fall through, the recurring yeast infection that the doctors can't figure out—that I can barely look her in the eye. These are things I shouldn't know. These are things that I'd play close to my chest, that I wouldn't talk about at work, that I'd leave the office and find a pay phone on the street to discuss. I'm always painfully aware that the flimsy wall between us is like a scrim and if you shine the light on it from the right direction it disappears completely.

I'm surprised, then, when Allison sticks her small blond head over the barrier and says, "Vig, can we take a meeting?"

This request is so out of left field that it takes me a few seconds to process it. Even though she has addressed me directly, even though she has used my name, I assume at first that she's talking to someone else. There must be another Vig present. I look up, expecting to see this other Vig standing beside me, but I'm alone in my cubicle. I stop typing.

"Can you spare a few?" she asks, her head tilted in a friendly angle. "This shouldn't take too long."

Since I have overheard almost every conversation she has had for the past two years, I know this isn't true. Everything Allison does takes too long. The abrupt, expedient nanoconference that the senior editors rely on to keep things moving along smoothly doesn't exist in Allison's universe. She is vulnerable to long digressions and often finds herself a million miles away from her point. Instead of beaming herself back to the beginning, she painstakingly retraces her steps. I don't know how the people on the other end of the line deal with it, but sometimes I have to get out of my seat and take a walk to the water cooler just to get away.

Although I have a mountain of work to get through before six, I'm too curious to say no. Allison's interest in me is unprecedented, and I can't take the chance that it will happen again. There are very few things I enter into thinking "once in a lifetime," but I think that now as I stand up.

"All right," I say, looking up at her expectantly.

"Not here. Do you mind if we...?" She gestures with her head.

I'm not used to her showing any sort of discretion and for a moment I fear that she's going to fire me. But this moment is fleeting and I toss away the thought. Allison is an associate editor just like I am; she doesn't have that sort of power. In fact, she has no power at all.

Since I don't mind, I follow her down the hall. The *Fashionista* offices are dark and dreary and the only natural light can be found in private offices behind closed doors. We walk past Reception and through to the advertising side. I've never been over here before and I am instantly struck by how nice everything is. The surfaces are shiny and the lighting is soft and not quite fluorescent. We make several twists and turns and arrive at a swinging door that says Ladies' Room. Allison enters a code and opens the door. We are in the executive washroom, which has three pristine stalls and a small carpeted lounge area with a black leather couch. Sitting on the couch are Kate Anderson from Accessories and Sarah Cohen from Photo. I am thoroughly disconcerted by the couch, the carpet and the company. Although not so very far from home, I feel like I've stumbled down the rabbit hole.

"Hi," I say, puzzled and a little bit uncomfortable, as though I am sitting at the wrong table in the lunchroom. I'm years past this and resolve to shake it off. I look at Allison for an explanation. She in turn nods at Sarah and Kate, who both jump to their feet.

"Thanks for coming," says Sarah, putting her hands on my shoulders and pushing me down onto the couch. I reluctantly take a seat.

"Why am I here?"

"You're the linchpin," says Kate.

"The linchpin?" I repeat.

"Yes, the linchpin," agrees Allison.

"The linchpin?" I say again.

"The pin that linches it," explains Sarah.

I examine all three with curiosity. "What pin am I linching?"

"Our plan," says Allison.

"Your plan?" I ask.

"Our plan," Allison says with satisfaction.

"But which plan?" I'm forced to ask, as if she has so many different plans that I can't keep them all straight.

"Our ingenious plan to take down Jane McNeill."

Jane McNeill

You know Jane McNeill. She is a familiar type—tough but good. She might have an abrupt manner, but she knows her job and sells magazines. You'll learn a lot from her, kid.

Don't believe it. There is nothing good about her. Her temper is short, and her patience is like a shot of smooth whiskey—gone in one gulp. Kindness is an affliction that weak people suffer, and if you take a week off after your mother dies, she'll roll her eyes in front of everyone, as if your personal indulgence is a great inconvenience to her. She delights in humiliating you in front of the entire staff, and when you actually know the answer to an out-of-left-field question about, say, hemlines in the fifties, and can form an intelligent response, she will reach deep into her bag of tricks until she finds something you know nothing about—like what Martha Washington wore to George's inauguration. Meetings are tense and awful and you always feel as though you're arguing a case in front of the U.S. Supreme Court on a topic you know nothing about—quick, list three reasons for the silkworm strike in Upper Volta. (This is a trick question; silkworms aren't unionized.) She is an anxiety-dream factory and you're the well-oiled cog that keeps it running smoothly.

Jane is rarely in New York, but her presence is logarithmic and can be measured like an earthquake. When she comes into the office two days in a row, the devastation is a hundred thousand times worse than if she had just dropped by for one. Small villages crumble, and your self-esteem, already compromised at several stress points thanks to shoddy workmanship, disappears completely in a cloud of dust.

You suffer her abuse for two endless years before finally getting the promotion that the managing editor had been dangling in front of you like a carrot on a stick for more than eighteen months. ("If you can just hold on a little longer, Vig.... An assistant editorship at *Fashionista* goes a long way.") It's only when you are about to smash your computer with a hatchet and walk away from the rubble that Jane calls you into her office to inform you of the good news. You are still at the magazine and you are still subjected to the slings and arrows of her outrageous temper, but you are no longer on the front line. There is another detail-oriented self-starter at your desk and it's now her job to absorb the blows. She's being paid to be your shield. You are so glad not to be her—and so ashamed at the relief you feel—that you avert your eyes whenever you pass the desk.

Jane does sell magazines, but that has to do more with the susceptibility of the public than the freshness of her ideas. Every year, at her insistence, we run an article on the classic style of Jackie O or the effortless grace of Grace Kelly as if these things haven't ever been done. But they have. You've seen all the pictures before, only alongside better-written text.

The secret to Jane's success is aligning herself with up-and-coming magazines that are already on the rise and then taking credit for their inevitable increased sales. She's done it before at *Face* and *Voyager,* and she will do it again when the next big thing appears on the horizon. She has a genius for self-promotion and a sort of ruthless glamour that appeals to the publishers of glossies.

You're not the only one who is counting the days.

A Plot Takes Shape

The bathroom on *Fashionista*'s editorial side isn't the sort of place where I go to sit down and get comfortable. It's a busy spot with lots of drive-thru traffic and little privacy. The stall doors are cut low, and you can see the foreheads of your co-workers as they zip up their jeans. If you want a moment alone, your best bet is the elevators. Sometimes you get one to yourself for all twenty-two floors.

Allison, Sarah and Kate seem quite at home here. While I watch the door, waiting for strange executives to enter, they slide onto the counters and fluff their hair in the unflattering mirrors.

"Now is the time," says Sarah.

"Now is the time?" I ask, struck by how much I don't know. I don't know why now is the time, I don't know how I can be a linchpin and I don't know what plan they've devised to bring down Jane.

Allison nods and avails herself of one of the myriad hair-care products that litter the counter. She leans forward, sweeps her hair over her head and spritzes. Today she is wearing gray linen pants and a white sleeveless blouse. The outfit should look elegant and svelte, but on Allison it looks like something she threw on because everything else was in the wash. Brushing the bangs out of her eyes, she says, "Now is the time to strike."

I take my eyes off the door. We've been in here for ten minutes and it hasn't opened once. I'm beginning to believe it never will. "All right," I say.

"We have a window of opportunity," explains Kate.

"A window?" I watch Allison flip her head over again and give her hair another spritz. When she rights herself, she looks exactly the same, only redder.

"A small window," clarifies Sarah, just in case I assumed the window was wide and spacious.

"There's no way Marguerite Tourneau is going to last long as editorial director," says Allison, putting the hairspray down, the last spritz having done its job. "You just know Jane is going to oust her within two months."

Sarah rolls her eyes. "Two months? Ha! I give her a week."

"Longer than a week," says Kate. "More like a month."

"A whole month?" Sarah is doubtful.

"It must take at least that long to get her hiring papers through Human Resources," Kate explains, logically. "You can't fire someone before you've officially hired them."

This reasoning satisfies the three of them and they turn to look at me. I'm sitting on the couch, my back against its supple leather, minding my own business. Linchpin, ingenious plan, small window, time to strike—I've been paying attention. I don't know why but I have.

They are staring at me with hungry, expectant looks in their eyes. "What?"

"Will you help?" they say in unison, like they're a cheerleading squad.

"I don't know. What's the plan?"

Allison looks at the other two. Kate conveys no with her eyebrows. Sarah backs her up with a less discreet shake of the head. Allison sighs. "We can't tell you the plan until you agree to help."

I never go blindly into situations. Awful things always happen. "I can't agree to help until you tell me the plan."

My immutable will irritates them and they glare at one another, speaking whole sentences with their eyelash flutters. I'm tempted to excuse myself, to give them a moment alone in order to have this discussion in private, but I'm too comfortable and I stay firmly affixed to the couch. I have no doubt of the outcome. They can flap their eyebrows all they want, but sooner or later they will tell me the plan. They have to. I'm the linchpin.

Allison Harper

Allison Harper is an unlikely beauty editor. Her ordinary appearance doesn't match anyone's image of glamour. She tries, though, wearing the right strappy sandals (Jimmy Choo) and the right pants (Emanuel Ungaro) and the right lipstick (Lip Glass by MAC), but something about the finished product refuses to pull together in the right way. Even though the elements are there, even though on a mannequin the look would be impeccable, something about her humanity throws everything off.

At thirty-two, Allison is three years older than I am. In recent months her usually upbeat disposition has taken on a particularly dour bent. She was passed over again for a senior editor position—they head-hunted from another top glossy—and she's starting to realize things. She's starting to realize that her future might not work out after all and that despite a pair of fine eyes, she's not an Elizabeth Bennett. Allison Harper isn't the heroine of her own story. She is, instead, a secondary character, a Charlotte who will trade her dreams for compromises that may or may not work out. That past life regression conceit that might have led her to assume she was Cleopatra is fading. She's starting to realize she was nobody, a nameless slave whose existence passed unrecorded.

It's an awful, uncomfortable thing to watch and I take the long way to the bathroom to avoid her cubicle. On late nights when the offices are almost deserted, I hear her on the phone with her best friend relating the day's trespasses. There is a mystified quality in her voice as she explains how she wasn't assigned the Girl Talk feature ("So tell me about your beauty regimen: Is it eyeliner mascara or mascara eyeliner?") or even the Style Wise Man interview ("If you had to choose between leather and suede, which would you pick and why?"). In angry tones she tells Greta that she was given yet another advertorial piece that will be yoked together from industry press releases. This is not what she went to Columbia for.

Allison blames Jane for her career's inertia, which is a reasonably accurate assessment. Jane doesn't make decisions based on skill and merit like other working professionals. She hires beautiful editors who can't write and fires ugly ones who can. She chooses her assistants as if selecting a fashion accessory, and we are all a matched set: tall, thin, straight chin-length brown hair.

The magazine is run like a seventeenth-century French court. You don't speak unless spoken to. You avert your eyes in Jane's presence. Her need for subservience is almost pathological, and if it weren't against OSHA rules (see under "repetitive stress injuries"), she would no doubt have us genuflect. Her interest in *Fashionista* will last only as long as its growing readership does and the second there is a dip in sales, she will be gone. She will be off this leaky ship, and the magazine will start the long slide into insolvency. Witness the now defunct *Voyager* and the struggling *Faces*. Investing in good people and laying the groundwork for years of successful magazine publishing is not part of her plan. After Jane the deluge.

It is little surprise that the peasants are revolting.

The Linchpin

I'm the linchpin for two reasons: Jane respects me and Alex owes me a favor.

"No, he doesn't," I say.

"Yes, he does," Allison contradicts.

"No, he doesn't," I say again. As a lowly associate editor, I'm little help to anyone, even myself.

"Yes, he does. Last May's makeover issue," an unseen Sarah calls out from one of the stalls.

"Last May's makeover issue?" I'm trying to remember some fleeting interaction with Alex Keller but nothing comes to mind. Nothing comes to mind because we've never interacted.

A toilet flushes and Sarah emerges, zipping up her ankle-length capris. "Last May's makeover issue," she says definitively, turning on the taps to wash her hands.

The May issue featured a special make-over-your-life section, which ran alongside the regular assortment of bashes and balls, but Keller stayed in his corner and I stayed in mine. "He doesn't owe me a favor."

"Carla Hayden," Kate says, and looks at me expectantly.

"Carla Hayden?" The name sounds vaguely familiar but I don't know why. She could be a famous actress, a Tinseltown hairstylist or a new *Fashionista* employee. Names inhabit a small, rarely used portion of my brain.

"Carla Hayden," says Sarah with a nod. She dries her hands on a paper towel, tosses it into the trash and throws herself onto the couch next to me. I'm accosted by her perfume, a flowery confection that smells expensive.

"Short, a little pudgy, dishwater-brown hair," adds Allison, as if these details are the sort that will jog my memory.

As far as I'm concerned this describes half the world. I stare at them blankly.

"She was a May makeover," Kate says.

Sarah turns to me with a frustrated sigh. "You put her in a Chloe bias-cut dress and gave her blond highlights."

"Oh, the Chloe," I say, recognition striking at last. It's their fault that it took me so long. If they'd had the presence of mind to bring the May issue with them, we could have sorted this out five minutes ago. "Her name was Carla Hayden?"

"Carla Hayden Keller," says Allison.

"Carla Hayden Keller?" I repeat.

"Carla Hayden Keller," Kate nods.

"You mean he's married?" I try to imagine the sort of woman who would wed a bad-tempered, wart-faced troll. Short, pudgy and dishwater-brown didn't seem the type.

"She's his sister," corrects Sarah with a laugh. "She dropped her last name to throw Jane off the scent."

"His sister?" Keller never gave the slightest indication that he had siblings, so we didn't factor any into his life story. It seems bad-mannered—and typical—of him to start throwing them around now. "I didn't know he had a sister," I say, cross. We should have known about a sister.

"He has two," Kate declares.

"The bastard," I say, trying to make sense of this development, which was at odds with what we already knew about him. Sisters should have been a civilizing force on the young Alex. "They must be older. They must be older and domineering and mean like Cinderella's stepsisters."

Sarah shakes her head. "They're younger."

"Damn." I don't know how such an awful man can have younger sisters. It just doesn't seem possible.

"So you get why he owes you a favor?" asks Kate.

I do twenty to thirty makeovers a year. Nobody has ever treated it like a favor. "No."

"You changed her life," Sarah says.

This is precisely the sort of silly nonsense we propagate in our magazine but it's not true. Your happiness doesn't really depend on the type of eyelash curler you buy. "I changed her hair."

"Two days after leaving here with her blond highlights and Chloe dress, Carla Hayden Keller got a job as a host of *Generation Y* on the Metro channel. At a Metro function, she met renowned corporate financier Alistair Concoran, who fell instantly in love with her. They got married two months later, bought a house in Westchester and are even now expecting their first child," Allison says with a wide smile.

"So you see," says Kate, "Alex Keller owes you one."

Alex Keller

Everyone in the office has a Keller story. Although no one has ever seen the confirmed misanthrope, we've all had our share of run-ins. He is always slamming the phone down in disgust or sending rude e-mails with impatient replies or dashing off abrupt little notes that cut interns to the quick.

He keeps his office door closed. You never see light shining through the frosted windows, and if you didn't hear the constant disco beat emanating from behind his door, you'd assume the room was empty. When you have something for him, you follow the prescribed delivery system. You place it in his in-box, knock twice and walk away. Turn around a second later and it's gone. The whole process is cloaked in mystery, and you feel like Dorothy leaving a broomstick for the Wizard of Oz.

Alex Keller is the events editor for *Fashionista*. Every month he fills a dozen or so pages with pictures from premieres, galas, benefits and openings. All happy parties are alike and when you look at the layouts you can hardly tell what distinguishes a Givenchy fete from a breast cancer fundraiser. Take the cookie-cutter genericness of every wedding you've ever attended, add a few thousand candles and you have Alex Keller's section. Only the names are different.

The candid snapshots, which vary only slightly from the ones in your high school yearbook, are usually accompanied by blocks of text describing the bash. Keller's snappy writing style—always chatty, frequently punny and seldom dull—mimics the Page Six gossips, only without the insinuations of sex and greed.

Since his life, tinged with glamour, offers no justification for his hostility, we are left to speculate. We are left to theorize about his parents (weak father, domineering mother), his childhood (fodder for bullies), his stature (Napoleon complex) and his sex life (nonexistent). The hostility he feels toward his fellow human beings can only be explained one way: He's a short man with unresolved rage issues who isn't getting any. Since Keller has never come out of his burrow to dispute this conclusion, the tales have grown more and more fantastic over the years. A mythology has sprung up in place of a person, and we are so intimately acquainted with the details that sometimes we forget that they are entirely fictional.

This is what happens when Sarah, Kate and Allison formulate their plan. They fail to take into account the fact that Alex Keller might not be an angry dwarf looking to avenge himself on an emasculating mother figure.

The Plot

I don't think *respect* is the word to describe how Jane feels about me but I keep that to myself. I want to hear what their plan is, and they are on the verge of telling me.

"It was Allison's brilliant idea," says Kate, "so she should decide."

Allison smiles and blushes. She's not used to her ideas being called brilliant. "I don't know," she hedges, turning to her fellow fashionistas. "We said earlier that we'd only tell her if she agreed to help."

"But she will help," insists Kate, who is all for spilling the beans. In a room full of cautious conspirators, she is a fool ready to rush in. "Once she knows the plan, she'll help. I'm sure of it."

Sarah doesn't look convinced, but she has ceded responsibility to Allison and is quite happy with her abdication. "I'm cool with whatever you do."

Allison breaks under the weight of autonomy and turns to me. "All right, but you have to swear that if you don't want to help that you won't tell anyone about our plan."

I consent to this because I'm reasonably sure that their plan amounts to nothing more than putting Nair in Jane's shampoo and waiting for her to resign from the humiliation of being bald.

"There is a show coming up, in a gallery in Soho," Allison says slowly. She's still not sure she's doing the right thing. "It's by one of those young British artists, Gavin Marshall. He's the sort who fills plastic inflatable furniture with cow entrails and calls it art. His newest work is a series officially entitled Gilding the Lily, but the British press called it Jesus in Drag. It's exactly what it sounds like," she explains. "He dresses up Jesus statues in women's haute couture. Although the show was a huge success in England, it was highly controversial and no style glossy over there would touch it. But we're going to convince Jane to do a story on it anyway. There will be an uproar and calls to boycott, and the publisher will have to fire her to appease our advertisers and religious conservatives."

"How are you going to convince Jane to do the story?" I ask. Their plan is actually interesting and creative, but I have little faith in its successful execution. Jane McNeill might be a tyrannical egomaniac, but she didn't fall off the turnip truck just yesterday. She's put out enough magazines to know what makes dangerous copy. She's worked in this business for enough years to realize that most celebrities won't relish being in the same issue as Christ in Christian Dior.

"That's where you come in," says Sarah.

"Me?"

"You," Kate says.

"Me?" I repeat, almost appalled. I can't imagine why they think I have influence over Jane.

Allison nods. "You're the linchpin."

I'm tired of hearing about my linchpinness and stare blankly.

After a moment of silence, during which she debates how much of her plan she wants to reveal without my acquiescence, Allison continues. "We need you to get Keller to agree to stick Gavin Marshall's opening party on the schedule for November parties."

"And make sure he puts down lots of celebrity names," Kate adds. "Jane won't be interested unless there are lots of celebrities involved."

Although all it takes is one A-list player to get Jane's attention, this plan is seriously flawed. "She won't be convinced."

"That's only phase one," says Allison.

"Phase one?"

Sarah nods. "There are other phases."

"How many?"

Allison closes her eyes and reviews her plan silently. "Four," she says, when she's done counting. "There are four phases. Phase two is your bringing Marshall to Jane's attention."

"Yeah, but you've got to do it very casually. She can't know that you want her to know about him," Sarah adds.

"We want Jane to think that she's uncovered a secret," Kate says.

Now I'm reserving judgment. "To what end?"

"Well, if she discovers, quite by accident, of course, that the new editorial director is planning to propose that *Fashionista* sponsor a party for Gavin and maybe do a story on him, then she's going to want to steal the idea from her," Allison says.

Although this sounds like typical Jane behavior, there is one thing wrong with their logic. "But Jane would look into Gavin and realize instantly that he's too controversial for us to touch."

"She would if one of us were to suggest a party for Gavin," Sarah agrees, "but she wouldn't if she thought the idea was Marguerite's."

I realize there are things here I don't know. "She wouldn't?"

"They've been rivals for more than fifteen years," Allison

says. "They were associate editors together at *Parvenu* and competed for interviews and stories and scoops. They both had their eye on a senior editor position and when it opened up, Marguerite got it. After that, Jane was given all the crappy assignments and she blamed Marguerite. Six months later she left."

This collection of facts amazes me. "How do you know all this?"

Allison smiles. "Number one rule of warfare: Know your enemy."

I didn't realize we were at war.

"So you see, if we can convince Jane that Marguerite is planning something behind her back in order to score points with the publisher, she'll do whatever she can to undermine her," Kate says calculatingly. "And whatever reservations she might have about the suitability of the project will be quickly crushed by her belief in Marguerite's interest."

"She won't be thinking clearly," Sarah insists. "All she'll be doing is watching her back, waiting for Marguerite to strike."

"I guarantee it," Allison says.

It's impossible to guarantee anything, but sometimes you can hedge your bets. Bringing down Jane McNeill does not seem like a sure thing to me. Although their plan is good—considerably better, in fact, than I'd given them credit for—it depends too much on human variables. No one knows how Jane is going to react to Marguerite. More than a decade has passed since their *Parvenu* days, and Jane, once a lowly associate editor, now heads the most successful women's magazine in history. These are the things—time and success—that heal old grievances.

I tell the fashionistas that I'll think about it for a day or two and get back to them, but I'm only being polite. I'm not a cabalist, and as much as I'd like to bring down the current regime, I'm not the sort to take up arms.

Your Silly Life

Dot Drexel speaks in magazine headlines. Her sentences are always declarative and you can positively feel the capital letters hurling toward your head.

"Skate-Skiing: Your New Favorite Sport," she says, as I enter her office. Although she's been a senior editor at *Fashionista* for five years, Dot's office is pristine and tidy and unencumbered with personal effects. If she had to sneak out under the cover of darkness during some military coup, she could do so in seconds and leave nothing behind. She wouldn't be weighed down by plants and picture frames and the quirky, useless things that clutter other people's desktops.

I sit down and search my brain for an old favorite sport that skate-skiing has supplanted. I draw a blank.

"Forget snowboarding," she says, handing me a brochure with snow-covered peaks and après-ski fireplaces, "here's the sexy new alternative the stars are racing to learn."

Although snowboarding never really made an impression on me and is easily forgotten, I somehow doubt that the sexy, new alternative will take up permanent residence in my mind. My psyche is a revolving door for trends. "All right."

"Excellent," she says, pleased by my amenability. "Give me five hundred words on the Hippest Fashions to Skate-Ski In. Call the designers and get a list of celebrity clients. We'll only shoot those outfits with names attached. Start with Versace. I think they have a line of outerwear. And for That Perfect Touch of Whimsy, call Sanrio and see if they make Hello Kitty skate-skies. We want to hold on to our under-twenty-fives."

The nanoconference is over and I get up from the chair. I stand up and marvel that I even bother sitting down at all. "I'll get right on it," I say, as though I'm Lois Lane and skate-skiing is a threat to the citizens of Metropolis. What we do is not journalism but sometimes I forget.

"And what is skate-skiing?" I ask before leaving the office. Usually I feign familiarity with esoteric topics during these meetings and then run to Google for elucidation the second they're over, but not today. Today I don't feel like playing. Today I want to have things explained. I don't know what to attribute this odd occasion of orneriness to, but I wonder for the very first time if I'm reaching the end of my tether. Five years might be all I can stand of nothing.

Dot sighs heavily at my ignorance. "The Most Fun You're Not Having," she says definitively, before picking up the telephone.

But she's wrong. Skate-skiing is not the most fun I'm not having. The most fun I'm not having is nothing so innocuous as a sport that combines the heart-healthy endurance of cross-country with the stimulating thrill of alpine.

Getting To Know You

Marguerite Tourneau Holland Beckett Velazquez Constantine Thomas calls me into her office for a talk. Since Christine, Kate and Allison have already gone before me, I'm expecting the summons and don't leave for lunch until it comes. Then I walk down the hall to a small office that shares a wall with the elevator shaft. You can hear the lifts going by.

This is not Eleanor Zorn's old office. Eleanor had a large corner suite with a comfortable sitting area and wide windows that overlook both Sixth Avenue and Forty-ninth Street. She had bright spots of sunlight in the mornings and the iridescent glow of Radio City Music Hall in the evenings. Marguerite has none of that. Her office is so tiny, it can barely accommodate a desk and chair. There is no place for a couch or a coffee table, and for the moment visitors have to sit on a plastic folding chair that is missing its fourth leg.

Marguerite has a window, but it's the sort you find in nineteenth-century French adventure novels, the type that reminds you of the world outside but doesn't let you see it. All you can see are brown panels from the building across the street, and the view itself hangs on the wall like a piece of modern art.

This is further evidence of Jane's vehement dislike.

Although this meeting has been advertised as an informal chat, I've brought half my file cabinet with me and several old issues of the magazine. I don't know what to expect and I want to be prepared.

"Bonjour," she says, holding an antique watering can. She's in the middle of watering her plants. This is only the afternoon of her second day, but she has already imprinted herself on the little office with African violets and flowering geraniums and wandering pathos, and her imprint has the comfortable aura of perpetuity. Her window ledge looks like it has always been a greenhouse.

"Hello," I say, sitting down. The plastic chair wobbles under my weight, and I grab on to the desk for stability. I notice then that she has several magazines opened to articles of mine. My one stab at journalism, fifteen hundred words on the care and presentation of teeth, is on top.

Marguerite follows my gaze. "Yes, I was just reviewing some of your work. This one here is *très magnifique. La Fashionista* needs more informative pieces like this, don't you think?"

"More pieces like that one wouldn't hurt," I say cautiously. Jane only asks your opinion in order to pick it apart and I expect this behavior from all my employers.

"Excellent," she says, sprinkling water on the last plant, a thriving azalea, before taking a seat. "Why don't you draw up for me a list of ideas of useful articles that you think might be right for *Fashionista* and I'll see what I can do."

Although I relish the idea of writing practical, useful articles instead of celebrity fluff, I refuse to have my head turned. I know a campaign promise when I hear one. "All right."

She smiles. "You've been here how long?"

"Five years."

"And you started as Jane's assistant?"

"Yes, for two years."

Marguerite raises her eyebrows. "Two years! How did you put up with that ha— I mean, two years, what a long time to be someone's assistant. I know mine never stay above fourteen months. Onward and upward, you know." She considers me for a moment. "You and Jane must be *très* compatible."

I shrug. *Compatible* is the wrong word to explain my and Jane's relationship but there is no right word. With Jane, things can't be described; they can only be experienced.

"*Bien.* I hope we'll get along just as well. I plan to be here for quite a while." She turns to her window for a moment. "I've been in Sydney for so many years that I'd forgotten how energizing this city is."

"How many years were you there?" I ask, to make small talk, to learn more about her, to enjoy the novelty of pleasant conversation with a superior.

Her answers are long and I stay in her office for twenty more minutes. When I leave, she reminds me to type up a list of article ideas and I assure her that I haven't forgotten.

Marguerite is friendly and approachable, and although I can find no cracks in her sincerity, I'm not convinced. Her efforts to get to know the staff seem genuine, but there's enough here to make me suspicious. Marguerite seems too much like a soldier gathering information behind enemy lines, and I realize that Jane's behavior might actually be in keeping with the situation. Just because you're paranoid doesn't mean they're not after you.

Jane Carolyn-Ann McNeill

We get the memo first thing on Wednesday morning. Marguerite has been in the building for less than forty-eight hours and already Jane is taking the offensive. Already she is cutting trips short and sending out directives.

"What do you think this means?" I say, leaning against the thumbtack wall that separates me from Allison. It's the first time I've ever stuck my head over the partition to make conversation, and she looks up in surprise.

"What's that?" she asks.

"It's a memo from Jane."

"I haven't even glanced at it yet." Curious now, she reaches into her overflowing in-box, removes the top layer and reads the memo aloud. "Please note herewith that *Fashionista*'s editor in chief Jane McNeill will be using her full given name of Jane Carolyn-Ann McNeill on all official and unofficial *Fashionista* documents. Thank you for your compliance in this matter."

"She had Jackie send it out to every media outlet in the city."

Allison smiles. "Someone, although I won't name names—and, yes, I do mean *names*—is feeling threatened." Because she thinks that I'm wavering, she lowers her voice and says, "The time to strike is now. We'll never have such an excellent opportunity again. Think about it." Then she straightens her shoulders and returns to the morning paper, the picture of innocence.

I sit down at my desk and try to focus on the piece I'm working on. It's an article about engagement rings for the wedding issue, which is fast approaching. Harry Winston, always willing to have their diamonds shot on either the red carpet of the Dorothy Chandler Pavilion or the pink burlap of a *Fashionista* layout, has turned oddly shy. When we requested pictures of several stars' engagement rings, they wrote back with descriptions only. The result is an awkward feature that reads like an anthropological study. Scientists are reasonably sure that Madonna's Edwardian ring resembles this one pictured here. Jennifer Aniston's ring with 4.5-carat emerald-cut diamonds may have looked like this ring from Tiffany's. It's as though these rings are dinosaurs and we're piecing together the historical record from their bones.

I'm trying to make the description of Anne Heche's ring seem like something more than pure speculation when Dot calls my name. She is standing at the entrance to her office with a pile of magazines in her arms. "Your Next Meeting—Eleven O'clock," she says, before disappearing behind a closed door.

I sigh, bored with conjecture, and reread Jane's memo. Although it's a long way from agreeing to sponsor a highly visible and controversial gallery exhibit, changing her name is a prime example of irrational behavior. For the first time, I think that their plan might work. Their plan might prevail, evil might be deposed and *Fashionista* might one day be a happy place to work.

Allison is right. I am wavering.

Drinks at the Paramount

Maya orders a cosmopolitan tumbled. The bartender stares at her uncomprehendingly until she scoffs and says, "In a tumbler. I'd like a cosmopolitan in a tumbler." He gives her another look before walking away to put vodka, Cointreau and cranberry juice into a cocktail shaker. "And no sugar on the rim," she calls after him. "In my ongoing quest to identify, isolate and eliminate the elements in my life that are no longer working for me, I've recently settled on white, unrefined sugar," she says, cutting a sliver of brie and putting it on a cracker. "I'm slowly letting carbs back into my life."

The bartender places the tumbled cosmo down on a napkin in front of Maya, puts a gin and tonic in my general vicinity and disappears. We are in the bar at the Paramount hotel. We always seek shelter here when bad things happen to Maya. Cosmopolitans are her comfort food.

The last time we stepped foot in the dark, low-ceilinged room was scarcely a month ago. Maya, whose agent, Marcia, was moving to a new agency and not taking her with her, had been in serious need of comfort.

"Yes, those are actual tears of frustration that you often hear about but rarely see," she had said then, pathetically handing me her dear-Maya letter.

But it wasn't just dear Maya. "Who's Dylan?" I ask, although I have a suspicion. I have a reasonable idea what happened. Marcia, in her haste to dump old, unproductive clients, had been remiss in tailoring her form letter. The part where it assures its reader that it has been a pleasure working with her was suppose to assure Maya, not someone named Dylan. "Can you believe that?" she says, her voice a sad whine. Her head dropped forward, depositing amber curls onto the bar. "I wasn't even given the dignity of my own letter."

"At least you know you're not the only one she dumped," I pointed out.

"That's true," she said, not prepared to laugh but no longer teetering on the edge of tears.

Although I'm not that good at comfort, I recognize success and continued in the same vein. "And it turns what should be an out-and-out tragedy into an absurdist comedy."

"It is a tragedy," she said, finishing her cosmopolitan in three gulps. This is why she hates martini glasses; she can't take gulps without spilling cranberry juice all over her Donna Karan blouses. "I'm back to square one. I'm standing exactly where I stood eighteen months ago, only I'm eighteen months older."

Thirty loomed large in Maya's mind. The landmark birthday wouldn't have been a problem if she still had an agent. But the marker was rapidly approaching—she only had fifteen days left to find new representation. It seemed unlikely that she would and so she has tensed her shoulders in expectation of a heavy blow. This is the sort of thing that happens when you set objectives for yourself and try to achieve things. Goals are the real enemy.

Despite all my hard work, tears welled up in Maya's eyes and she backslid into heaving sobs. I understood her sorrow. For a little while, she had stood apart from all the other magazine freelancers with manuscripts under their arms. For a little while, she'd been distinguishable. Now she was tossed back into the chorus line, where we all look alike.

I ordered another round of drinks, handed her some tissues and began muttering platitudes about things happening for a reason. I thought she'd had too much vodka to notice that I suddenly sounded like a greeting card, but she wasn't that drunk. She wasn't too drunk at all and she refused to let me offer mass-produced comfort, although that is what I do best. So I started slinging mud. It's the last defense of the helpless. "You're really better off. She was an awful agent."

Maya balled the tissues in her fist. This was not what she wanted to hear. "She was a good agent."

"And how many books did she manage to sell for you?"

Now I'd just thoughtlessly reminded her of her failure not just to keep an agent but to make a sale as well. Fresh tears began falling, and although she started the sentence with something resembling composure, by the end her words were scarcely more than a whimper. "Marcia got my work read and rejected. I can't ask for...more...than...th-that."

"Pooh," I said, dismissive of her logic. You can and should always ask for more, especially when you've set goals for yourself. "You'll find another agent and she'll be better than Marcia. Just you wait. The next one won't call you Dylan."

She realized the truth of this. It is extremely unlikely that the next agent—if there is a next agent—will also have a client named Dylan. "But what if I never find another one?"

I told her not to be silly, and after several more attempts at lifting her spirits with upbeat and optimistic inanities, I realized she wanted to wallow. I realized she wanted to cast herself into the thick swamp of disconsolation and loll there in the mud. I had no right to deny her its soothing coolness, and threw myself in alongside. They tell you that finding an agent is harder than finding a publisher, but Maya knows that's not true. As hard as getting an agent is, snagging a publisher is many times more difficult. And you can't do it from the back row of the chorus line.

***

We are here now because Maya broke up with her boyfriend.

"It's over," she said when I picked up the phone. No hello, no how are you, just it's over. Thank God.

"What about the ring?" I asked.

"I don't give a fuck about the ring."

"How does it feel?"

"Awful."

"Wanna get a drink?"

"Be there in fifteen."

It was the middle of the day, but I didn't care. I'm nobody's assistant and operate under the supposition that I should work when I want to. I often sneak away during periods of downtime to go shopping or see a movie in the theater next door. All I have to do to lull suspicion is keep my computer on, leave my jacket hanging in the corner and light a candle.

I'm almost done with my gin and tonic when the bartender reappears to ask if we want another round. This is the great thing about the Paramount. They never let you finish a drink.

"I just have to accept the fact that it isn't going to happen," she says, after the bartender has left. "I love him and I'll miss him but I can't keep doing this. I don't know why he bought that stupid ring but he clearly never had any intention of giving it to me." A tear slides down her cheek. Not being wanted always hurts.

The ring is a two-carat diamond that Maya found five months ago in one of Roger's kitchen drawers. For two weeks she was giddy and impatient and excited. For two weeks she lived life with an excess of energy. For two whole week she expected every single moment to pop. But nothing happened. Five months later, it's clear to her that nothing is ever going to happen. The engagement ring is Roger's pistol on the wall and Maya is tired of waiting for the third act.

I didn't like Roger Childe from the very beginning. He

introduced himself to me as an entrepreneur, and the contempt I felt was swift and complete. "Entrepreneur" is a term magazine writers ascribe to you; you don't ascribe it to yourself, especially not when you're the president of a Jersey City dot-com that your father bankrolled.

He had other pretensions—name-dropping A-list players, wearing monogrammed sweaters, using the word *cinema* in mixed company—but Maya didn't mind. All she noticed were his handsome face and his lovely compliments and his coordinated J. Crew separates.

But it wasn't just his mail-order-catalog perfection that put me off, although having both the Barn Jacket and the Fisherman Cable Knit didn't help. He had a prep-school patina, which lent him an air of entitlement that seemed entirely out of place in the early twenty-first century. He knew all the right people and went to all the right places and could buy all the right things and his life would no doubt follow all the right formulas.

Maya was dazzled by his confidence. Before she lost her agent, she'd seen Roger and herself as a top-one-hundred power couple in the making. She'd change the way a generation thought with her books, he'd change the way a generation behaved with his software, and *New York* magazine would spotlight them in a glossy cover shoot that made her look beautiful and edgy.

"A month ago it was no big deal that he hadn't asked me to marry him," she says, "but I'm thirty now and can't live my life like a carefree twenty-something. I've drawn up terms of reference."

"Terms of reference?" Three gin and tonics have slightly muddled my brain, but I'm reasonably sure I've never heard the term "terms of reference" before.

She reaches into her leather backpack and withdraws a sheet of white paper. It's crumpled and creased and she runs her hands over it several times, trying to flatten it. The corners still curl up.

"Today," she announces in almost sententious tones, "is the first day of the rest of my life. Here is a year-by-year breakdown of what I hope to accomplish in my fourth decade of existence."

But the breakdown really isn't year by year. It's more month by month and in some severe cases day by day. The first term of reference— "have talk with Roger to see where this is all going" —has minutes attached.

"He was very evasive," she says, when I ask how the talk went. "I just wanted to know if he thought there was a point to all this. I mean, I didn't need the ring right there and then, only a word or two of encouragement. But he kept hemming and hawing and saying things like 'We'll see,' as though I'm a car he's not sure he wants to buy."

He is weighing the pros and cons of marrying Maya. He is looking at all the available information and trying to decide if she'll be a credit to him. Will his name gain luster in association with hers? He doesn't know yet. Maya's an incomplete stock report.

This is the level of calculation Roger works on, the sort you read about in Edith Wharton novels and don't believe exists anymore. He is like a great sculpture. He can make things that are hard—like his heart—seem soft. But all you have to do is get close enough to realize the truth. All you have to do is touch him to discover differently.

"It was a mistake from the beginning," I say, pushing the crinkled proof of her insanity to the side. I don't want anything to do with her terms or her references. The answer to one thwarted goal is not forty more. It's like trying to cure a hangover with Jell-O shots. "Rule number one—never date a man named Childe."

"I know, I know," she says, putting her head down on the bar. "It's just asking for trouble, isn't it?"

I agree that it is and order another round.

My 102nd Day

I was in my third month as Jane's editorial assistant when the fax machine arrived. It came by UPS, which refuses to leave packages in front of apartment doors, so even before the beeping and squealing modern convenience entered my home, it was already a great inconvenience. In order to get it, I had to walk over to Washington and Houston, wait twenty-five minutes as they looked for it in the back and then carry it home in my arms.

Nobody told me the fax machine was coming, and when I asked Harvey, the office manager, what it was about, he shrugged, looked abashed and mumbled something about needing to order staples from the catalog. I wasn't completely clueless. Jane had taken to calling me late at night and telling me to fax documents to her, to the publisher, to writers, to designers, to her parents. When I'd remind her that I didn't have faxing capabilities, she always seemed vaguely stunned, as if I were subsisting without the basic requirements of life, like food and water. She righted that injustice ("No, you don't have to thank me. Giving is what I do") and instantly began treating my apartment as *Fashionista*'s downtown annex.

The midnight requests began to pile up ("It's still lunchtime in Tokyo") and after a week of the graveyard shift, I stopped answering the phone. Jane would leave long, suspicious messages—"Pick up, Vig. Are you there, Vig? Vig, if you're there, this is very important. The future of the magazine rests on it. Don't play with me, Vig. All right, Vig, here's what I need you to do as soon as you get home, if you are indeed away from home and not listening to this message as it comes in"—dictating letters that I was to type up, print out and fax to studio execs and event planners immediately. But I never typed up, printed out and faxed a letter to a studio exec or event planner immediately. I always waited until I got to work the next day. Jane never noticed the difference.

Then one day she started faxing me work. She started faxing me contracts and articles and expecting me to have everything done by the next morning.

She'd say, "Where's that expense report? I need it by ten."

She'd say, "Give me those spreadsheets I sent over last night. I've got a meeting first thing."

She'd say, "Bring the invite list to Publicity right now. They're waiting for it."

As soon as I realized what was going on, I put a stop to it. I disconnected the fax machine and looked baffled when Jane asked me what was wrong with it. Six hours later there was a repairman at my door. He immediately diagnosed the problem—the dangling plug was a dead giveaway—and reminded me that most appliances need electricity to run. I submitted silently to the humiliating lecture, and the next time I interfered with the fax, I opened it up and pulled out a wire. Another repairmen was sent with undue haste. He was mystified as to how the circuit came loose. Was I sure I didn't have any mischievous nieces and nephews who liked to play with colorful wires?

Several months passed like this, with me breaking or jamming the machine like it were a parking meter in front of my house that I refused to pay, and Jane became increasingly skeptical. She became more and more suspicious, and although she laid numerous charges at my feet, she could never make them stick. When the motherboard short-circuited quite inexplicably ("I'm quite sure, sir, that I don't know what that orange sticky stuff is"), the repairmen shook their heads in disgust, called the machine a lemon and walked away.

After that, Jane made threats but she never delivered. There was much talk of faxes but she knew better than to give me another one. I was no longer an amateur. I was now a seasoned pro and what I knew about fax machines could keep them in disrepair for years. Far better to avoid a showdown altogether than to come up short twice in a row.

Wavering

Maya works with strangers. She freelances at a variety of magazines and although she toils alongside the same people month after month, she barely exists to them. She hasn't been introduced en masse in a big, splashy staff meeting, and her life and times are of little interest. When she sneezes, no one says bless you. When she comes in with a sexy tan, no one asks where she's been. When she wears a cute new sweater, no one compliments her.

"If it were just any sweater, I wouldn't have expected anything," she explains, finishing off her third cosmopolitan.

Through the wood slats that cover the Paramount's semi-circle windows, I can see light from streetlamps. It's almost dark. I'm flirting with the notion of going back to the office to turn off my computer and perhaps blow out the candle when the bartender sweeps by and delivers fresh drinks. I stay firmly rooted to the spot. If Christine doesn't feel compelled to extinguish my candle as a product of her Midwestern only-you-can-prevent-forest-fires upbringing, then the cleaning woman will.

"But this wasn't just any sweater," she continues. "It had little beads and pink slivers of sequin sewn around the edges. It was darn cute."

"Not a word?"

"Not a word," she says sadly. "And I had the whole conversation planned in my head. They'd say, Cute sweater. I'd say, Thanks, I picked it up at the Donna Karan outlet outside Ithaca. They'd say, Oh, you were in Ithaca this weekend? And I'd say, Yes, I was visiting a friend. We went tubing. Them: Tubing? Me: Yes, it's like skiing but much more repetitive."

Maya used to freelance for *Fashionista*—I had hooked her up with the copy chief—but she jumped ship after a few months because she couldn't stand the way we do things. She couldn't stand having to clear every single word or comma change with the editors and writers and researchers. And she hated having to justify in the margin each correction (dangling modifier, sentence-verb agreement, predicate nominative case). Copyediting is deadly dull work, the sort that requires a mind-numbing attention to detail, and it's thoroughly unglamorous. *Fashionista,* with its system of checks and balances, somehow found a way to increase the tedium of the job.

"It was warm in the office, but I kept my sweater on, hoping that someone would notice its cuteness."

"Almost all hope is cruel," I say carelessly.

Ordinarily Maya would contradict me but today her usual optimism is dulled by rejection—Roger's and Marcia's—and she nods forlornly.

A prolonged silence follows.

"I'm involved in a plot," I say out of nowhere. This thought has been circling my brain for almost twenty-four hours now and it has to go somewhere. It has to be expressed or permanently crushed.

"Hmm?" Consumed by her own misery, she's forgotten my presence.

I'm reasonably sure that there is no one from *Fashionista*

in the bar, but I scope out the perimeter just to be certain. I lean over and whisper. "I'm involved in a plot to bring down the editor in chief."

Maya's eyes bug out. "A plot?"

"A plot."

"What kind of plot?" she asks, leaning forward. Maya is genuinely interested. My talk of plots has managed to break through her wall of self-pity.

I give her the rough outline of the plan and she stops me to ask details. "Gavin Marshall?" she says, as if trying to re-call the name. She draws a blank.

"I've never heard of him, either. But he's a big deal over in England," I say. "I looked up a few articles about him today. He's the son of an earl. He grew up in a mansion that's a na-tional landmark. I think his great-great-grandfather was the prime minister during the Crimean War. He went to all the best schools—Eton, Oxford and the Royal Academy of Art," I say, running off a list of his advantages. "I think the only hardship he's ever had in his life was convincing Daddy to let him mutilate a cow in the Victorian plunge pool."

Maya is quiet for a moment. She's putting it all together and trying to come to a conclusion. "Do you think it'll work?"

I laugh. "Not a chance. I'll most likely get fired over the whole mess, but I'm leaning toward it anyway." Having said these words aloud, I'm overcome by an unexpected emotion. Although I haven't felt it in a while, I know it's excitement. Nothing else feels this way.

"You'd risk your job?"

I nod enthusiastically. "Don't get me wrong. I'm as sur-prised as you. When I woke up yesterday morning, I was pretty satisfied with my job."

Maya takes a sip of her cosmo and tilts her head. "What's changed?"

An excellent question. "I'm not really sure. Somewhere be-tween talking to a new editor who's receptive to ideas that are typically un-*Fashionista* and meeting with one of my editors who gave me another classic *Fashionista* assignment, I've become disgusted with my job. We don't *do* anything. We take the same three strands of yarn every month—celebrity, fashion and beauty—and weave them into different patterns. It's so deadening," I say, recalling today's assignment to track down famous skate-skiers. The topic is new, but the copy is old, and after several days of talking to publicists and personal assistants, I will produce five hundred words on why you should be trading in your old snowboard. The article will have too many adjectives and several exclamation points and it will make you wonder if you're really missing out on something, but don't be fooled. It's just rhetoric. It's just *Fashionista* trying to convince you that celebs, like blondes, really do have more fun. "Do you remember how excited I was when I got this job?" I ask.

Maya nods. Of course she remembers. I'd been sleeping on her couch at the time.

"We'd only been out of college for two years, but it felt like I'd been fetching coffee for the editor of the *Bierlyville Times* for more than a decade. Back then, I didn't think there was anything in the world more glamorous than living in Manhattan and reporting on celebrities." I take a sip of gin and tonic and sigh heavily. "How's that for Missouri-bred naiveté?"

Maya doesn't comment on my Midwestern simplicity. She was raised in a Connecticut suburb less than forty minutes away, and there was never anything glamorous about the big city. It was just a place to go on Saturday nights to get drunk. "Fight the power," she says, raising a fist in the air in a half-hearted display of revolutionary fervor. "And if mutiny doesn't work out and they fire your ass, don't worry. You can go freelance. I'll help you get started—there's plenty of work."

Despite the fact that she works with strangers, Maya is always upbeat about freelancing. She's like one of those immigrants who comes to the New World and writes letters home about untold wealth and success. In the past, I've been resistant to her lavish claims. I know the streets aren't paved with gold. I know that most people aren't prosperous in the land of prosperity. I know this and I cling to my Old World ways. But sometimes you have no choice. Sometimes events propel you across oceans. Working at *Fashionista* is starting to feel like a potato famine.

It is now six o'clock and the trickle of people who have been coming in for the past hour suddenly arranges itself into a crowd. A man wearing Gucci slippers squeezes in between our chairs and starts waving his hand in the air in a desperate bid for attention. Theatrics like this rarely work in New York City bars.

"Get the check," Maya says, but I'm already one step ahead. I've already made eye contact with the bartender, and at this moment he's tallying up our tab.

Maya protests but I insist on treating. Although I've played the scene lugubriously out of deference to her feelings, this has been a celebration for me. Roger is out of our lives. And even though seventy-five dollars is a substantial portion of my drink budget for the month, it's a small price to pay for the pleasure.

In the lobby, Maya vanishes into the bathroom, and I stand in the corner, watching people check in. A large group of Japanese tourists has just arrived and while the men are waiting in a cluster for room keys, their wives are milling around. Some are at the newsstand flipping through magazines; others are sitting in the lobby. The lobby itself is full of misfits—riveted aluminum lounge chairs, long lime-green benches that cut the room in half, wide orange wingbacks with brothel-like flourishes, armchairs with pictures of dogs silk-screened on. These are discordant objects that shouldn't come together. They shouldn't come together and anywhere else they wouldn't, but somehow they do here against this gray backdrop.

Lynn Messina

Maya reappears a few minutes later. She steps out of the bathroom and is almost instantly accosted by a Japanese woman who wants her to take a picture of her and her friends, who have arranged themselves on the grand staircase. Maya complies happily, although her picture-taking skills are somewhat compromised by the copious amounts of alcohol she's consumed. She covers the lens with her thumb. The Japanese women are too polite to comment and they thank her appreciatively, but they stay in formation. After we leave, they'll call to one of their friends over by the magazine racks and ask her to take the shot.

Phase One

Despite the dramatic improvement in Keller's sister's life after her inclusion in our makeover issue, I don't believe Keller owes me a favor or that he'd even acknowledge such a debt if it did exist. With all this uncertainty in mind, I decide to meet with him in person. I don't want to have this conversation over the phone. I don't want to conduct it over e-mail. I want to read his face and see how he reacts to my suggestion. Sometimes that's the only way to know if you should advance or retreat.

I call his assistant, Delia Barker, to set up an appointment.

"Alex is booked," she says into the receiver. "I can put you through to his voice mail."

I don't want his voice mail. "Are you sure he doesn't have one single minute to spare in the next seven days?"

"Alex is booked," she chirps again. "I can put you through to his voice mail."

She sounds like a cuckoo bird, like an automated device that only tells you the time. I hang up the phone and walk over to her office just to make sure she's flesh and blood. Delia is sitting there in her vanilla-scented room with her thick, black hair in a ponytail. She sees me in her doorway and takes out a calendar. "Alex is booked," she says. "You can look for yourself."

I accept the calendar and peruse his commitments: lunches, openings, junkets, meetings, photo shoots, jacket fittings, more meetings. Delia has filled in something for every minute, but it's not just the next seven days. It's the next seven months. This can't be real. There has to be another set of books here, the set that you don't show to the guys from the IRS. I stare at her consideringly. It's obvious that Delia isn't going to stray from the party line. Alex is booked. She can put me through to his voice mail.

Crushing a sneer, I thank her for her help and think about other courses of action. Taking Delia's advice would be the logical choice, but I don't. Instead, I position myself in the supply closet across the hall and wait. I have calls to designers of outerwear to make, but I don't let that bother me. I'm focused on one objective and one objective only—to have a face-to-face with Alex Keller.

Five hours later I'm still waiting. Lydia has been in here twice to get padded envelopes and timesheets and each time, she looked at me funny. Each time she came in, I'd grab a box of staples and try to look casual as I stared at it with intense fascination.

Constant surveillance demystifies Keller's delivery system. After the second knock, Delia sticks her head out of her office and takes the item from Alex's in-box. She does this quickly, with an economy of movement, as though each time she's going for the world record. Blink and you miss it.

I'm ready to call it quits when I hear Delia tell a senior editor that Alex is in an extremely important meeting, but he'll give her a call as soon as he's out. I perk up at this. If Alex is in a meeting now, then he has been in a meeting all day. This doesn't sound right—there was no talk of meetings when I tried to make an appointment five hours ago—so I wait until Delia leaves her desk. I watch her disappear into the ladies' room and let myself into Alex's office.

I'm hoping to interrupt an extremely important meeting but the office is empty. He left the computer, the lamp and the stereo on. He even placed a half-finished cup of coffee on his desk. The coffee is a nice touch but it doesn't fool me. I know exactly what he's doing. I've done it myself many times but never on a scale this big. Whereas I light the candle and step out for a few hours, he's stepped out for a career.

Although I have nothing but a half-drunk cup of cold coffee to go on, I know I'm right. There is no other explanation for his phantasmal existence, for the way he is rarely seen but often heard.

I exit the office before Delia gets back—Delia, the accomplice who tells lies and falsifies documents for him—and return to my desk. Staring up at me are twenty photos of engagement rings, a list of designers who make outerwear, and the telephone number for the Sanrio headquarters in San Francisco. I have thirty-two new e-mails, the message light on my phone is blinking and there are four Post-it notes from Dot, each one more illegible than the last. Thanks to my spy stint, I'm now hours and hours behind. I won't leave here until after nine o'clock.

I sit down with a heavy sigh, thinking that if I had an assistant who was willing to cover for me, it's doubtful that I'd ever go to work either.

Phase One Continued

Christine is rhapsodizing about kumquats.

"It's like this," she says, her voice full of wonder. "The soft-shell crab is to the lobster as the kumquat is to the orange." She looks at me expectantly.

I nod to show her I understand the analogy, but she just shakes her head at my tepid response. I don't really *understand*.

"One more time," she says, "follow me here. The soft-shell crab is to the lobster as the kumquat is to the orange."

I shrug. "You eat the exoskeleton."

"Close enough," she concedes before bursting out with the right answer. "You eat the skin! Isn't that just the gosh-darniest thing you've ever heard?"

I'd like to say that I've heard things gosh-darnier but that would be a lie. "Yes, it is."

"Here, have one." She gives me a kumquat. "They're a revelation."

It's spongy and sweet and when I bite into it juice squirts onto my lips, but there's nothing revelatory about it. "It's good," I say, underwhelmed and not trying to hide it.

Christine's disappointed with my reaction but she rallies. "Last night we made frozen kumquat soufflé with apricot coulis. It was delish."

I say, "Frozen kumquat soufflé?" to be friendly, to encourage conversation, but I really don't have the time for either kumquats or conversation. It's Friday, and I've several things to do before the weekend, the least of which is finding Alex Keller's address. I don't know how I'm going to do this. He's not listed with information, so I will have to sneak into Human Resources or somewhere equally unwelcoming and look through files.

But despite this, I ask questions. I take a moment to show interest because I know few people who have dreams and it seems wrong not to nourish their hopes.

From her detailed description, a frozen soufflé sounds like nothing more exotic or complicated than vanilla ice cream served in a white ceramic bowl, but I just nod and smile and refrain from comment. I've already disappointed her on the kumquat front and don't have the heart to do it again.

While she's explaining the intricacies of making apricot coulis—first you stew the apricots, then you add sugar—I'm trying to decide what to do next. I'm trying to figure out which is more important: keeping my job or liking my job. Breaking into Human Resources and rifling through their files will produce the address of Alex Keller, but it will more likely yield my instant dismissal. And to what end? Keller won't agree to help. He won't offer his services with a carefree smile and a happy glint in his eye. Even if I do manage to get my hands on his contact info without suffering personal harm, nothing will come of it. As soon as I knock on his door, Keller will tell me to get lost before viciously slamming it in my face. I've been on the receiving end of too many of his voice mails to expect anything less.

This is the perfect excuse to extricate myself from the plot, and I consider telling Allison and the fashionistas that the whole thing is off. I consider jumping ship and making them find someone else to be their linchpin. Alex Keller is too much of a risk; he's the sort of long shot that tumbles empires and destroys fortunes.

But even though I have the entire withdrawal speech formulated and written in my head, I don't deliver it. Bringing down Jane McNeill might just be a pipe dream but it seems wrong not to nourish it.

My 15th Day

My first quarrel with Alex Keller was over the color copier. He'd left a sheet of white paper in the feeder, which I removed and placed next to the machine.

"Don't do that!" he yelled, as soon as I answered the phone.

Since the only thing I had done was pick up the receiver, I naturally concluded he meant that and immediately hung up. A second later the phone rang again. Clearly he was a hard man to please.

I let it ring four times before picking up. "Hello," I said pleasantly, as if I didn't know who it was.

"Don't you ever hang up on me again or I'll have your job," he said, angrily throwing his weight around.

Although I hated all sorts of confrontation and was only an editorial assistant, I refused to cower in the face of threats. "Whom do I have the pleasure of speaking to?" I asked disingenuously. Although I didn't yet know his voice or his telephone number, I'd heard enough stories to make an educated guess.

"This is Alex Keller. I'm the events editor at this magazine and I was in the middle of using the copier outside the kitchen when you hijacked it. You took the article I was photocopying. It's a very important document and I can't have people like you touching it. Don't do it again."

I rolled my eyes. Although I hadn't bothered to read the article before moving it—gingerly!—to the side, I saw enough to know that it wasn't the Declaration of Independence. Magazines are a completely disposable medium. Nothing we touch is very important.

"I thought you were done," I said, compelled to defend myself.

"Until you see me removing my documents from the feeder, I'm not done!" he announced, as though he were visible to the naked eye, as though he didn't move through secret passages and priest holes.

There were four other copiers on the floor. "Okay."

The phone slammed down. He didn't say goodbye.

Keller never says goodbye and he snaps at you whenever possible and, rather than leave messages on your voice mail—because you're too wily now to pick up the phone when you see his extension on the display—he sends you blistering e-mails telling you what to do.

And he never thanks you. So when on those rare occasions you need something from him, you're always polite and you always send a thank-you—as a reminder, as a dig, as an act of passive aggression. You know being thanked over e-mail bugs the hell out of him. You know this because the first time you did it, he wrote an e-mail back telling you never to thank him again. He already gets too many effing e-mails.

You write "okay" and hit Send.

More Phase One

Stacy Shoemaucher is a friendly-looking woman with chin-length black hair and faded lipstick. She's wearing a double-breasted light blue suit, the sort that makes her figure seem frumpy and her complexion sallow. If she weren't an employee of Ivy Publishing, she'd be an ideal candidate for next year's makeover issue. We're always looking for frumpy and sallow.

Her desk is pleasantly disheveled, and the walls of her office are decorated with those earnest and vaguely embarrassing posters that you expect human resources people to have, the ones with nature scenes that say things like "The mountain only seems taller up close" and "Success is more afraid of you."

Stacy gestures to a chair and I take a seat across from her at the small round table in the corner. I must seem a little hesitant to her—this is my first trip to Human Resources—so she smiles encouragingly. Her lips curve warmly and her eyes crinkle in an amiable way, and when she asks, "What can I do for you?" I believe that she actually wants to help.

"I'd like to report a section C."

Her smile wavers. "A section C?"

"Yes, a section C, subset 2."

"Are you sure?" she asks.

"I'm sure," I say.

She sighs heavily, the amiable crinkles disappearing completely. "We take dress-code violations very seriously here." Then she retrieves a form from the filing cabinet along the wall and lays it on the table in front of her. She isn't prepared yet to give it to me. "Are you quite sure they weren't shoes? With the fashions today, sometimes it's so hard to tell.... And *Fashionista,* such a trendy place. One time we had an editor come in complaining about a co-worker wearing a bikini but it turned out it was just Betsey Johnson hot pants." She lets out a nervous laugh.

"They were slippers," I say emphatically. "I'm positive."

With great reluctance, she hands me the form. Since I read the employee handbook from cover to cover before coming down here, I'm very familiar with the form and I fill it out quickly.

She peruses the document. "Everything seems to be in order. If there's nothing else...?"

"Actually, would you mind checking his file for me? I'm very much afraid this is his *second* such infraction."

Jumping to her feet, she digs through the cabinet filled with personnel files and withdraws Alex Keller's. "I don't believe it. Nobody violates the dress code twice!"

His file is thin. There is nothing in it except his résumé, emergency contact information and a card with his current address and telephone number.

"He has a spotless record," she says proudly.

Although I'm trying to memorize a long series of numbers—47386405074#11A—this grabs my attention. "Are you sure?" I almost snatch the file from out of her hands.

"That his record is spotless? Of course, I have it right here. There's not a complaint in it, except your Section C, subset 2, which will not be officially entered until after we conduct a full investigation."

"But that's not possible," I say. Alex Keller has been pissing people off for six years. How can there be not one complaint in his file?

Although I didn't mean to imply that she's on the take, that's exactly what I've done. Her eyes narrow suspiciously. "And why not?"

"He's belligerent and antagonistic and seems to have a serious problem controlling his temper," I say, listing a few of his many failings in an effort to put her at ease.

Her features lighten but she's not appeased. "If you have a specific incident in mind, you can make a formal complaint now."

I have several specific incidents in mind and would like nothing more than to spend the rest of the day lodging complaints against Alex Keller, but I can't linger. The numbers are already fading from my memory.

The Maine Filibuster

Every morning Anna Choi comes into the office, itemizes her clothing and sums up her look with a pithy statement. Today she is Ellis Island retro. Pants: Antique Boutique, $45; shirt: H&M, $11; coat: Hasidic overcoat from Williamsburg, $30; headwrap: Bendel's, $220; shoes: Fausta Santini, $72.

Although she is making fun of the Public Eye, an item in the local weekly that asks people on the street these very questions, Anna faithfully adheres to the dictates of self-conscious funkiness found therein. Her pants are almost always from a flea market, her shirts are almost always from the bottom of the secondhand bin at Domsey's, and nine times out of ten she's sporting one outrageously expensive item, which is usually something small like a belt or a purse.

Anna is the editor of *Fashionista*'s Home Front section and it's her job to write about celebrities puttering about in their French country kitchens. She visits their homes, spends two hours touring their grounds and taking notes on the way sunlight pours through skylights, and then returns to her three-hundred-square-foot apartment in the East Village. Because her tenement barely has a kitchen, let alone a place for pots, pans and oven mitts, Anna is a closet fetishist. Her mouth waters at a glimpse of neatly stacked linens in a narrow space. Her heart beats faster at the sight of dry goods in a pantry. These are the temples she chooses to worship in, and every month her editor has to cut five hundred words on walk-ins and shelving systems and coat hangers.

Home Front is a lush section, with exquisite photographs of beautiful celebrities in white fluffy robes eating croissants on hydrangea-drenched verandas or kissing in wooden boats on their lily ponds or playing Bach's third concerto on their baby grand pianos. Flipping through the section, you get the sense that these moments are more than posed, they are staged. They are practiced scenes that don't quite exist beyond the click of the Canon Rebel EOS 5 and you can't help but feel that the participants themselves look at the photos with the same longing you do. It's like Cary Grant wishing he were Cary Grant.

Despite the breadth of homes covered—ranches in New Mexico, villas in Malibu, town houses in Manhattan—there is a remarkable sameness about the articles. It's as though everyone has a 200-year-old circular stone shrine in the backyard or a statue of Nefertiti in the driveway. Anna does a good job of mixing it up, of making this library of leather-bound first editions seem like the first library of leather-bound first editions she has ever seen. Her writing is strong, and she delights in giving celebrities free rein and then gleefully reporting the glittering bon mots they let fall from their lips. Inevitably an actor will show her the spot on the side of a hill where he stands and belts Hamlet's "too too solid flesh" soliloquy at the top of his lungs. With enough rope, anyone will hang himself.

Although it's three-thirty and the cannonball has already left Penn Station for the Hamptons, we're having a Friday afternoon meeting. This is an unprecedented event, and Anna, like everyone else in the room, is thoroughly unprepared. She has a short list of celebs whose publicists have pitched her their homes but they're not quite A-list, and at the mention of an *All My Children* star, Jane's lip curls in disgust. We do not cover soap opera actresses.

"What else?" asks Jane, checking to see if it's four o'clock yet. She's not the only one whose eyes are repeatedly drawn to her watch. Half the room had expected to leave by three to get to their summer shares in time for pre-dinner cocktails on the deck.

Anna glances down at her notes, and although she is now nervous, she looks as impeccable as ever. She's wearing an overcoat so tattered and torn that even the Hasidim threw it away but she still looks perfect. On her, frayed cuffs are an accent. "That's all for now. I'll know more on Tuesday," she says, a subtle reminder to our intrepid editor in chief that this meeting is impromptu and unplanned. "I expect the publicists to get back to me after the weekend."

Jane is the sort of person to leave publicists and editors hanging over long weekends, but she doesn't accept that type of behavior from others. She huffs angrily now, looking very much like she wants to vent her spleen on Anna, but she holds herself back. Marguerite is in the room. She's sitting across from her with a friendly smile on her face and Jane seeks to mimic her behavior. For a nanosecond Jane wants to be liked. It's for all the wrong reasons, but it saves Anna a reaming.

She turns her attention to a summer intern. "You there, with the pimple, what are you working on?"

The mortified college junior mutters and sputters for a few seconds before mumbling something about high-top sneakers. The other intern in the room, who has a carbuncle the size of the Liberty Bell on her nose, tilts her head down, trying to hide her face. She is wishing desperately that she could disappear.

Jane called this meeting after discovering that Marguerite planned to catch the last flight to Bangor, Maine, which leaves Kennedy at four. A multimillionaire land developer has invited her to his private island for a weekend party, and Jane is determined to put a damper on the festivities. Marguerite was free to miss the emergency meeting, of course, but she chose to stay for political reasons. She knows that her position at *Fashionista* is still precarious. Jane herself planned on being on the express train to Montauk, but thwarting Marguerite's weekend plans is more important than her own. Now she'll have to take the jitney and suffer the traffic on the L.I.E. or take one of the later trains, which stops at Forrest Hills and Baldwin and Seaford and Copiague and Bridgehampton and all the stops in between. Jane is the first person to cut off her nose to spite her face.

By the time Jane finishes tormenting spot-riddled teenagers, she has only fifteen minutes left to kill. She will not allow this meeting to end a second before four. Leaving nothing to chance, Jane wants to make sure that even if Marguerite hops on a magic carpet, she still won't catch that plane. Her assistant, Jackie, who has been on the phone with the airline since two o'clock, is under strict orders to report any delays the moment they happen. Jane will keep us here as long as long as it takes, even if she has to read names from the telephone book until midnight.

"What about article ideas?" Jane asks, looking around the table. "I believe I sent out a memo asking for three fresh article ideas from each of you by this afternoon's meeting."

This is a complete fabrication—since this meeting was not conceived of more than ten minutes before it was called, no memo went around—but nobody points this out. We all sit in our chairs averting our gazes and hoping someone else raises her hand. The atmosphere is very much like freshman English, with none of us quite sure of the symbolic importance of the bell jar.

Marguerite steps up to the plate. "I have a few ideas for the upcoming wedding issue."

Giving Marguerite the floor was not Jane's intention and

she glares at her nemesis. "I'm sure you do, but I would rather start with the junior..."

"We should do a feature on bridesmaid dresses," she says, as if Jane weren't still speaking. Jane, who has never been confronted with this tactic, trails off into stunned silence. We all notice and try desperately to hide our smirks. Some of us don't succeed but Jane is too angry to notice.

Marguerite continues, seemingly oblivious. "I was thinking about how people always say that you can wear your bridesmaid dresses again. Even with the most hideous dresses, someone, usually the bride, insists that if you cut the hem and dye it black, it will be a lovely cocktail dress. But nobody ever does. What if we got five or six bridesmaid dresses and gave them to designers—Michael Kors, Tom Ford, Marc Jacobs, Donna Karan—and asked them to make them wearable?"

"I've got six dresses in my closet ready to go," announces Christine. "Just say the word."

There is general agreement around the table. You don't get to your late twenties without wearing at least one pink dress with a sweetheart collar.

"I have an awful Maid Marian gown in forest-green," says Allison. I know all about her Maid Marian gown in forest-green. Allison spent weeks and weeks trying to change her sister's mind. First she reasoned, then she cajoled, finally she begged. It was all for naught. The elder Harper was determined to have her medieval-style wedding, despite the fact that jousting was made illegal at the turn of the eighteenth century. As I learned from many hours of eavesdropping, you can always find someone willing to get on a horse and dodge a five-foot lance for a few hundred bucks.

"Maid Marian?" an editor asks, amazed by the depths to which a bride will sink. "Gee, and I thought the Empire-waist periwinkle-blue thing my cousin made me wear was bad."

Allison laughs. "Please, I'd kill for an Empire wai—"

"It's an interesting suggestion," says Jane, trying to draw attention away from Marguerite's very good idea, "but there are strict rules in this company about utilizing our own people for anything in the magazine."

This rule applies to using Ivy Publishing employees in layouts, not their cast-off bridesmaid dresses, but Marguerite has a better idea anyway. "Of course, Jane," she says, as if she is expecting this objection, "I'm aware of the company's rule. But I thought we could turn to our readers for dresses."

"Our readers?" Jane asks, thrown off by the concept, as if she's unsure who these people are.

"Yes, we can have a contest of sorts and ask our readers to send in photos of their ugliest bridesmaid dress," Marguerite explains. "We'll select the ten worst and give them to designers."

"That's an excellent idea," says one of the photo assistants, whose enthusiasm for the project momentarily overcomes her good sense. If you want to last at *Fashionista,* you do not offer compliments to people Jane is trying to skewer with her eyes. "We can get before and after shots of them."

The annual wedding issue already has one layout with regular women wearing bridesmaid dresses. There is no way Jane will allow two. She feels the same way about regular women as she does soap opera actresses. As far as she's concerned, soap opera actresses *are* regular women.

"Yes, an interesting idea and I'm sure it would be perfect for your average Australian." Jane gives Marguerite an artificial smile. It's the only kind she's capable of. "However, here at *Fashionista,* we're not dressing kangaroos. Our readers are a little bit more sophisticated."

"Our readers weren't kangaroos," Marguerite says pleasantly. She's trying to appear as if the insult doesn't bother her, but her hands are clenched tightly at her side.

"Right, of course. Wallabies, then. Regardless, your idea is cute but I'm afraid it's just not right for us. If you stay around long enough, you'll probably get a feel for what is *Fashionista* and what isn't *Fashionista.* For the moment, I think *Fash-*

ionista is escaping you. Read a few more issues and get back
to me."

Marguerite smiles tightly. "That's all right. I'm willing to
take another stab at it. I believe the memo said three ideas?"

Terrified, with good reason, that the loathed editorial director might come up with another impressive suggestion,
Jane demurs. There are only three minutes to go. "No, I'm
sure I said only one. Let's give someone else a chance." She
looks around. "Lydia?"

"How about camouflage fatigues? They're a trend du jour."

Trend du jour is one of Lydia's favorite phrases and she
uses it without any sense of self-conscious irony, as if some
current styles really are more current than others.

Jane nods. These are the sort of ideas she likes—ones that
aren't from Marguerite and that we've done before. She likes
to trod familiar ground and it's tough to blame her. Our readers, who she has a hard time remembering, don't seem to
mind what we write about as long as we show pictures of
famous people. Lydia will find three examples of stars sporting the camouflage look and that will be that. "Good. Go
after it. Who's next?" Since I'm sitting next to Lydia, Jane's
gaze naturally settles on me. "Vig."

Although I always have a few ideas swimming in my head,
I know these aren't the sort that Jane will like and I try to
think of a trend du jour to toss out. Then I hear the sound
of change jingling—a sure sign that Jane's assistant is near. A
second later, Jackie is standing in the doorway nodding discreetly to Jane. The last plane for Bangor has closed its door.
This meeting is over. "Well," I say, "I thought we'd do a piece
on—"

Jane interrupts me, as I knew she would. She's already
standing up. "That's very nice, Vig, but I've got to run. I have
an important appointment that completely slipped my mind.
See you all Tuesday," she says, before remembering Marguerite. She will not leave us alone with her and her dangerous bridesmaid ideas for long. "Ah, I mean Monday. See

you all Monday." She darts out the door and the rest of the staff waits a respectable five heartbeats before following close on her heels. They dash to their desks, grab their suitcases and wheel their compact one-pieces out to the elevators. Five minutes later I'm the only one left on the floor.

Superwoman

Maya thinks that I'm only attracted to emotionally unavailable men.

"Workaholics, cheats, mama's boys. It's a freak show of guys who can't make a commitment and you're the ringmaster," she said after my last relationship ended unceremoniously in the produce aisle of the Associated supermarket on the corner of Bleecker and LaGuardia. While I was watching Michael debate the relative merits of green bananas—sure, he wanted a banana now but would he want one in three or four days when this bunch finally ripened—the unfeasibility of the relationship hit me. The uselessness of the entire thing hit me like a blast of heat from a very hot oven, I said goodbye and walked out of the store alone. Michael didn't notice. He was too busy reassuring the bananas that it wasn't them, it was him.

"It's like a superpower with you," Maya continued. "Being able to find emotionally unavailable men at fifty paces and through concrete walls is what you bring to the Hall of Justice. I mean, if there's a room full of single well-adjusted men, wholehearted and unscarred, you're inexorably drawn to the only one who just broke up with his girlfriend of four years in the parking lot."

This much is true. I met Michael at one of those serial dating evenings that Maya dragged me kicking and screaming to the week before Valentine's Day. He was there to pick up his sister. But it's not a superpower. Or if it is, then it's a silly power, the sort someone thought up after all the good ones were taken. I'm like a Wonder Twin without Gleek and the mass appeal of seventies kitsch.

"There must be some way to harness your power," she added, with a laugh. She is only half joking. "Like, maybe we can rent you out by the hour to women who want to know before they expend all that time and energy if their relationship is going to go anywhere. Ooh, maybe we can get large groups of women to gather with their men in one place, like Tupperware parties. We'll line them up and have you go down the row to see who you are attracted to." She gave me a considering look, as if I were there in the trenches with her, devising a business plan. But I wasn't. I was in the real world where my superpower isn't good for anything but pain and disappointment. "Then we'd have to charge by the man, I suppose, although we will, of course, offer volume discounts."

Maya rattled on in the same vein for several minutes more, discussing T-shirt designs and Oprah appearances, but I was no longer listening. I was no longer paying attention, because a procession of former boyfriends was marching through my head with considerable force. Michael, who was unable to commit to a green banana. Scott, who refused to even use the word *date*. Ethan, who always called me Jevig, after his old girlfriend Jennifer. Dwight, Thaddeaus, Kevin, Rob. It was a long parade of also-rans. "New topic," I said, taking the napkin away from her. She was sketching our logo—Cupid with a crossbow aimed at his own heart—on a napkin.

But I'm thinking of Maya's words now. I'm recalling her scathing business plan now because of Alex Keller's sandy brown hair and his light green eyes and his welcoming smile. I'm instantly attracted and have enough sense to know that this cannot be good.

Man and Myth

I'm unprepared for Alex Keller's enthusiastic welcome. I've come here straight from work, despite reservations and other things I'd rather be doing, and I'm all ready to sweet-talk my way into his apartment. That he would simply open the door and invite me in is not on a list of possible outcomes, and I stare at him for several seconds uncomprehendingly.

"You're here," he says, grinning widely. "Great. Come in." He's wearing tan cutoffs with a maroon T-shirt that says Springfield Civic Center Ice Crew. The shirt is old and torn and looks like some ancient papyrus scroll that will disappear into a cloud of dust if you touch it. He is barefoot. "You're a little early but I'm almost ready. Please sit down."

Alex Keller's living room is sparse—dark blue couch, thirteen-inch TV, aged telephone stand—and is dominated by a recently refinished wood floor hidden partially by a small light blue area rug. Since my host is gesturing to the couch, I walk toward it. I walk toward it and notice as I get closer that its diagonal position has created a storage space for an assortment of small appliances, including an iron, a blender

Lynn Messina

and an old-fashioned rotary telephone. The jerry-built closet leads me to conclude that he, like Anna, doesn't have closets. I admire his bravery. Catercorners are the provenance of the rich and you don't often see catercornered bookshelves and sofas outside of magazine pictorials, the sort that *Fashionista* specializes in. You have to own a five-story town house in order to be able to spare the floor space the arrangement requires.

"Quick should be back any minute now," he says, carrying sneakers and socks into the kitchen, where he sits down on a wooden folding chair. My perspective affords me a clear view of his kitchen with its black-and-yellow wallpaper and pint-size fridge, and I watch him pull on his socks, the muscles in his arms bunching in response to the activity. Alex Keller has biceps. I'm not expecting this. Despite its deteriorated state, the T-shirt holds up. "A neighbor is helping out in the meantime."

There is a misunderstanding here. It's not me he's expecting. I've known this from the moment the doorman downstairs let me go up without asking my name. I'll tell him who I am but not right now. Right now I want to watch him put on his sneakers. The novelty of a friendly Keller is seductive and I'm loath to bring the experience to an end. In a minute I'll tell him my name. In a minute I'll reveal all and his pleasant countenance will turn sour and pinched and he'll start throwing obscenities at my head. That moment can wait.

"You'll like Quick," he says, tying the laces of his Adidas into double knots. "He's got large puppy-dog eyes that melt your resolve every time."

I don't know if Quick is a beloved pet or a beloved son. Keller's spotless record only revealed his address and telephone number; it didn't list dependents. "All right," I say, to be vague.

Keller smiles. He has a great smile, a little shy and dimpled. "But you have to be strong. A little discipline never hurt anyone."

Hearing Alex Keller, ordinarily an id on the rampage, expound on the benefits of discipline, breaks the spell. Despite his dimples and his biceps and his lively green eyes, I open my mouth to introduce myself. But before I get a chance, the doorbell rings and Keller jumps to his feet. "There's the boy now."

Keller disappears around a corner and I hear him chatting with a neighbor. "Did he give you any trouble?"

"Nope, he's a darling," answers a soft, breathy female voice. "It's a beautiful day and we had a lovely time at the park sunning ourselves."

"Great. Thanks again for your help."

"My pleasure. Are we still on for dinner tomorrow?"

Although I can't see her, I know this woman is curvaceous and blond with a cute nose and heart-shaped face. All breathy women are.

"Of course," he says. "How's eight?"

"Come by at seven and I'll serve cocktails," she offers. There's a flirtatious lilt to her voice that I'm very familiar with. You can't go to the Beauty Bar or Man Ray on a Saturday night without hearing it, which is why I stay far away from such trendy places.

"Sounds good. So I'll see you then," he says, winding down the conversation. "And thanks again for helping out."

"Really, it was my pleasure."

Of course it was. What woman wouldn't want a man who looks like Keller in her debt?

I hear the door close and prepare myself to meet Quick. If he's a boy, then it's just as well that Keller is a bad-tempered, emotionally unavailable co-worker with multiple personalities, because my skills with children, especially little ones, are undeveloped.

Quick turns out to be a chocolate Lab. He is large and consumes more space than a catercornered couch. His movements are ponderous and deliberate and he seems to be considering each step before he makes it. He is wagging his tail in greeting, but it's like an oscillating fan on slow. There is nothing swift about him.

"An odd choice in names," I say because it's the first thing that pops into my head, but I'm not sure if this is the sort of thing you can say to a besotted dog owner.

Keller smiles, revealing the devastating dimples and shyness. I can feel myself staring with a sort of gape-mouthed stupidity and I try to pull myself together. Emotionally unavailable, I chant in my head. Emotionally unavailable. The legendary bad temper, nowhere in evidence, doesn't seem so important.

"No, Quick isn't very quick. He's seven now, but even when he was a puppy he never had much energy," Keller says. "I took him to the vet to see if he had low blood pressure or an overactive thyroid or something like that but everything checked out okay. I think he's just a very lazy dog who prefers to stay in one place. Like Nero Wolf, without the mystery-solving capabilities."

I don't know if Nero Wolf is a real character or a fictional one, so I don't pursue it. Instead I say, "Why Quick then?"

Hearing his name, the chocolate Lab meanders over to me and leans his body against my leg. I pet his soft fur gently, even though I'm not sure if he's seeking affection or using me as support.

"It's the other kind of Quik—the chocolate drink with the cartoon rabbit. We had two dogs named Pepsi and Sprite while I was growing up. I wanted to keep the beverage thing alive," he explains, "and Snapple or Shasta just didn't seem right."

"Shasta?"

"Shasta, Fresca, Tab. I dug deep and tried them all out. He was Yoo-hoo for a few days but that didn't play well at the dog run. It sounded like I didn't know my own pet's name. I could feel the other owners judging me. I think one lady was about to call the ASPCA and report me for doggy abuse."

I'm surprised that a man who has done everything possible to alienate the people he works with on a daily basis would care what strangers think. But then again, it's not like he actually works with us on a daily basis. I scratch Quik's back and his tail makes a halfhearted sweep. I know I should tell Keller who I am but my moment of resolve is crumbling.

Emotionally unavailable. Emotionally unavailable.

"All right, boy," he says, picking Quik's leash off the floor and tugging him gently in the direction of the door. "Come on, one more walk. Let's go introduce your new friend Kelly to all your other friends at the dog run." Keller winks at me. "We don't use *d-o-g-w-a-l-k-e-r* because I don't want him to feel abandoned."

"All right," I say, charmed by this logic.

He hands me the leash. "Here, why don't you take him? You guys should get to know each other."

I take the leash, wrap it around my hand a few times and tug on it authoritatively. I'm trying to look like a professional, but Quik isn't fooled. He yawns at me with long yellow teeth and leads the way out of the apartment.

I follow Quik to the elevator and push the button while Keller locks up his apartment. I look at my watch. It's almost five-thirty and I wonder for the first time when the real Kelly is supposed to show up. I know I should say something but by now there are other factors at work aside from his dimples and biceps. And it's more than just the stunning embarrassment I'll feel when I reveal the truth. Quik is involved now. He and I are getting to know each other. I can't callously abandon him.

At Seventy-fourth and Broadway, Keller's apartment is just a block and a half from Riverside park. During the walk over, Quik behaves and makes it look as if I'm leading him, even though it's really the other way around. For a dog with no energy, he is certainly strong.

"He gets along with everyone, except Julie Andrews's walker," he says as we cross West End Avenue.

It's a beautiful mid-August day, the sort summer brides pray for—sunny, warm, breezy and gentle. I breathe deeply and absorb summer. You don't need a house on Fire Island to enjoy the season.

"Julie Andrews's walker?" I ask. I don't know why I'm surprised. When you live in New York, you are surrounded by celebrities. They stand on street corners with you while the light changes; they wait behind you in line at Balducci's.

"Yeah, I don't know why he doesn't like this little feller." He pats Quik on the head affectionately. "From what Adam tells me—Adam is Quik's previous friend—the guy took an instant dislike to Quik. So don't be offended if a short troll-like man scurries off in the opposite direction with a poodle. I think he has unresolved issues with his mother."

This description fits the Keller of myth so well that I whip my head around and look at him intently. I'm trying to detect some hint, some small indication that he knows who I am, but there is nothing. His green eyes are staring ahead at the tree-lined park.

"Here we are, boy," he says to Quik, as we open the first gate of the dog run. The dog's temperament remains even. It does not quicken with excitement or slacken with dread.

We are in the fenced-off area but I'm wary of letting Quik go. There are so many dogs running around, so many bouncing, athletic, robust, energetic dogs darting to and fro that I begin to fear for Quik's safety. Does he really come here every day?

"The first rule of good parenting," Keller intones wisely in my ear, "is knowing when to let go."

I have never met a man in my dating demo who knows any rules of parenting let alone the first one of *good* parenting and I stare dumbly at him. Emotionally unavailable, I tell myself. Emotionally unavailable.

Keller bends down on one knee and unhooks Quik's leash. Rather than run like a child for the monkey bars, Quik meanders over to a corner in the shade and lies down. Nap time.

We sit down on a green bench along the fence where other pet owners and dog walkers are sunning themselves and talking. We are upwind and unmolested by the scent of urine.

"So, do you think you can handle him?" he asks, closing his eyes and turning his face toward the sun. I'm left to marvel at his handsome face with impunity and find myself almost pining for the other Keller, the ogre who roars at villagers for stepping into his swamp.

I'm silent because I don't know what to say. Yes, I think I can handle Quik, but even though I hate my job I'm not quite ready for a career change. I'm not quite ready to give everything up, but Keller tempts me very much. He makes me want to quit *Fashionista* so that I can take his dog to the park every day.

"Like I said on the phone, you come highly recommended and I trust you implicitly with Quik. I know your schedule is pretty full already and you're insanely busy, but it would only be three days a week. And you don't have to take him out for hours and hours." He laughs. "As you can see, Quik doesn't do much here that he doesn't do at home."

This is almost true. Quik is lying on his side sleeping but he has company. A collie-golden retriever mix has sidled up next to him. They both look peaceful.

"I'll have to check my schedule, of course," I say evasively, glad that he has given me something to cling to. "I don't think I'm that busy but I shouldn't commit until I'm sure."

This is the right answer. Keller smiles. "Fair enough."

"What happened to Adam?" I ask, in the silence that follows. I know I should fess up now but I don't want to end this. I've never sat in the dog run on a breathtakingly beautiful day with a handsome man who knows the first rule of good parenting. It might never happen again.

Connecticut Small Talk

Maya lives in the Future, in a sleek silver thirty-five-story building on the corner of Third Avenue and Thirty-second Street. It looks like one of those pictures of the twenty-first century that you used to see, the sort that depicts nuclear families in their polyester jumpsuits enjoying life on Mars. Its Experimental Prototype Community of Tomorrow quality is what attracted Maya in the first place. Enamored of all things kitsch, she was hooked the second she wandered past it on the way to the movie theater. Other people see the town houses on Bedford or the towers on Central Park West and lose their hearts but not Maya. Maya needs a steel-plated facade, a space-age lobby and the word *future* spelled out in red letters in that clunky old computer font.

A one-bedroom in the Future does not come cheap and Maya has had a steady stream of roommates, some better than others, all of whom have lived behind a thin artificial wall that went up as quickly as it will come down. The L-shaped living room lent itself to graceful subdivision and the resulting spaces are not large but certainly comfortable enough to justify the rent.

Maya lives on the fringe of two neighborhoods. She's almost Gramercy, not quite Murray Hill. Getting there is a challenge, especially when you're coming from an apartment on the Upper West Side, and even though she e-mailed me the schedule of construction the MTA is doing on the N and R trains, I'm surprised to find out that they're not running from Times Square. I arrive at her dinner party a half hour late and with a sad bouquet of dying daffodils in my grip. I meant to bring wine, but when I couldn't find a liquor store I grabbed a bunch of flowers from a Korean grocer. I considered and dismissed the idea of buying a bottle of twelve-percent merlot at the supermarket. There are worse things than showing up empty-handed.

Answering the door in oven mitts and her mother's cast-off apron, Maya welcomes me with an exuberant hello and sends me to her bedroom to drop my backpack. Her bedroom is small and fits only her bed (double) and dresser (makeshift collection of plastic milk crates piled one on top of the other and secured with duct tape). The walls are white, bare and smooth, a pile of paperbacks congregate in a confused crowd at the head of her bed and clothes hang from a metal rod installed on the back of the door to accommodate the overflow from the narrow closet. Next to the bed is a paint-splattered garbage-picked stepladder that serves as a nightstand. A picture of her family—mother, father, brother, other brother, Grandfather Harry—rests next to an alarm clock.

The disheveled, half-finished, seams-still-showing bedroom is in sharp contrast with the living room, which is unnaturally neat and organized. Maya didn't just scour estate sales and flea markets for the right blend of Eames and Sears, she internalized a philosophy. The result is a living room that has the disturbing sterile air of an Electrolux commercial. You never touch anything because fingerprints on the Formica are like a reproach: You really should be wearing white elbow-length gloves.

I duck my head into the kitchen with offers of assistance, but I'm handed a stack of cloth napkins and sent away to do busywork. Folding napkins and placing them next to plates is not the sort of helpful I want to be, but I content myself with making odd, fanlike creations that resemble abstract swans. Today the card tables are set up on the sleeping side of the Sheetrock wall. Maya's roommate, a small Indian woman who worked as a pastry chef in one of Manhattan's finest French restaurants, had recently returned to her hometown in Goa with fifteen hundred dollars of Maya's money. She'd opened envelopes addressed to Maya, extracted checks and deposited them into her own account. This theft, coming in the wake of two major disappointments—agent and boyfriend—hardly registered on Maya's radar. Her only complaint was that Vandana had spelled *deposit* wrong, adding an *e* at the end.

"I'm a copy editor, for God's sake," she said. "It offends me on a professional level."

This is why she's having a dinner party tonight. Temporarily free of the constraints of communal living, she wants to revel in the novelty of going to bed with dishes in the sink, of having people over until four in the morning, of leaving three card tables smack-dab in the middle of the room. I can relate to the giddy feeling of temporary freedom. Before my roommate moved out two years ago, I cherished those evenings when I had the place to myself.

With seven swans swimming on the table, I can distract myself no longer and reluctantly submit to Connecticut small talk in the living room. Maya's high school friends are pleasant. Sophie, Beth, Tina and Michelle (in descending height order, which is how they always arrange themselves) are pleasant and blond and have politics but the wrong kind and employ the sort of social graces that earn the approval of people like Emily Post and Queen Elizabeth II. They make me uncomfortable. Their conversation is always town and country, and even though I don't know who these people are, they continue to drop names as if they're pistachio shells. Mrs. Frothingham-Smythe, no doubt a social scion in Greenwich, doesn't play well in New York City and anecdotes about her son's shocking behavior (refusing to join Ashley Bennett in mixed doubles!) don't carry the same narrative weight. I stifle a yawn and glare at the kitchen door, willing Maya to stick her head out and say she needs help killing the fatted calf.

I'm sitting next to Greg, Beth's fiancé, a meek Walter Mitty type whose vivid inner life is not a determined fact. His stare is often blank and empty, and it's very easy to assume that he's not piloting an eight-engined navy hydroplane in his mind.

"How are you, Vig?" he asks me, revealing that he knows my name. We have been thrown together a few times at Maya functions, but this is the first time he's ever addressed me directly.

Before I can answer, Beth, who is sitting adjacent to me, breaks off her story about Edna McCarthy's highlighting disaster (zebra stripes!) and says, "Yes, how are you, Vig?" Her voice has a convincing touch of sincere concern but I'm not fooled. She is only asking because the manual says she should and she's not about to be outmannered by her timid fiancé.

"I'm fine. Things are busy at work," I say, giving the sort of stock answer you do to aunts and uncles you only see at Christmas and Easter. "How are things with you?"

I direct this question to Greg, but he doesn't answer. He's been with Beth for so long that he doesn't open his mouth or take a deep breath or even formulate a thought. He knows the routine too well to bother with these things. "Greg has some very exciting news." She pauses here to give me a second to prepare myself. "He just got a promotion. Say hello to Slokam-Beetham's new junior VP of marketing management."

"Congratulations," I say, although I don't really believe this position exists. It sounds like nothing.

Beth beams. "Thanks. We're so happy. It's what we've been waiting for. Now we can start looking at houses."

I ask the requisite follow-up question—"Oh, where are you going to look?"—even though I know the answer. They're going to look within five minutes of Beth's mother, in Riverside, in Cos Cob, in Old Greenwich.

While Beth rattles off the expected response with one curve ball, Westport, tossed in for good measure (now that Martha has moved!), I glance at Greg, whose expressionless face suddenly reminds me of a goldfish staring dumbly at the world outside its glass bowl. Jump out, I want to say, jump out and breathe the air. But I don't. I won't interfere in things that I know nothing about. Maybe fresh air will suffocate him.

The conversation turns to topics outside my demo (18 to 35, urban, single) like fixed-rate mortgages and quality of schools and property taxes and I excuse myself. There are some things I cannot listen to, even to be polite.

In the kitchen, Maya is grating manchego. "How's it going out there?" she asks, sprinkling the cheese on the asparagus tartlet appetizer.

"They're having a very grown-up discussion about school districts. Beth is reciting reading-level statistics and percentages of kids who go on to college. It's making me very depressed," I say, leaning against the counter and watching her work. "Are you sure you don't need help?"

"Here. Lightly season the salad." She hands me a pepper grinder. "I know. It gets to me too sometimes—the house, the SUV. I don't get it," she says, putting the appetizer into the oven.

"It's not that," I insist, but it is that—at least partly. I don't want the house in the suburbs and the gas-guzzling SUV and the uniform green lawn and the smug satisfaction of having a guest room. Space, just like everything else, is a commodity, and sometimes it comes at too high a price. But I envy their clear-sightedness. I envy the confident way they know what they want. The people in the other room are immaculate; there isn't a speck of doubt on them.

"What is it?"

I'm incapable of doing anything lightly and the salad suddenly looks speckled. I take out the leaves hardest hit, mostly the top layer, and throw them in the garbage when Maya isn't looking. Then I toss the salad with orange plastic tongs. "I don't know. I think it's their certainty. They know what they want," I say, trying to put my finger on it, "and they're going after it without paralyzing themselves with too much thought."

"They want to be their parents. It's not something they think about," she says dismissively. Then she inspects my handiwork, wipes her hands on a striped dish towel and withdraws a bottle of red wine from the cabinet. "You lasted more than a half hour," she observes, uncorking the cabernet sauvignon after a small struggle. "I expected you to come hide in the kitchen long before now."

Although Maya is still fond of the old high school gang, she can't spend too much time in their company without wanting to hit her head against a brick wall. There is an unremitting sameness about who they are: investment bankers and lawyers and insurance salespeople and accountants.

"It's the world's one crime its babes grow dull," she said one night over Midori martinis—tumbled, of course.

We were in the lounge at the Soho Grand hotel, dwarfed by giant lampshades and bathed in golden light. "Yes," I said, although I think the world has many more crimes than this.

"It's a poem," she explained, "that always reminds me of my friends from high school.

> Let not young souls be smothered out before
> they do quaint deeds and fully flaunt their pride.
> It's the world's one crime its babes grow dull
> its poor are oxlike, limp and leaden eyed.
> Not that they starve but starve so dreamlessly.
> Not that they sow, but that they seldom reap.
> Not that they serve but have no gods to serve.
> Not that they die but that they die like sheep.

"They're not so bad," I say now, thinking now how easy it is to starve dreamlessly.

Maya laughs, assuming I'm only being polite, and pours the wine. But it's more than a reflex, more than just instinctive diplomacy, that sparks the statement. Childhood friends are continuity, uninterrupted connections between selves, and you hold on to them. You hold on to them and you love them, but sometimes they're not quite comfortable. New York City and Greenwich are like the Galapagos and mainland Ecuador. There's a wide gulf between the two, and a different language has developed over time.

Terms of Reference, August 19: Cultivate Hustle

"Hustle?" I ask, squinting my eyes to make sure I read the word right. Maya has given me my own copy of her new life manual. She reduced the font to seven point, printed out three months' worth of terms and bound the fifty pages together with a thin blue ribbon. The end result is a book with print so small it's like the condensed version of the OED—you need a magnifying glass to read it.

"What's this?" I asked earlier, when she'd handed me the crude notebook.

"It's the pocket edition. You're my sponsor," she said in a tone that suggested she was spelling out the obvious.

"Your sponsor?"

"Yes, my sponsor. It's your job to keep me on track," she explained, as if giving herself a keeper were an everyday experience. "I'm like an alcoholic and these are my steps to recovery. When you think I'm straying from my core objectives, you have to reel me back in."

I accept the responsibility of sponsorship because I don't believe it's a long-term commitment. Maya will get bored with accountability and regimens within a week and move on to something else. This is her way. In the dozen years I've known her, there have been many first days of the rest of her life.

"What does 'cultivate hustle' mean?" I ask now, laying the book on the table—the pocket edition is too thick for a pocket—and starting the long cleaning process. Maya's small kitchen doesn't have much counter space and to compensate she stacks dishes and puts them on the floor. She wants to leave them on the floor overnight but I can't do that. I can't sleep knowing mice are treating her kitchen like the fairground in *Charlotte's Web*. I put a pile of salad plates into the sink.

"You know hustle," she says, watching me with disapproval. It's her house and her dinner party and there is no way she can let me clean up without feeling agitated. I use my thumb to scrape off dried cheese and Maya huffs angrily. My every action is like a rebuke. "Here—" she pushes me aside and puts on yellow rubber gloves "—let me do that."

"I know hustler."

Maya gives me a disgusted look and explains. "Since I no longer have an agent and quite possibly might never get a new one—"

"Don't be ridiculous. You haven't even started loo—"

Maya interrupts with a dripping yellow hand. "Uh-uh. August 15," she says.

Her comment is nonsensical and I stare at her for a second. "What?"

"Terms of reference, August 15."

I find August 15 and read aloud. "Face reality."

"Check," she says. "The reality of the situation is that I don't have an agent and there's the very real possibility that I'll never have an agent again. I've got to deal with that." She squirts blue dishwashing liquid onto a sponge. "Actually, I did deal with it, four days ago. I've moved on to new challenges."

"But, Maya, you're going to get a new—"

"Buh!" she says, raising her hand like a traffic cop's. "I'll have none of that soul-destroying optimism in my house, only clear-eyed cynicism tempered with despair."

"That sounds horrible," I say, appalled.

My clear-eyed honesty earns me an annoyed look. "Vig, you're my sponsor. Either support me in everything I do or let me find someone else."

Neither option is acceptable, so I change the subject. "You were explaining hustle...."

"Yes, since I no longer have an agent and quite possibly might never get another one, I need to find a satisfactory backup career in case bestselling author doesn't work out. I can't copyedit all my life."

Copyediting is one of those tedious jobs you're glad someone else has to do, like data entry or toll collecting, and I'm not surprised that Maya wants to get out. Editors treat copy departments as though they are necessary evils that must be endured—like traffic on the way to your summer share—and I'm amazed that she's lasted this long.

"What do you want to do?" I ask. This is the question I ask myself almost every morning when I wake up and the answer always escapes me. I don't know what I want to do. I don't know what I want to be when I grow up, so I stay at *Fashionista* year after year hoping one day blinding inspiration will strike. Maya is different. She's always known the answer and suddenly it doesn't seem fair that she find a second dream before I find a first.

Maya shrugs. "I'm taking suggestions. I'm supposed to know by August 30, so please get your ideas in by the twenty-eighth at the latest."

There is now a clean stack of dishes next to the sink along with bowls and serving utensils and I pick up a towel. I don't know where anything goes, and I start opening and closing cabinets until I see something familiar.

"In the meantime," she continues, "I want to try writing magazine articles. That's where hustle comes in. I need to be more proactive in pitching ideas. Waiting for you to become editor in chief and start assigning me stories doesn't seem to be working."

"I didn't know you were so invested in my career," I say, a green plastic colander in hand. I'm staring at the cabinets, trying to remember which one has the plastic bowls. This is like a game of Concentration and I'm losing. "What magazines are you going to pitch?"

"It seems like a good idea to start with the ones I copy-edit for. I know people there."

Maya works mostly for women's magazines such as *Glamour* and *Cosmo* and *Marie Claire*. Their field of interest is small and articles travel a limited circuit from sex and relationship back to beauty and health. I can't see Maya embracing any of these things. "You know you're just going to be writing stories about antioxidants and ten ways that it's okay to change for your man."

She makes a pained expression. "It's never okay to change for your man."

I point a spatula at her. "Terms of reference, August 19— Stop thinking independently."

"You're not helping," she says, rinsing a red, green and yellow plate. Maya's collection of dishes has been culled from flea markets and thrift stores across the country. No two plates are alike, but they all have pictures of pretty flowers on them.

I *am* helping. This is what she asked of me: clear-eyed cynicism. "Look, even if you do manage to shrug off the label of copy editor—and I'm not saying you will; these magazines pigeonhole you early and they pigeonhole you deep—you'll be bored out of your mind. I know you, Maya. Test-driving sunscreens is not the sort of thing that will get you out of bed in the morning. It's unsatisfying and dull and so dour and humorless that you might as well be writing stock reports for AT&T," I say angrily. Service items are fact-gathering missions; they're black and white. Maya is Technicolor. She's a Matisse painting and Venetian glass.

This isn't what she wants to hear, and she takes her anger out on a defenseless whisk. It is bent in all the wrong places by the time she's done cleaning it. "It's a beginning," she says, her temper under control now. She tosses the deformed whisk into the drying rack. "I have to start somewhere and this is it. I'll cultivate hustle, write a few articles for women's magazines, put together a portfolio of clips, make a name for myself as an ingenious writer who makes even dull topics interesting and then wait for the good assignments to pour in. A couple of hundred words on which suntan lotion provides the best UVA and UVB protection is a small price to pay. All I have to do is cultivate hustle. It'll be fine," she adds in a calm voice, as though she is comforting me and not herself, "you'll see."

I'm not so sure I will see but I don't say anything. I only hold my hand out for a wineglass and wipe it dry with a damp cotton towel. Maya is convinced that small changes ripple across the pond of your existence. She believes that they snowball into massive alterations that affect everything. But life is not like that. You are not an airline. You can't remove a single olive from every salad served in first class and save one point two million dollars.

An Idea Germinates

Roger's cell phone is programmed to play the theme song to an obscure Swedish children's television show that aired for two years in the early seventies. Childish but not Swedish, Roger exuberantly showed off his new ring one night over dinner, playing the quickly grating tune over and over again until the couple at the table next to us quietly asked him to stop. Embarrassed, Maya averted her gaze, I hung my head in shame, and Roger spent the rest of the meal talking with food in his mouth and complaining in between telephone calls that people don't have manners anymore. It seems that some people never did.

I hear the familiar la-da-do-dada now and cringe. The Met is crowded with summer tourists and the European portrait rooms are thick with sweaty people in fanny packs, but I know that if I turn around I'll see him. He is right behind me, and between *Portrait of a Man* and *Portrait of a Bearded Man,* I'm cornered. I hold myself still like a leopard in the underbrush and hope he passes, but I have no camouflage.

My summer dress is bright blue and I stand out like a beacon against the old Dutch masters.

Roger says, "Vig darling," and I turn around. Since he and Maya are no longer dating, I'm not required to affect pleasure. I'm not required to affect anything at all, and I give him a look of pure disgust when he raises a hand to indicate that he'll be off the phone in a second. I did not come to the Met to stand in Roger Childe's waiting room.

I point across the room to indicate the direction in which I'm going and walk away. My instinct is to scurry out of the building, but I settle with hiding behind a pair of German-speaking tourists who are admiring a Rembrandt. Next to me a woman is drawing the picture with thick gray charcoals and I'm distracted for a moment by her skill. I'm also sketching austere portraits, but I'm using a No. 2 pencil. I've never done this before and my clumsy fingers don't glide across the paper. They stumble and limp and sometimes even fall. I feel self-conscious and silly, but I refuse to let these wayward emotions quell my enthusiasm.

I'm here because I want to be Technicolor. This is the revelation that struck me last night as I was railing against hustle and drying colanders and putting away dishes. I don't want to write boring service items either. The world is so much more interesting than the type of teeth-whitening strips you use.

Enter Pieter van Kessel, a young Dutch designer whose fashions borrow liberally from Rembrandt and Frans Hals. His fall show impressed me and stayed with me and gave me dangerous ideas above my station. I squashed them, of course. I crushed them ruthlessly beneath my heel because up-and-coming designers are not the sort of thing *Fashionista* covers. Rising stars are not in our cosmos. At least not under the Jane regime.

But suddenly I'm eager to plan for the best-case scenario. It will mean going back to Keller's apartment and braving his anger and calming him down enough to gain his compliance. It will mean researching a story idea that has very little chance of coming to fruition. But this is how it has to be done. I still don't believe in the cultivation of hustle, but you can't wait for the world to come to you. You have to go after the things you want. And I want van Kessel. I want to meet him and talk to him and write about his designs. I want to publish a story about the making of a superstar *before* he plays to packed stadiums.

My moment of distraction is fatal. While I'm contemplating the woman's clean lines and my future, the German-speaking couple moves on to the next painting and I'm left without cover.

"Vig," Roger says again, either oblivious or unoffended by my hasty retreat. He's off the phone now and holding the hand of a beautiful redhead in a skintight leather dress. Roger is a creepy guy, the sort who thinks up catchy nicknames for serial killers or peeks into the women's bathrooms, but I don't think of him as the type to go for skintight leather dresses. J. Crew only makes tasteful jackets.

Roger is of medium height and build and is plagued by a persistent acne problem that is exacerbated by encroaching baldness—his hairline is receding, followed closely by an army of pimples that cannot march fast enough across the plains of his scalp to keep up with its retreat. Accutane did not help and only made spending time with him and Maya unbearable. Roger is quiet and introspective when he's drunk.

"Sorry about that, Vig," he says, kissing me on the cheek. When he and Maya were dating, there were no cheek kisses or darlings. "I was leveraging information. It was a very important visit."

Roger believes that language is something you bend to your will instead of the other way around. He changes nouns into verbs and invents new usages. He thinks he's revolutionizing the English language but he's not. He's just speaking nonsense.

"Vig darling, meet Anthea," he says, introducing me to his companion, whose eyes are so large and round she seems right out of a Margaret Keane painting.

I offer my hand. "Hi, I'm Vig Morgan."

She takes a second to read and interpret my gesture before grasping my hand. Her grip is so loose and cold that for a moment she seems dead. "Hi."

"Vig's a friend of Maya's."

"Oh," she says in such an arch manner that I naturally conclude that the only Maya she knows is Roger's psycho bitch ex-girlfriend.

"She's an editor at *Fashionista* magazine," he adds, giving me more context.

Anthea looks interested. "That should be cool."

"Yes," I say, because it should be.

"Anthea works in a shop on Twenty-second. It's called De-Mask," he says casually. "Ever hear of it?"

DeMask is one of those sex shops that sells everything from inflatable butt plugs to male chastity belts. I'm not intimately acquainted with the establishment, but I've seen their ads in the *Village Voice*. "The Mask? No, I can't say I have. Do they sell costumes?"

Roger is annoyed by my ignorance and is about to elaborate but Anthea giggles. "Yes, sort of," she says, before adding, "If you ever need one, you should drop by. All our latex originates in Europe."

"In Europe?" This is not an area of the fashion industry I'm familiar with, but I know that a European pedigree is always a selling point.

"Yes, we've got outlets in Germany and Amsterdam."

Roger is not happy with this friendly chitchat. Now that DeMask is a friendly costume shop with Old World charm, he doesn't want to talk about it. He looks impatiently at his watch. "Look at the time. Anthea and I have to engine. We've got somewhere we need to be." He places his hand at the small of her back before leaning in to kiss me again. I'm prepared this time and dart my head in the other direction. His lips meet air. "It was so lovely to see you. You will send Maya my love, won't you?"

There is an awful victorious gleam in his eye. He is expecting me to go running back to his ex-girlfriend of four days with the tale of how he's now dating a drop-dead gorgeous woman with large breasts and a yen for whips and chains, but I don't. I tell Anthea goodbye and return to taking notes on the Delft School. I never say a word about the meeting to Maya.

Still Phase One

Alex Keller opens the door with an angry sneer on his face. Although he's still devastatingly appealing, his posture is more in keeping with what I've come to expect from him and it puts me at ease. Now I'll be able to clear up yesterday's misunderstanding.

"Who are you?" he asks, raising his voice and leaving me in the hallway where the neighbors can listen. "Why are you sabotaging my dog's happiness? What have I or Quik ever done to you that you need to ruin his life?"

I open my mouth to explain, but he doesn't let me. Keller is on a rampage, treading familiar ground, and will not be interrupted.

"Do you have any idea how hard it is to find a dog walker you can trust? Any idea? Do you have a dog?"

I assume this is a rhetorical question, like the last one, and don't answer.

"Well, do you?" he presses, his voice raising thunderously.

"No."

"Do you have a cat?"

"No."

"Do you have a fish?"

"No."

"Are you a pet owner in any way, shape or form?"

"No."

"So you know absolutely nothing about the care and supervision of domesticated animals. You have no idea the damage you've done, do you?"

"No."

"Do you have any idea how hard it was getting that appointment with Kelly in the first place? She's extremely busy and only agreed to see me as a personal favor to a friend. As a *personal* favor to a friend and I wasn't here when she stopped by for our *scheduled* appointment. Do you know what she did when she found I wasn't here? She left a short, abrupt note with the doorman informing me that she doesn't have time to play games and that she'll have to deny herself the pleasure of my custom. And don't be naive. Her use of 'pleasure' was completely facetious."

It occurs to me that I wouldn't want anyone walking my dog who routinely used the word *custom,* but as it was so clearly pointed out to me only seconds before, I'm not a pet owner in any way, shape or form.

Keller takes a deep breath. He's steadying himself. "Now, if you will excuse me. I don't see why I should be afflicted with your presence any longer." He closes the door.

Over the years, Keller has behaved appallingly and no doubt voodoo dolls, hexes and incantations have all been implemented on his behalf, but I'm not a plague on anyone's house.

I knock on the door, hoping that he'll at least come back and stick his eye against the peephole without my having to lean against the bell. I'm here to ask him a favor and am well aware that alienating him further won't help my cause. Still, I'm prepared to do it. I'm prepared to stand on his doorstep and pound on his door and shout his name. I'm prepared to do anything. Jane's downfall, once a part-time fantasy that sustained me during fourteen-hour days, is now a cherished goal. It *will* come to pass.

A dark shadow, which I assume is Keller's eye, covers the hole, and I adopt a posture of deep contrition, stooping my shoulders and looking abashed, even though the image he's seeing of me is warped and tiny.

"I want to apologize," I say, knowing the door is thin. The neighbors are watching *All in the Family* and I can clearly hear every word Edith says. "Please."

He doesn't respond but nor does the shadow move. "I'm very sorry and I would like a chance to explain my motives. I'm distraught to discover what a mess I've made." I don't know what distraught looks like, so I content myself with more pronounced contrition. I tilt my head down. "Please, I didn't mean to sabotage Quik's happiness," I insist, trying very hard to sound sincere. I'm not quite convinced that anyone's happiness has been sabotaged, but saying so at this juncture doesn't seem wise. I decide to wait a few minutes, at least until I've passed the threshold, before instigating a more clearheaded discussion about the dog's daily care and supervision.

Keller opens the door. "Who are you?" he asks, his voice even and well modulated. I'm no longer worried that the neighbors are listening.

"Vig," I say, cringing and preparing myself for the onslaught of curses that are going to be rained on my head.

Instead of raining curses, he furrows his brow. "Vig what?"

Vig is not a common name and it's inconceivable that he knows another one. "Vig Morgan. We work together."

"At Walters and Associates?" I can see him running through the faces he sees all the time at the office. Mine is not one of them.

Walters and Associates? "No, at *Fashionista*."

"Oh," he says, momentarily disconcerted. A faint blush creeps up his neck. He knows that I'm intrigued. He knows

I'm interested and want to hear more about the firm of Walters and Associates. He stares at me silently, carefully considering his next move. Finally he opens the door and steps to the side. "Come in."

Delia's First Job

Alex Keller is a franchise. He's like V. C. Andrews, except he isn't dead and his morbid plots only twist around movie stars. He has no plans to trademark his name.

"Delia's been editing the section for the last two years," he says. "She does everything. Researches events, generates ideas, takes publicists out to lunch, hires writers, writes stories, approves layouts, draws up contracts, selects photos, edits articles, sets deadlines, plans the editorial calendar."

"You don't do anything?" I ask, striving to keep the censure out of my voice. I'm trying not to sound appalled, as if I found deception on a scale this large commonplace, as if I don't think it's something that just governments do.

He shrugs. "I make it possible."

This isn't enough. "That's all?"

"I meet with Lydia from time to time to keep up appearances."

"From time to time?" Disdain creeps into my voice. What he's describing isn't a job, it's a hobby, the sort of thing rich

people do between lunching at the Plaza and buying diamonds at Tiffany's.

"Once a month, sometimes twice."

"And Delia is cool with this?"

He's surprised by my question. I can tell from the way he
raises his eyebrows and stares at me. "Why wouldn't she be?"

"She does the work—you get the credit," I say, highlighting what I think is an obvious point. But nothing is ever as
obvious as I think.

"Please," he says with scorn, as if Delia were some sort of
social or political cause he didn't subscribe to, like Cartographers for Social Justice. "Delia is completely independent.
She plans her days to best suit her, not me. She takes long
lunches, comes in late and leaves early whenever she wants
to. She works quickly and efficiently and doesn't have to look
busy when there's nothing left to do because she works too
quickly and too efficiently. She isn't subjected to the whims
of a tyrannical boss. I don't ask her to get coffee, make my
lunch reservations, pick up my dry cleaning, stay until nine
o'clock to answer my phone or sort through a pile of receipts
to itemize my expenses."

I'm not immune to the allure of independence and self-
sufficiency and the freedom from tyranny. When I was young
and fresh out of college, this is the sort of job I thought I
would have. This is precisely the sort of job I thought I'd have
before I realized that administrative assistants don't actually
assist in the administration of things. They only make photocopies and fill out expense reports and distribute memos.

"Most of the important decisions are left to her," he says,
outlining more of the advantages of his franchise system. "She
has all the responsibility of a high-pressure job but none of
the accountability. It's an ideal environment to learn about
magazines in. Plus, she's a shoo-in for the events editor job
when I leave. Actually, she'd have the job already if Jane
weren't such a stickler about age. Fortunately for me, there's
no way she'd give my job to someone so young, even though

Delia can do it with her eyes closed. But in a year or two, there'll be no stopping Delia. I'll have to step aside or get run over."

Delia is twenty-three. She's the sort of go-getter over-achiever that corporations all over America look for when they're recruiting go-getter overachievers. She completed her undergrad degree at Fordham in three years and, because she wasn't ready to leave her friends yet, she stayed on another year to get her master's. The editorial assistant job at *Fashionista* was the first one she interviewed for and because both Alex Keller and the managing editor had liked her instantly, she was offered the job within twenty-four hours. She is one of those people who will be profiled in an NPR piece before she is thirty. *New York* magazine will include her in a "Thirty Under Thirty" article. She will be running a major publication, if not the world, before a dozen years pass.

I don't have the same hang-ups with age that Maya does— I've never had an agent or goals or a boyfriend for more than six months—but Delia Barker makes me feel old. She makes me feel like the game is already over, like twenty-nine is not the jumping off point that other people say it is, like my life has fallen short of its potential. She is that subtle reminder that you were never intelligent enough, never beautiful enough, never clever enough. You were just always you and that barely covered the cost of admission.

No one has ever worried about my running them over.

How to Build a Better Career

By day, the mild-mannered Alex Keller is an architect.

"Well, not an architect exactly. But I'm close. Only one year of school left," he says, in response to my amazed statement.

I'm wandering around his apartment, taking everything in. This time the bedroom door is open and I duck my head inside, noticing the drafting board in the corner, the shelves full of architecture texts, the models made from plywood that line the floor. I draw the obvious conclusion.

"One year left?" I ask, flipping through a book on structural support. It has been liberally marked up with a pencil and a yellow highlighter. There are calculations in the margins that look like the formula for cold fusion.

"One year." Although he's trying his best to hide it, Keller is nervous. He doesn't know a thing about me and yet here I am, forcing his deepest, darkest secrets from him. This was not my intention. I meant only to come here and ask for his help in overthrowing Jane, but something more interesting has suddenly thrown itself into my path and I'm not about to walk away from it yet.

When I realized his phantomness was the product of extended absences and not smoke and mirrors, I'd assumed that he was doing something useless with his free time. I'd figured he was out shopping or at home watching bad daytime television or sitting in a darkened movie theater in the last row daydreaming of things he'd like to do. It never occurred to me that he was actually doing those things.

"How long?" I ask.

"How long?" He draws his eyebrows together in confusion.

"How long," I say, nodding. "As in how long does it take to become an architect and how long have you been scamming *Fashionista?*"

He flinches at the word *scam* and stares at me for a long time, trying to decide how much to reveal. It's obvious from his stance that he doesn't want to tell me a thing. He doesn't want to reveal any of it, but he has enough sense to know when it's too late to close the barn door. Vig Morgan is a reporter, even though she never actually gets to report on anything. My decoder ring might be a little rusty from disuse but I still know how to follow a lead. With one call to Walters and Associates, I could discover the entire truth. Keller would be hard-pressed to come up with a convincing lie and would know better than to tell me he was working on a story. *Fashionista* only covers interiors and we don't care why a house stands as long as it does.

"That's a tricky question," he says after the silence. "Cooper Union's program is five years for a bachelor's degree, but they accepted all my distribution requirements from my first undergrad degree, so that brought it down to four years. However, four years is for a full-time student, which I wasn't in the beginning."

I don't know if he's being intentionally evasive or simply burying his response under a mountain of detail. "That doesn't answer my question."

He looks at me with innocent green eyes. "Yes, it does. It takes four years to become an architect."

"You've been scamming Ivy Publishing for four years?"

"Actually, I've been availing myself of their generosity for more than five years, but only on a part-time basis," he says, as if this caveat excuses his behavior. It doesn't. Nor does it explain Delia.

"How long has someone else been doing your job?" I ask.

Keller disappears into the kitchen and returns with a beer. "Do you want?" he asks, holding up a bottle of Beck's.

"Sure," I say, accepting the drink. I'm standing awkwardly against one of the white walls and he indicates with a head gesture that I should take the couch. I look at it for a moment and then comply. Quik is lying on the floor next to the couch and he thumps his tail slowly as I lean down to pet him. Quik looks exactly the same as he did the day before and not at all like a dog whose only chance at happiness has been destroyed.

"I'm sorry about yesterday," I say sincerely, feeling bad about the damage I had unwittingly done. "I didn't mean to screw anything up for you. I just came by to talk about something and never got around to it because I was having too much fun hanging out with you and Quik."

"That's all right," he says, sitting on the arm of the couch with his beer. "Quik's a charmer. Kelly will come around. If not, we'll find someone else. It's not a disaster."

Although this is what I think, I'm not convinced that he really does. Just a half hour before he was railing at me for the awful turn I'd done his dog and now, because I know the truth of his identity, he's trying to be agreeable.

He takes a gulp of Beck's before launching into the story of his perfidy. "Delia has been doing my job full-time for almost two years. My assistant before her, Howard, only did half of it. At that point, I was still telecommuting. I'd write, assign and edit articles between classes. I used a lot of writers from the West Coast because their hours were more amenable to my schedule. I could juggle the two things easily and the quality of the section didn't suffer at all."

I'm not surprised he could do both. The events section isn't brain surgery. The two-hundred-word blurbs on celebrity events are completely formulaic. You start with a sentence describing the room—flowers, candles, a few yards of hot-pink silk draped over giant Oscar statuettes. Then you get four or five gushing quotes from celebrities. If it's a D&G party with a high school theme, you ask about their favorite subject. If it's a Jaguar auction to raise money for AIDS research, you ask about their first car. If it's a premiere for an action blockbuster about a shopping mall overrun by a tidal wave, then you ask about their worst shopping experience. Finally, you conclude with some zippy kicker that's cute and smart. It's fluff, complete and total fluff, and someone like Alex Keller can do it with his eyes closed.

"Things got harder when I started the externship two years ago," he continues. "It's a really intense learning environment and suddenly I didn't have time to make the calls and edit the articles. I had a stack of homework this thick and actual projects to work on. It was exciting and overwhelming and when Howard handed in his notice, I thought it was all over. I figured I'd have to suck it up and pay for school myself. But then Delia came in for an interview. She was the first person I saw." Keller is more relaxed now and he smiles at me without the tight lines around his lips. I don't know if it's the confession or the alcohol but something here is good for his soul. "Delia is a dynamo. I knew she'd be perfect the second she walked into my office in her requisite navy-blue interview suit. She had the experience—three years running the student paper at Fordham—and the intelligence. She got her undergrad and master's in eighteenth-century literature in less than four years and completely on scholarship. She was outgoing, had a winning smile and said all the right things. I knew the publicists would love her. And I was right. They do. It's been an ideal arrangement."

"Pay for school yourself?" I ask, when he's done lavishing compliments on Delia.

He looks away, not ready to confess all despite the beer.

"What did you mean, pay for school yourself?"

"Tuition reimbursement," he answers, his voice soft.

"Ivy Publishing is paying for your architecture degree?"

He has the grace to blush. "The company is very generous and will reimburse you for up to three courses a semester. It's in the employee handbook."

This is true. Ivy Publishing is paying for Christine's classes at Peter Kump and the French Culinary Institute. But it's not the same. She shows up for work every day. "It says that because they know you can't possibly carry a full course load and work a full-time job at the same time."

Keller shrugs. "Apparently they were wrong."

I can't argue with this logic. "Didn't someone notice that you were taking classes in the middle of the day, all day?"

"A summer intern once asked me about it, but I took her to a party to kick off some boy band's world tour and that was the last I heard of it."

"That's contributing to the corruption of a minor," I say, only half serious.

His eyebrows draw together again. "No, it isn't."

"You offered her a bribe."

"She was over eighteen." He finishes off his beer and returns to the kitchen to throw the bottle into the recycling bin. "I was about to take Quik out when you arrived. Fancy taking him for a walk again?"

"This is going to take some getting used to," I say, getting to my feet. I very much fancied taking Quik for a walk again.

Keller hands me the leash. "Not at all. You're a natural. I had no idea you weren't a professional yesterday."

"That's not what I mean." Quik shows no enthusiasm at the prospect of fresh air and remains still as I attach the lead. "It's going to take me a while to get used to your being nice. You're an ogre in the office."

"Well, I wouldn't want to foster a friendly environment where people feel comfortable just dropping by my office, would I?" he explains with a self-mocking smile. "And I'm not that bad, am I?"

"You freaked out on me once because I used the copier outside your office," I remind him.

"Only a fool comes between a man and his favorite copier. Itchy has never let me down," he says with his winning smile, as if my overly sensitive nerves were to blame and not his infamous hair-trigger temper. "Clearly you have no idea how frustrating it is to actually take time out of your life to go into the office and not be able to find a working copier."

No, I have no idea how frustrating that is, I think, as he opens the door and leads Quik into the hall. I have to take time out of the office to go into my life.

My 529th Day

Jane's editing style is thorough and compact and consists of passing around your article to other editors to get their feedback. She distributes the raw copy after she's torn it apart with her red pen and her soul-destroying fragments (stupid idea, dumb phrasing, pointless and useless) and the other editors cannot help but see your humiliation. They can't help but see it, and rather than buoy your self-confidence with a polite word or two, they second Jane's comments with exclamation points and heartfelt yesses. By the time you get the story back, you feel like a zebra whose eviscerated carcass has been picked over by vultures.

Since Jane's assistant doesn't do anything other than assist her, I wasn't assigned an article until my first week as an assistant editor. This was something I'd been waiting for for two years, and my enthusiasm did not dim when I learned that it was just one of those hairdo stories, the sort that provides step-by-step directions on how to copy Nicole Kidman's Oscar look. My enthusiasm remained high and I painstakingly translated the stylist's instructions for *Fashionista*'s audience ("Apply quarter-size dollop of Bumble and Bumble Prep to palm and smooth over hair"). The piece was stream-lined (no articles) and never once strayed from the point (all Nicole's hair, all the time), but still Jane found much to crit-icize. She didn't like a single thing about it, and when I fi-nally managed to breathe some life into my deflated ego and type up a second version, she flattened me again, this time with her complete indifference ("And why are you wasting my time with this?").

In the end, the Nicole hair piece went to print in its orig-inal form. When the fact-checkers sent over the edited ver-sion to the stylist, he had so many problems with it that he called me up personally. He rang me up himself to discuss it and we ran through every line. It turned out that the things Jane deemed pointless and useless ("Twist ends and tuck them under") were vital bits of information, without which the hairstyle wouldn't work. The small sense of satisfaction I felt was short-lived. With the next article already on my docket (actual Mother's Day recipes from actual celebrity mothers), it was open season again on Vig.

What I didn't know then was that it is always open sea-son on Vig. Although Jane can't be bothered to read most of the copy we publish, she takes a special interest in mine. Whenever she's frustrated or at loose ends, she calls up a story I'm working on and tears it to shreds. She's like a bored five-year-old with a butterfly's wings in her grasp. With one fierce tug, she grounds me.

Phase One: Accomplished (Finally)

Circumstance and his own intractability force me to blackmail Keller.

"This is my first time," I say, as if apologizing for the lack of resolution in my manner, "so bear with me. And please let me know if I'm not doing it right."

This isn't how I meant to gain his compliance. I had a speech all prepared in my head—in times of crisis, all citizens must do their share to alleviate tyranny—that I delivered with the right amount of patriotic fervor. I could practically hear the "Battle Hymn of the Republic" humming in the background.

Alex Keller was unmoved. "Sorry," he said with a regretful shake of his head. His disappointment seemed genuine. "I can't help you out. I'd like to but Jane McNeill is my greatest ally in the help-Alex-become-an-architect scheme. A new editor in chief might actually want me to show my face at staff meetings or call me into her office at the last minute. With one more year of school left, I can't run that risk. Jane's indifferent editing style really works for me."

"But it makes for an awful magazine," I protested.

He watched as Quik bared his teeth at a frisky Chihuahua who wants to play. The indolent chocolate Lab wasn't having any of that. "The public doesn't think so. Sales are up."

This is true. "All right. But it makes for an awful work environment."

"Then don't go into the office," he said, as if the help-Alex-become-an-architect scheme is something anyone with a little willpower could implement, like an exercise routine. I'm amazed the whole thing hasn't come toppling down on his head before now.

"You know that's not an option," I said impatiently, my voice rising. The woman next to me, who was doing the *Times* crossword while her Chihuahua harassed Quik, looked at me with a puzzled expression. I shrugged.

"Then get a new job. How long have you been there?" he asked.

"Five years," I mumbled, suddenly feeling as though I'd been there four-and-a-half years too long.

"Well, then," he said, as if this answer explains everything, "I don't think a new editor in chief is the change you're looking for. Jane is the system. Either you work within it or you get out. That's the choice you have."

That was what I believed until a third option presented itself. "You owe me. I changed your sister's life," I announced almost peevishly. This is precisely the sort of stupid thing you say when you're being thwarted, and it made Keller laugh.

He laughed with such exuberance and genuine humor that Quik actually got up and dragged his lazy carcass over to investigate.

It was in the wake of this humiliation that I settled on blackmail.

"This is a first for me, too," he says now, my extortion attempt only amusing him further. "But we're both reasonably intelligent people. I'm sure we'll figure out the procedure sooner or later."

Gangster movies have not prepared me for this reaction. He is supposed to straighten his shoulders and draw his eyebrows together in righteous anger and insist that he'll never give in to a scoundrel like me seconds before giving in. "You help us bring down Jane and I won't say a word about your double life." I'm only bluffing. Regardless of how this works out, I won't say a word about his double life. However, he doesn't need to know that. "Either way you play it, things are going to change. Now, there's no guaranteeing that a new editor in chief will require your presence more than Jane does. However, if I tell Human Resources about your scheme, they will fire you. *That* is guaranteed."

Keller nods. "And what do I have to do?"

"Just add an event to the list of parties you plan to cover in future issues."

"Yes, but what are the details? What event, what month?"

"November. It's an opening party for an exhibit called Gilding the Lily. The artist's name is Gavin Marshall. And you might want to throw in a few A-list celebrities to convince Jane that it's a really huge event. I'll take care of the rest," I say, an awful feeling of guilt cluttering my nerves. It's tougher to be a hardened blackmailer than I thought.

"That's it? Just put Marshall on the November party schedule?" he asks, as if outlining the terms of a contract. "And in exchange you won't tell anyone about my double life? That's all I have to do?"

Although I feel awful about extracting a promise under duress, I say, "That's all you have to do."

"All right. And what's to stop me from telling Jane about your devious plan to orchestrate her downfall?" he says, turning the tables on me.

My heart drops in its cavity as I realize I've given too much away. There is nothing to stop him. There is nothing at all to stop him from telling Jane and getting me fired. With our destructions mutually assured, I look at him across the bargaining table. I'm contemplating all possible futures and wondering which one would suit me best. Getting fired from a job I can't seem to quit isn't a tragedy. I smile recklessly. An itchy finger doesn't belong on the activation button of an A-bomb.

"Never mind then," I say, deciding in the end to step away from global thermal nuclear war. There is no point in antagonizing him further; Keller isn't the key player we thought he was. He's so infrequently in the office and so rarely does his job that the plan could go forward without his help and without his knowledge. We just needed to get Delia on board. Delia would no doubt welcome the opportunity to move up the editorial ladder without Jane's prejudices holding her steady on the bottom rung.

"Never mind?" he asks suspiciously.

"Never mind. You've effectively outmaneuvered me, so never mind." I smile to let him know there are no hard feelings. "It was always a long shot anyway."

Keller pats Quik on the head and sits beside me silently for a while. The woman with the Chihuahua stands up and calls, "Here, Cookie. Mummy wants to leave." But Cookie isn't ready to leave. Although her owner may have finished the Saturday crossword puzzle, Cookie isn't done with her game and continues to chase an overly groomed black poodle around the perimeter of the dog run. With a frustrated sigh, the woman puts down the newspaper and scurries after her dog. Keller and I watch, neither one of us trying particularly hard to hide our amusement.

"I'll do it," says Keller, when the woman has Cookie by the leash again.

I'm so involved with the scene that I assume I've misheard him. "What?"

"I said I'll do it."

"Why?" I'm not prepared now for total capitulation. When I introduced the subject a half hour ago I thought it was a very real possibility but after the blackmail and the counterblackmail, I abandoned hope.

Keller smiles. "Three reasons. One—it can't work. Two—I've had a good run. Three—Delia deserves better."

"You don't know the whole plan," I say, feeling oddly defensive. You shouldn't insult things you don't understand.

"I have a pretty good idea," he says, "but that wasn't the real deciding factor. The only way I've been able to rationalize having Delia do my job for the last couple of years was believing that I was just keeping the seat warm for her. A new editor in chief might give her the promotion she deserves."

"That's exactly what I was thinking."

"I know."

I look at him, startled. "You know?"

"You're transparent, Vig. You give everything away with your face."

This is something I've never been told before and I don't quite believe that I'm transparent. I'm capable of great subterfuge and guile. But since he has agreed to help, I don't press the point.

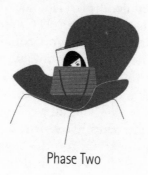

Phase Two

Jane's office is like a pizza parlor. The walls are covered with snapshots of celebrities who have wandered in off the street. Everywhere you look it's Jane and Brad, Jane and Meryl, Jane and Julia. With her arm draped around some famous person's shoulder and her lips smiling in that "we're buddies" way, she looks just like Famous Ray, only without the tomato-paste-splattered white apron.

These photos are vaguely unsettling and whenever I enter her office, I avert my gaze. I always keep my eyes fixed on the view outside, on the lights of Radio City Music Hall and away from the pulsating naked ambition that adorns the walls. Jane is like one of those changelings on soap operas who shows up on some special night claiming to be the il-legitimate daughter of the wealthy land baron. She's an ambitious climber. She wants to be one of the beautiful people. She wants to see and be seen. She wants Page Six to document her every move. She wants to turn her head away from rabid paparazzi.

"What, what, what!" she spurts angrily, when I step inside.

It's not yet eleven-thirty, but Jane's temper is already frayed. Her morning was kicked off with a telephone call from Marguerite, who just wanted to let her know that the private Cessna that was flying her in from Bangor was running a little bit behind schedule. Prince Rainier of Monaco had an important business meeting in D.C. and needed to be dropped off first. Marguerite, who could do nothing but bow her head in the presence of royalty, promised to be in the office no later than noon. This is not the sort of news that kicks off a good morning for Jane. It robs her of the smug satisfaction she had been feeling all weekend and enrages her. There is nothing she hates more than having her plans to thwart thwarted.

"What, what, what!" she says again, determined to take her ire out on anyone who has the misfortune to walk through her door.

"I have coverlines for the November issue," I explain, although she knows exactly why I'm here. Jane never sees anyone unless their purpose is stated, vetted and okayed.

"All right, all right. Bring them here." She is waving her pen in the air like some sort of maniacal sketch artist.

I tighten my grasp on the manila folder and approach her desk. My palms are a little sweaty and my heart is beating abnormally fast. This is it. With Jane on the warpath because of Marguerite's Maine sojourn, there can be no better moment to strike.

I'm holding several folders, as if I've just come from one meeting and am about to go to another. I lay all of them down on her desk and open the top one. "Here they are," I say, my voice stiff. I'm not worried that Jane will notice anything. Her powers of observation are limited to herself. I cough and try again. "It's this page. Right here."

Jane picks up the sheet of paper. She will make a great show of reading it and carefully considering each coverline but none of this will make an impression. None of this will penetrate her indifferent skull and in a week or two I will be called into her office and taken to task for not showing her coverlines. It's a stupid routine, one that I won't miss when Marguerite is in charge.

After grunting a few times, she nods her head dismissively. I pick up my stack of folders but I don't get a proper grasp on them all and the contents of the bottom folder spill all over Jane's desk.

Jane scoffs in annoyance. "What a clumsy mess you are," she says.

"I'm sorry," I say, gathering up the papers. I leave the memo for Marguerite for last. It's right beneath Jane's nose and sooner or later her eyes will connect with her nemesis's name. I move slowly to give her more time.

"What's this?" she asks, finally taking the bait.

"It's just a memo."

"Don't be stupid. I can see it's a memo from the way it says memo in large black letters across the top." She puts on her glasses and scans it quickly. "What's the Gilding the Lily exhibit?"

"Uh, nothing," I say evasively. "Just something Marguerite asked me to look into."

Jane nods and purses her lips. "Why?"

"Why?"

"Why did she ask you to look into it?"

"You'll have to ask her," I say, hoping that she will do nothing of the sort.

"I'm asking you. Why is Marguerite looking into this exhibition?"

"I don't know. She *might* have said something about it being the sort of thing that *Fashionista* should support," I say hesitantly. "She thinks our name needs to be out there more."

"She does?"

"Yes, I believe she said that wherever a celebrity stands posing for shots, our name should be there behind them."

"Really?"

"She said it would boost sales and impress the publisher."

"So, she's trying to impress the publisher, is she?" Jane asks, almost under her breath.

"I don't know," I say, watching her carefully. I can see her mind turning and I know exactly what she's thinking. After five years, she's almost an open book.

"That's all, Vig. Shoo," she says, dismissing me. When I don't leave, she gives me a cross look. "What, what, what!"

"The memo." I hold out my hand.

For a moment she looks as if she won't give it back. "Stupid distraction," she says, balling up the memo, tossing it into her trash can and ostensibly returning to the pile of work in front of her.

I leave the office. Phase two complete.

An Idea Takes Root

Jackie is angry because at her doctoral defense they put her on the defensive.

"It was a terrible, awful, horrible experience that I never want to talk about," she says, bringing up the topic over corned beef sandwiches.

I'm happy to discuss movies or weekend plans or this month's Celeb Watch section, but she has other ideas. She is still fresh from the battlefield and wants to show off her wounds.

"It was just devastating. They kept asking me the same questions over and over again, changing the wording each time and I kept saying, 'No, I don't know the Marxist implications of bell-bottoms,' 'No, I don't understand what Hush Puppies have to do with the value of the Japanese yen,' 'No, I didn't study the economic ramifications of the Triangle Shirtwaist fire.' And why would I? My thesis was on the literature of fashion. What does that have to do with money?" She sighs heavily and bows her head, as if she's just lived through the ordeal again here in a midtown deli. "God, the

way they just kept pounding me with the same question—
it was brutal," she says with a shudder, as though this were
some sort of interrogation technique used on prisoners of
war and not an everyday teaching method designed to help
students realize they already know the answer.

Jackie is *Fashionista*'s only Ph.D., and Jane gets a kick out
of having an overeducated assistant. For her, it's like having
the winner of the Westminster dog show fetch her morning
paper. Jackie's original plan was to get her feet wet in corporate America while waiting for a position to open up in
academia but now she's not so sure. Now she's thanking her
lucky stars that she has a job far, far away from those cruel
tormentors in their ivory towers.

Jane, of course, is receptive to the idea of Jackie staying.
She can't lord her doctorate-assistant over everybody's head
if she doesn't have one. "She says there's a future for me at
the magazine."

There is a future for Jackie at the magazine, but things
move slowly at *Fashionista* and Jackie will have to put up with
a lot before she can grab the brass ring of career advancement. I slurp the last ounce of my soda. "I'm getting another,"
I say, waving an empty Coke can in the air. "Do you need
anything?"

She nods and extracts a dollar. "One piece of Bazooka."

"My treat," I say benevolently. "Consider it a graduation
present."

"Thanks." She smiles and slides the dollar across the table.
"I'll take four quarters then."

I sigh and take the money, admitting that I walked right
into that one. Jackie isn't running out to do her laundry or
looking for a metered space to park her SUV. She's collecting change. She's collecting it because an episode of *Oprah*
informed viewers that saving all your coins can net you fifty
dollars a month. Taking this advice to heart, Jackie has made
the pursuit of change a full-time occupation and sometimes
you see her counting pennies at her desk when she thinks

no one is looking. She now wears cargo pants and weighs her pockets down so heavily with pieces of eight that she sounds like a Salvation Army Santa. The jingling serves as an early-warning system and most times you can duck into an empty cubicle to avoid her.

Although she tries hard to be liked, Jackie is a difficult person to spend time with. This is her first year in New York and she wears her pricey Brooklyn Heights apartment and entry-level salary like a cross. She believes her suffering is more acute than yours, that she's the only one in Manhattan who doesn't have enough money. But the truth is that nobody here has enough money, and after a while, you get tired of her attitude. You get tired of her air of persecution and the way she looks at you—with a combination of fear and suspicion, as if she's Marie Antoinette and you're a blood-mad peasant.

I steel myself for another twenty minutes of thesis talk and poverty laments and return to the table. The only reason I'm here is because of Jackie's access to Pieter van Kessel. She comes from a family of fashion-industry insiders, which is how she got a position at *Fashionista* before one became available. Her mother, a well-known designer for Christian Dior, called up Jane and asked if she had a job for her daughter. Emily, Jane's old assistant, who barely finished college with a 2.8, was fired on the spot.

"So, I was thinking of trying to get an interview with van Kessel for one of the winter issues," I say, broaching the subject cautiously and hoping I'm not as transparent as I feel. I've made lunch seem like a spontaneous thing, like the thought hadn't crossed my mind before we bumped into each other by the elevators at 1:27, but the thought had crossed my mind. It had been zigging and zagging through my brain for hours, and I'd been listening to her jingle-jingle all morning, waiting for the sound to fade. When it finally did, I jumped out of my chair and raced after her.

"Yeah?" she asks, interested. "You think he's good?"

Although Jackie has spent the past five years studying how clothes affect cultural and social identities in different societies, she doesn't know a thing about fashion. As far as she's concerned, an Empire waist is France after Waterloo. She only went to Pieter van Kessel's show because her mother was in town and she only invited me along because she needed someone to act as a buffer. I sat in between the two mademoiselles Guilberts and ran interference until the show started. The lights dimmed and the clothes captured my attention and I left Jackie to fend for herself. As I watched black ball gowns with wide ruffles and silver blouses with flounced sleeves go by, mother and daughter hissed at each other like angry cats. I leaned forward to give them better access.

"I think he has potential," I say, not wanting to rave and gush and give myself away. I've never been this excited about a story before and I'm afraid. I'm afraid that if Jackie or Jane or the fashion gods learn of my enthusiasm, they'll take Pieter van Kessel away.

"That's what Mother said, but I didn't see it."

I'm not surprised. She never once turned her eyes toward the runway. "Your mom should know. She's been around designers for years. How did she hear of van Kessel?" The show had been amazingly low-key. There were a few fashion photographers there, and aside from us and a well-known critic from the *Times,* there wasn't any press.

"His partner used to be John Galliano's right-hand man. Hans sent Mother the tickets," she explains. "He was the small guy who she was talking to after the show. Remember, he was wearing the red velvet smoking jacket and you said he looked like Hugh Hefner?"

Few people leave Dior and one of fashion's superstars to toil alongside a nobody in a dirty basement on the Lower East Side. "That was bold."

"Mother called it career suicide," Jackie says, change jangling as she crosses her legs. "You shouldn't have any trouble getting an interview with Pieter. Mother said the turnout at the show was a disappointment. He'd probably be happy that you even know his name."

I'm not so sure of this. In my experience, designers, even up-and-coming ones, expect you to know their name. They tend to live in hermetically sealed universes in which everyone knows who they are and is wowed by their ideas and flattered when they condescend to talk about their work. "I don't know..."

"Sure he will," she says, impatient now with the topic. We haven't talked about her for almost fifteen minutes and she's starting to wither from the lack of attention. "I'll call Mother and she'll arrange something with Hans. Don't worry about it." She looks at her watch. "I've got to get back to the office. I have to call my travel agent and book a flight to Athens for Christmas," she says with a sigh, as if spending a week in Greece were a hardship. "I promised Mother that I would do it today."

"Athens?" I ask, as though I don't already know everything about her vacation plans. There are few untrod paths with Jackie.

"Yes, Mother wants to go island-hopping. I wish I could look forward to it but I can't. My sister, who always makes these outings bearable, just had a baby, so she won't be coming. It will just be my mother and me and lots of blue water. And the worst thing of all is that Athens is one of my favorite cities and I would love to hang out for a few days after she leaves but it's too expensive. With my rent and salary, I always have to be mindful of my pennies. Mother is paying for the airfare, but I'd have to foot the bill for room and board if I stayed on, which means getting an efficiency in a dreary little pension in the worst part of town. I still have several months to save, but I have to be so careful. My apartment isn't stabilized or anything and even though I've only been there a few months, I'm worried about what they're going to raise it to next year. I mean, I'm already stretched so thin that I can barely afford to use the telephone. Can you believe how much they charge for local calls?"

This is the noise that accompanies me along Fifty-first, down Sixth and up the elevator to the twenty-second floor, but I'm not listening. Jackie's self-involved monologue is only background music. In my head, I'm already writing an article on Pieter van Kessel.

Too Much of a Linchpin

Allison's conversations with her dad are not so much dialogues as lists of complaints.

"The restaurant's host came over while we were still eating dessert and asked us to leave because they needed the table," she says, relating her recent experience at Pó, one of those tiny eateries in the Village that you have to make reservations a month in advance for. "We'd been there too long."

Pause.

"An hour and a half."

Pause.

"No, I know that's not long. And we had gotten the six-course tasting menu."

Pause.

"Yes, the six-course tasting menu has six courses."

Pause.

"Oh, I did the math all right. It comes out to fifteen minutes a course. I don't see how we could have eaten faster. And after five courses, it's no wonder we were a little slow with dessert."

I've heard the Pó story several times today already, although this is by far the most streamlined version. She is not
telling him what she ate (shaved cucumber salad, shitake
mushroom ravioli, pan-seared salmon, braised lamb, assortment of cheeses and warm chocolate cake with cinnamon
ice cream) or the restaurant's pedigree (once owned by TV
chef Mario Batali, who now owns the restaurant across the
street from where she lives. No, it's not very good. They put
snails in everything). She is just telling him the facts. Allison
never lingers over phone calls to Dad. Their relationship is
cursory and abrupt and fulfills a sort of mutual obligation
they both feel toward Allison's deceased mother.

"Of course I'm writing a letter to the owner," she assures
him. Writing letters is a huge part of the Harper routine.
Whether Allison actually composes these documents and
sends them out I don't know but she certainly pays lips service to the notion. "I'll cc the Better Business Bureau and
New York magazine."

Pause.

"Yes, I know. He was a complete bird brain."

This is the signal I've been waiting for and I call Kate and
Sarah to let them know that Allison will be off the phone in
a minute. I know this because, in the end, these conversations
with her father always come down to one of three vital life
lessons: people are bird brains, you can only rely on yourself,
everything is worse than you expect.

"All right. I'll talk to you then." Allison hangs up and
sighs. This, too, is par for the course. She would rather not
have these talks with Dad. They just make her miss Mom
more. Before she can pick up the phone to call Libby or Greta
or Carly to complain about being an emotional orphan, I
stick my head over the thumbtack wall.

"Meeting," I say.

Allison looks up at me in surprise, marveling at my timing. It does not occur to her that I hear every word she speaks.
I hear every syllable she utters, every drawer she opens, every

click she makes with the stapler. "All right. I'll just notify the others."

"I already called Kate and Sarah. They should be by in a second."

She looks at me sharply for a moment; then her eyes stray to the telephone. She's wondering if a second is enough time to talk about Daddy.

"Hey there," says Kate, approaching our cubicles eagerly. "What's up?"

"Progress report," I say, fighting a smile. This feeling of accomplishment, this sense of a job well-done, is new and odd and I want to savor it.

Allison's eyes pop out. "You've made progress?"

"That's what I'm here to report."

"What are you here to report?" asks Sarah, approaching with an iced cappuccino in one hand and a bag of biscotti in the other.

"Progress," I say again.

"Great, let's take this to the bathroom," says Allison, whose fear of being overheard is limited only to plots to bring down the editor in chief. Today she's wearing a beautiful pleated skirt, mesh sandals and a classic black V tee but somehow she looks shlumpy. The outfit is expensive and even if she bought the entire ensemble at Century 21—although I doubt very much she found that skirt in their picked-over racks—it still had to cost half a week's take-home pay. That's the thing with *Fashionista*. Its employees are indentured servants to their wardrobes.

The walk to the bathroom on the other side of the office is long and Allison fills the time with yet another rendition of dinner at Pó. This time she goes into minute detail of how the shitake mushroom ravioli was served and, although she's trying to discourage people from dining there, her diatribe digresses into an advertisement for the restaurant. By the time we get there, my mouth is watering and I have to ask Sarah for a biscotti.

It's odd to eat in a bathroom, even one with leather couches and plush carpeting, and I nibble on the cookie, trying to enjoy it. Sarah is completely at ease. She has the air of a woman who often takes breaks in luxury lounges adjacent to toilets.

Allison checks the bathroom stalls to make sure they're empty before raising the topic that is so dear to her heart. "Tell us everything. Has Keller agreed to help?"

I nod. "He said he'll put the Gilding the Lily show on November's calendar."

Kate looks at me. "Was he very hard to persuade?"

"He was a bit stubborn at first but then he gave in."

"How'd you convince him?" Kate asks.

"I reminded him that he owed me a favor since I changed his sister's life," I say, because there is no reason for them to know the truth. Keller's double life is not my secret to tell.

Sarah raises her eyebrows in surprise. "And that worked?"

Allison flicks her a look of distaste. "Of course it worked. I told you he owed her a favor. That's why she's the linchpin." Allison turns to me. "Excellent. Now on to the next phase. What we need to do—"

"I've already done it."

Allison is shocked. "What?"

"This morning I went into Jane's office with coverlines and accidentally spilled a folder with information about the exhibition," I explained. "Jane saw the memo and was all over it. I couldn't even get it back. She pretended to throw it in the garbage but I know as soon as I closed the door she fetched it out of the trash."

Sarah high-fives me and then giggles. "I can't believe we're actually doing this."

Kate is equally moved and sits down on the couch to contemplate a future without Jane. Only Allison isn't pleased.

"You left a paper trail?" she asks coolly.

I hadn't thought of it in those terms. "I suppose so. But it's just an unofficial memo. And it only has my name on it."

She nods slowly. I feel as though I'm being judged. "And you wrote the memo?"

"I did but I incorporated all the things you mentioned at our first meeting," I say, trying to appease her. Although we are a fashion and lifestyle magazine, we are owned by one of the largest publishing companies in the country and are tied up in corporate values. Project ownership is still a big deal. "I might have written it but it was basically your words. I can print you out a copy if you'd like to see it."

Afraid to seem too petulant, she assures me that's not necessary. "It's just that you should have talked to me about it first. I don't like being left out of the loop."

"When I heard that Jane was on the rampage because Marguerite spent the weekend in Maine with a prince, I decided to strike while the iron was hot." I look her in the eye. "I didn't intentionally leave you out of the loop."

Allison manages a thin smile. "Well, let's not do it again. When we formed this group we promised to work as a team. We're all in this together," she says, but what she really means is that they're all in this together and I've only been invited along for the ride because they had to. I'm the linchpin.

But that's the problem with us linchpins. We tend to be loose cannons.

The Bridesmaid Maneuver

Laurel Vega has an idea for a new magazine.

"I want to call it *Divorce,*" she says, showing Christine the mock-up. On the cover is a black-and-white photo of Elizabeth Taylor in the cinched-waist silk dress she wore for her wedding to Conrad Hilton, Jr. The coverlines are in pink and say things like "What to Wear to Wear Him Out" and "Courting Trouble" and "20 Divine Divorce Destinations."

Laurel is Dan Neuberg's assistant. Dan is the magazine's publisher and, although the staff has almost no contact with the publisher, we are often visited by Laurel, who finds the business end of magazines to be boring. She pines for editorial.

"The idea is to provide women with all the information they need to get a good divorce," she continues. "A magazine just for her. And it won't just cover the best clothes to wear to court—although we will of course have fashion layouts in every issue—but also the best lawyers and the best prenups and the best way to celebrate your new freedom." She takes out a graph she made with PowerPoint and indicates with her wooden pointer that the numbers are there. Christine is getting the full treatment but then everyone does. Like a magician with a street-corner act, Laurel can set up her presentation in three seconds flat. "Half of all marriages end in divorce. These women need advice: What should I look for in a private investigator? Which assets are in my name? How do I tell the children? I know you're afraid the subject matter will frighten the advertisers away but think about it. The target demo will be newly divorced working upper-middle-class women who are getting alimony. What does that mean?"

Christine has no idea what it means and she looks at me in mute appeal. I've already been through the *Divorce* pitch and know the answer.

"Disposable income," I call out, like a kid from the peanut gallery.

It doesn't occur to Laurel that she has a larger audience than one until now and her smile widens to include me. "That's right. Disposable income. Women who have enough money for the big-ticket items and the glamorous vacations to Bali. But that's not all. What else does it mean?"

Christine looks at me again and I shrug. This part is new to the presentation and I'm as baffled as she.

"New houses and new apartments. Ladies and gentlemen, these are women who are setting up new lives from the top to the bottom," she says, playing now to the last row, as if she were in some sort of a stadium and not a shantytown of cubicles. "The assets were sold off and the proceeds were divided. Now it's time to acquire new assets. Washers and dryers and stereo systems and couches and entertainment centers. Ladies and gentlemen, this magazine will sell by the millions and it will bring in millions. Thank you for your interest," she says before bowing.

Christine's good manners compel her to clap. She doesn't quite understand what she saw but it was entertaining and worthy of an enthusiastic ovation. Laurel's *Divorce* magazine presentation is a piece of performance art and, if the right people saw it, she would no doubt get a one-woman show off-Broadway.

"Thank you," she says again.

"What's up?" I ask, realizing she had to be here for some reason other than presenting her magazine idea to Christine. That is merely a fringe benefit.

"Nothing much. I'm just dropping this off for Marguerite," she says, picking up the garment bag that she'd laid on Christine's desk. "Do you know which office she's in? I went to Eleanor's old one but it's now a storage closet."

"Our new editorial director is in the tiny office next to the elevator shaft. Marguerite hung a large silver star on the door, so you can't miss it," I say.

"Silver star? We use name tags upstairs."

"For some reason maintenance hasn't gotten around to hers yet," I say, as though I really don't have a clue why.

"Maybe I'll put in a call." It's not her job to make sure things run smoothly down here, but Laurel likes to be useful.

"What's in the bag?" I ask.

"One of Tisha's old bridesmaid's dresses."

"Tisha?" Christine is reordering her files with an ear bent toward our conversation.

"She's Dan's oldest daughter." Laurel unzips the garment bag and shows us what Tisha had to wear to her cousin Judy's wedding, a champaign-colored dress with the sort of straight neckline that is most unflattering to large-chested women. Tisha is a double D and this dress must have made her chest look like the French Alps. "Marguerite said she's doing some story about bridesmaid dresses and wanted to know if one of his daughters might like a nice cocktail dress by Donna Karan. Tisha is gaga over the idea of having a one-of-a-kind original by a famous designer."

"Who wouldn't?" says Christine with a smirk, which looks oddly out of place on her lips. Although she usually takes things very seriously, she has been deriving a tremendous amount of humor from Jane's travails.

"I know. That's exactly what I was thinking. I'd have substituted my own dress, only I've never been a bridesmaid," she confesses. "Actually, I was tempted to run out and buy some hideous thing from the discount rack at Michael's Bridal but I held myself back." Realizing she has lingered too long, she straightens up. "Must get going. The door with the silver star?"

"Yep, the door with the silver star," I say, "although I think she deserves a gold one for this maneuver."

Christine laughs and returns to her filing cabinet.

The Factotum Strike

Marguerite has a quarter share in an editorial assistant. When Kylie isn't returning calls for Tom or typing up memos for Nora or ordering lunch for Pat, she's at Marguerite's beck and call. This rarely happens and you often see Marguerite at the photocopier, clearing the feeder with a pleasant smile on her face.

The previous editorial director had an assistant but the second Jane realized who the new hiree would be, she fired Cameron and eliminated the position. Within seconds, she had maintenance on the floor taking apart the cubicle and throwing away files. The only thing that remains of Cameron's existence are light streaks on the carpet, which make an outline of the former cube. These streaks are a rebuke to Jane. They are like traces of blood after Luminol is applied—evidence of a crime—and she has effectively tried with little success scrubbing the entire carpet to make it all one shade.

Having successfully denied Marguerite her rightful assistant, Jane underscores the victory in meetings by delegating a mountain of busywork to her and saying she should have her assistant take care of it. Marguerite always waves her hand as if she doesn't mind the partial-custody agreement, but she must feel the lost of status keenly. It's the difference between hiring someone to clean your house once a week and employing a full-time domestic.

"And last, the bridesmaid-dress story. I want to use only the top designers. My vision is of fashion-forward designs that we can shoot around town—the Staten Island ferry terminal, the Flatiron building. I want to go on location with these, not in the studio," Jane says, as if this story idea were hers, as if it had not been foisted upon her by a bitter rival. "Jackie, call the modeling agencies and find out if they have any clients with bridesmaid dresses in their closet. We can have a contest and let the readers send in photos but we're using models from Ford. Jackie, have T-shirts made up that say *Fashionista* and send them out to the first one hundred contestants. That ought to appease them. Anything else?" she asks, her eyes darting yet again to the stranger seated next to Marguerite.

Jane's not the only one who can't keep her eyes off the new person, but she's the only one who's nervous. Pleated trousers, practical shoes, puffed-sleeves blouse, a middle-aged softness around the middle—these are not the traits of a fashionista and Jane is afraid that this woman is from the corporate offices upstairs. The only reason she asked, "Anything else?" instead of finishing her last sentence as she walked out the door is she wants her leadership style to seem nurturing and supportive to an outsider.

"Yes," says Marguerite, "I'd like to introduce to the staff my personal factotum, Mrs. Beverly."

"Your factotum?" Jane spits out, as if trying a new food and finding it distasteful. "Your personal factotum?" It's clear from the way she repeats herself that she doesn't know what the word means. None of us do.

"She's going to help me out with whatever chores need

doing," Marguerite explains with a gleam in her eye. She knows that Jane doesn't know what a factotum is.

Jane looks at her with scorn. "You mean an assistant."

"No, Kylie is my assistant—" she finds Kylie and makes eye contact with her "—and a great job you're doing, to be sure. Mrs. Beverly is my factotum."

"Hmm, that must be a quaint Australian thing," Jane drawls condescendingly, although she's still uncertain what it does. "I'm sure all the best aboriginals have one, but this is New York. We're not a third-world trading outpost in the middle of nowhere."

"Actually, factotums are quite de rigueur at the moment," Marguerite says, less bothered than usual by Jane's backwater insults. "Terence Conran and Philip Johnson each have factotums."

Jane looks as though she'll scream if she hears that word one more time. "I'm sorry. We don't have enough in the budget to fund your fac—assistant."

"Please, there is no need to apologize," she insists with exaggerated magnanimity. "As I said, Mrs. Beverly is my *personal* factotum. I'll be paying her salary out of my own pocket."

"Oh, I see," Jane says as if she gets it; but she doesn't get it. She can't imagine paying for something like that—for anything really—out of her own pocket. A long pause follows as Jane considers tactics. It takes her a while to hit upon a strategy that isn't related to money. "It's a shame then that we have no room for her." She tries to give Mrs. Beverly a pitying look, but it comes out smug and superior.

Marguerite smiles. "There's plenty of room. I know just the space."

"There was never a cubicle there," Jane blurts out, like the madman at the end of *The Telltale Heart.*

"What?" Marguerite draws her eyebrows together.

Jane composes herself and says, "I mean, just the space?"

"Yes, that corridor by the freight elevator."

Jane shakes her head. "We can't put an office there. Your assistant would be a fire hazard."

Marguerite whips out a piece of paper, pushes it toward Jane and waits.

Jane picks it up and barely glances at it. "What's this?"

"A letter from the New York City fire marshal saying that putting an office in the north freight elevator corridor on the twenty-second floor of the Ivy Publishing building would not be a fire hazard."

"I see. Well, it will have to be cleared with maint...." She trails off as Marguerite slides another sheet of paper under her nose. This time Jane doesn't even pretend to look. She already knows what the letter says.

"I've cleared it with maintenance, Human Resources and the lawyers," she says, taking out supporting documentation for each claim. "I even ran it by housecleaning. They've assured me they won't mind emptying another trash can. I will, of course, be furnishing it at my own expense."

Jane's mind is working so furiously on her next move that you can almost see smoke pouring out of her ears. But there is nothing she can do at the moment. Marguerite has trapped her in a corner and her only recourse is to end the meeting. "That's all," she says to the staff, getting stiffly to her feet. *This is just a battle,* she's telling herself as she walks to the door. *This is just a battle but the war isn't over yet.* She is already scheming her next move.

By the time we come in tomorrow, she'll have hired a butler.

Your Life Gets Sillier

Dot thinks you can tell a lot about a person from the way they treat their windows.

"Don't Buy Drapes Until You Read This," she says, motioning me into her office with a zealous hand.

Since I have no plans to buy drapes and she isn't holding out something for me to read, I readily agree. "All right." I move a stack of magazines from the chair to the floor and sit down.

Dot smiles. "It's an idea for a new column—Your Best Feature. Each month we're going to highlight a different decorating feature and talk to three or four celebrities about their choices. First up: window treatments. Why a beige valance? Gingham or chintz? How do you feel about Levelors? That sort of thing." She pushes a folder across the desk. "I've written down suggestions. And here's the number of Perky Collins."

I know no Perkys. "Perky Collins?"

"Yes, She's the fabulous host of *Perky's Paradise,* a popular show on the Home and Garden network," she says, as if

Perky Collins were a common household name. She is not. A popular show on the Home and Garden network gets a .3 ratings share. That means about two dozen people are watching. "She's a very well-respected decorative scientist and she's done some groundbreaking work with color. Hue You Are—What Red Says About You."

Dot's phone rings, signaling the end of our meeting. I make an "I'm going now" gesture, which she completely misses because she turns her head to face the window the second I raise my arm. I leave with little fanfare and return to my cube.

Allison is away from her desk, so the area is unusually quiet and I stare at my phone, willing it to ring and provide me with a distraction. After five trancelike minutes, I admit that I have absolutely no magical powers and open Dot's file. I don't want to read about the new column idea because I already know what it will be like. All our monthly columns are the same. Girl Talk, Style Wise, Pajama Game—pick a celebrity and ask her trivial questions. If you were on a deserted island, what beauty product would you die without? What designer best captures your sense of style? Moisturizer or nail polish: Which is more vital to your well-being? Finish this sentence: I'd be naked without my....

Most of these interviews are done at a discreet distance—through a publicist, over the phone—but we always make it seem like we're sitting on the deck with Sean Connery watching a pod of dolphins frolic in the sea. We are peddling intimacy and exclusivity and the idea that you can't get there without us.

I open the file and, unable to distract myself further, start reading about the new column. Window treatments are just the beginning. Refrigerators (the inside scoop on what's inside) and beds (has the frill gone out of your marriage?) and gardens (growing pains) will follow in rapid succession.

Asking silly questions to rock stars and actresses—or rather their publicists and handlers—is just business as usual at *Fash-*

ionista. Light and frothy are our specialty and the only thing deep here is your mortification. And if you always feel like a reporter in a Noel Coward play asking, "So, what do you think of the modern girl?" you have no one to blame but yourself. There are plenty of useful magazines out there asking important, relevant questions that don't make you cringe. Go work for one of them.

Pinky

Maya is like Typhoid Mary.

She's being very careful—washing her hands regularly and keeping her hands out of her eyes—but she is still highly contagious and there's no telling how many co-workers she's infected.

"I don't think any," she says defensively. She's sitting on her couch with a cold, wet towel over her right eye. The left one is staring at me, red and drippy.

I'm here at Maya's request. She wants to practice pitching article ideas, but I'm a reluctant, unenthusiastic sounding board. The A to Z Guide to Antioxidants bores me and I quickly change the topic.

"You touch everything," I remind her. Copy is the center of trafficking. Everything passes through her hands. Every layout and article goes through her infected fingers and flirts with conjunctivitis. It's inevitable that someone catch it. That's why they make you stay home from elementary school when you come down with it in third grade.

"I told you, I kept my hands clean. I must have been in

that bathroom like sixty times today." She sits up and the cold compress slips off to reveal a second infected eye. This one is worse off. It's so puffy and swollen that it can barely see my disapproval. "I was in there so often I thought about bringing my chair and pencils in and setting up shop next to the sinks."

"You should stay home then," I say, the voice of reason. "By the end of the week there could be a dozen cases of pinkeye. Then how will you feel?"

"I can't afford to take a day off. You know that."

This is true. When you freelance there is nothing to protect you from yourself. There's no social safety net and you don't stay home for anything less than scarlet fever or rubella. "I hope you're at least going to the doctor." From her look, I can tell she's already raised and dismissed this option. "Maya," I say, outraged on behalf of a dozen magazine editors whose eyes will soon be red and puffy.

She glares at me with her demon eyes. "I looked it up on the Web. It'll clear up on its own."

"Really?" I'm doubtful.

"Yes. It's a viral infection."

"How long?"

She is absentmindedly playing with the fringe on a throw with her infected fingers, and she will now have to either wash the pillow or burn it like the velveteen rabbit. "Only four weeks," she mumbles.

The idea of Maya walking around Manhattan looking like a monster that escaped off a B-movie lot for four weeks makes me laugh. "Call the doctor. You might as well get it over with." Maya is reluctant because her health insurance, with its very large deductible, doesn't help with everyday scrapes and bruises. It's for when her appendix bursts or her kidneys fail or when she tears her anterior cruciate ligament in a skiing accident. "An office visit will run you a hundred bucks. A hundred bucks to alleviate suffering is a small price to pay. Plus, you owe it to your co-workers."

She grumbles a few words that I don't understand. I consider moving closer, but I don't want to run the risk of touching anything she's touched. "What?"

"My co-workers—ha!" she says forcefully. "Think about it. I don't know where I got this thing from. I haven't been anywhere except to the office."

This isn't quite true. Today is only Tuesday and she's had a whole weekend to pick up alien germs. I raise my hand to make this point, but Maya isn't taking comments.

"I probably got it there. I had to have gotten it there. You're so concerned about saving my co-workers from me and, for all I know, I got it from one of them. Yes, I bet that's what happened." She is warming to her argument now. "One of the editors has pinkeye and, instead of washing her hands and keeping them out of her eye and going to the doctor, she's been passing it along with little respect for human life. Tomorrow I'm going to hunt down the culprit and when I do...." Maya pauses, coughs and looks slightly abashed. "That's funny."

"What?"

"I didn't realize I was so susceptible to mob rule."

"A mob of one," I point out.

"Yeah, but if I can get myself so worked up, imagine how easily a passionate speaker and a dozen angry barefooted peasants holding scythes could do it." She looks disturbed by the idea, as if she just realized she would have been the first person to light a match in Salem.

"Now you're being ridiculous."

"Am I?" She tries to raise an arch eyebrow, but her ocular movements are impeded by the conjunctivitis. A thick mucus tear falls.

"God, I can't believe they haven't noticed. The copy chief or the managing editor should have sent you home."

Maya shrugs. "I work with strangers. Nobody looks at me. Half of them don't even know my name, even though it's written on every piece of paper I distribute. They stand behind me and say, 'hey, hey' until I turn around."

"Still, your eyes are freakishly red."

"It's not so obvious with my glasses on." She demonstrates.

The difference is minimal. Like Superman to Clark Kent. "How can't they notice?"

"Vig, I could go in with a hunchback and horns and nobody would notice. I work with strangers," she says, sounding wise and old like the village shaman.

An Idea Blossoms

Pieter van Kessel is tall and wiry and towers over everything around him. He's like the Sagrada Familia church rising over Barcelona and you suddenly feel like a two-story hacienda. His face, though gaunt almost to the point of hollowness, is handsome. He has dark brown eyes, the sort that stare at you steadily and seldom blink, and wears a neatly trimmed Vandyke, as if somehow compelled to wear his homeland on his chin.

"This is what I'm working on now," he says, showing me some sketches with his signature ruffles. Even though I wouldn't recognize a Dutch accent if it spit in my face, he speaks without a trace of one. He has no accent at all, like a Canadian, only without the revealing "aboats" and "ehs."

The interview with van Kessel was ridiculously easy to set up. Because she didn't want to talk with her mother, Jackie provided me with all her mom's coordinates—work, home, car, cell—and let me arrange everything. I was happy to re-move another person from the equation, especially one as needy as Jackie. Madame Guilbert was glad to help out and called her friend Hans on my behalf. Hans then called me, delighted by the prospect of appearing in *Fashionista* magazine—clearly he has never read it—and eager to set up a time for me to come by.

Hans is standing over my shoulder now, pointing out the brilliant details of van Kessel's designs, which their creator is hesitant to do, either from modesty or a fear of appearing immodest. There are two other people in the room—Dezi Conran, a petite woman with agile fingers who is rapidly sewing a skirt, and van Kessel's wife.

We are in the basement of a Lower East Side apartment building. We're right across the street from the tenement museum, where they bring you inside and show you the tiny quarters in which a family of ten lived at the turn of the last century. Not much has changed in a hundred years. This space isn't much larger, and although only van Kessel and his wife officially live here, Dezi and Hans and seven plastic mannequins rarely leave. It feels very crowded.

After hours of poring over fabrics and drawings and stitches and his ideas for the next collection, I suggest we return to the surface for a bite to eat. Outside the mercury has been steadily rising and with it the temperature in the basement. Sweat is pooling in the small of my back and around my collarbone.

Pieter picks a restaurant that is nearby, a dinerlike place that is always packed on nights and weekends. On a hot August afternoon at three o'clock, its booths are empty and the host seats us with an absent smile. Techno music is playing in the background, just below loud.

"If the next show goes well, we're going to need to find a backer," Hans says after we order, "but it will have to be someone we all trust, someone who's not going to use inferior-quality fabrics and will give Pieter creative control."

Pieter smiles demurely, his modesty with us at the table. "There is no need to jump ahead of ourselves. We'll see how the November show goes and then, if it's necessary, we'll worry about backers."

Before you can get the windows at Barney's, you need to find a financier who will invest in you. Only then will you be able to manufacture your designs, put them in department stores and sell to fashionistas. This is how you build a label.

The waitress comes by to take our order but I barely spare her a glance. I'm too busy scribbling illegibly in my notebook, which I've already filled with sketches from the Met and telephone interviews with van Kessel's former co-workers. When she persists, I tell her to bring me a hamburger.

When the waitress leaves, I ask if anyone has shown interest yet, and while Pieter is shaking his head, Hans jumps in and talks about the nibbles they've gotten. Everything is dependent on recognition. If they can get press and buyers to come to their next show, then they'll be able to create demand for his product.

Hans drops a few names of investment groups and, listening to him, I feel of fissure of excitement. This—Pieter, Hans, the mouthwatering clothes—is going somewhere. It's going places and here I am, in at the ground floor before the elevator even moves. In three months or six months, van Kessel will be a name fashion people recognize and talk about. In a year he'll be manufacturing dresses and selling them at Bergdorf's. This is my story and I don't want to lose it. *Fashionista* isn't usually interested in designers unless someone famous is wearing them, but I refuse to be discouraged by reality just yet. I will draw up a proposal and submit it to Marguerite. Already ideas are flying like butterflies through my head. I will do a piece on them now and then another one in twelve months. I will explore the effects of success on a designer and the people around him.

By the time I leave them two hours later, I can barely contain myself. I'm composing sentences in my head and dreaming of outlandish things. I don't just want to chart Pieter van

Kessel's experiences for a year, I want to chart them forever. I want to write a one-year-later piece ever year, like they do with sextuplets and in those Michael Apted documentaries.

The Delia Files

Delia comes over to my desk to assure me that I have her full cooperation.

"Alex filled me in on your plan," she announces loudly, not at all concerned by the possibility that the walls—or the thumbtack boards—have ears, "and I want you to know that I'm ready to serve the cause if there is anything you need me to do."

I raise my hand and indicate that her first assignment is to lower her voice. Even though Allison is at her desk talking about braised lamb ("That's exactly what I thought. I assumed I wouldn't like it, either. You should try it, though—delish!") I don't want to take a chance that she's listening. The last thing I need is for Allison to hear someone calling her plan my plan.

"Let's talk outside," I whisper, looking around to make sure Kate and Sarah are not nearby. "Come on."

She follows me silently through the office. I can tell that she's bursting to talk about it, and the second we get in the elevator she opens her mouth to speak. I cut her off with a severe shake of my head.

"Sorry to go all 007 on you in there, but I've always sus-pected that the elevators are bugged," I say, once we're out-side in the bright sunshine. We sit down at the fountain in front of our building with hundreds of other working stiffs in their suits and ties.

"Don't ever apologize for being too cautious," says the woman who has spent the past two years successfully hiding things from everyone she works with. "A) There's no such thing as too much caution. B) I don't know if those guards in the lobby can hear but they can certainly see. I once took my stockings off during the ride down, and when I got out on the first floor I got a few wolf whistles."

"Why not use the bathroom?" The man next to me is eat-ing a pungent tuna sandwich and I lean back to breathe in the fresh scent of chlorine, practically throwing myself into the water. The Ivy Publishing fountain doesn't do any tricks. It doesn't have a statue or a waterfall or intense dramatic lighting that makes it look like more than a reflecting pool gone awry. It's only at Christmas when they turn off its three halfhearted jets, drain the pool and put up a large tree that the space has any charm.

"It's more efficient," she says, untroubled by the smell of warm, rotting fish. "I try to multitask whenever possible, al-though sometimes outside factors make it impossible."

Delia doesn't look like a fashionista. Her clothes are neat, practical and affordable—light blue knee-length skirt from the Gap, dark blue cotton tee from Bradlee's—and they lack a sense of au courant catch-up. She bothers with very little makeup and wears the long, thick strands of her dark hair tied back in a French braid. She always carries a boxy leather briefcase that looks like the sort your parents buy you when you get your M.B.A. It even has her initials engraved in Hel-vetica on the gold-plated clasp. Everything about Delia shouts no-nonsense and efficient, and she seems like just the type of person who would take her panty hose off in the elevator to save time. I'm surprised she let the wolf whistles stop her.

Before getting down to business, I do a quick reconnoiter of the area, swiveling my head toward the tuna and away again, to make sure there are no magazine people eating lunch or smoking cigarettes. I see no familiar faces. "So Alex told you about the plan?" I ask, keeping my voice low. There is no reason to be careless. We are right in front of the building and Jane or Allison or Marguerite could walk by at any moment.

"Yes, and I think it's brilliant. I think you're brilliant," she gushes, although it really isn't gushing, because Delia is incapable of effusiveness.

"It's not my plan," I say, because I don't want to take credit for things I haven't done. "It's Allison's plan. They just brought me on board to help out."

Delia is not listening to a word I say. She's digging into her shoulder bag and extracting an accordion file. She hands it to me. "Here."

The file is thick and heavy, and since I'm not prepared for the weight, I almost drop it. "What's this?"

"It's my file on Jane," she says, mouthing the last word.

This is not what I'm expecting. "You have a file on Jane?"

She looks at me with perplexed eyes through horn-rimmed glasses. "I have a file on everyone."

"You have a file on everyone?"

"Yes," she says, as if this weren't something that just the FBI did. "I have a file on everyone."

"You have a file on me?"

"Well, yes."

"You have a file on Carter?" Carter delivers the mail and fixes the coffee machine when it starts dripping cold water.

"Of course."

I stare at her, trying to absorb this information. It's not the idea of Delia Barker with her lightning-quick reflexes jotting down bits and pieces of my life in her Nancy Drew notebook that bothers me. It's something else entirely. Not only is she doing her job and Keller's job, she's also doing J. Edgar

Hoover's job and the work of a small team of crack special agents. She's an overachiever in the classic mold and, watching her as she smoothes imaginary wrinkles out of her pristine skirt, I wonder what I'm doing in the magazine business at all. I don't have this drive or this determination or even this level of interest.

"You have files on everyone, including me and Carter?" I ask again, just to make sure I understand the situation clearly. She nods. "If I give you my complete name and a notarized signature, can I get a copy of my file?"

"No."

"Aren't you obligated to under the Freedom of Information act?"

Delia smiles. "The Freedom of Information act only applies to government agencies. I'm a private citizen."

I try another tactic. "I'll show you yours, if you show me mine." Although I don't know what a file should contain, I'm reasonably confident I could pull together a fairly inaccurate one by the end of the day.

She isn't interested in making deals and ignores my suggestion. "I've only just started a file on Marguerite and will get that to you ASAP. My general rule is to wait two months and then compile information. I don't have time to make files on everyone and had to draw the line somewhere," she says with a shrug, as if apologizing to all those people whose privacy she couldn't be bothered to invade. "It was the most practical solution. However, given the circumstance I believe making an exception for Marguerite is the most logical course of action."

"Of course," I say, as if the most practical solution weren't not to have files on all your co-workers. I open the accordion folder and withdraw a stack of papers. They are mostly photocopies and tear sheets from other magazines. I flip through the pile, pausing intermittently to scan headlines. There is enough reading here to keep me occupied for a week. I'm feeling a little bit overwhelmed.

"The information is arranged in chronological order, starting with the minutes of our first one-on-one meeting. I don't know if there's anything useful in there but I wanted to give it to you just in case." She laughs a little giddily and rubs more imaginary wrinkles out of her skirt. "This is so exciting. Really, if you need my help in any way, don't hesitate to call."

"All right." I consider telling her again that the scheme isn't mine, it's Allison, Kate and Sarah's but I don't. I don't want her to feel she entrusted Jane's file with the wrong fashionista. "Thank you again for all this information. I'll be very careful with it. No spilling coffee all over everything."

"That's just a copy. The originals are in my apartment." She glances at her watch and stands up. "I've got to go. 'Alex'—" she makes exaggerated quotation marks with her fingers "—has a conference call with some West Coast publicists in ten minutes."

Although the man with the smelly tuna has finally left and the day is suddenly beautiful and inviting, I get up as well. "How do you do that?"

"What?" she asks.

"Be Alex without anyone getting suspicious."

She laughs. "It's all him. He's a perfect darling about being an absolute monster to everyone. Nobody ever wants to talk to him and when I tell them that he can't make the meeting and sent me to represent him, there's always a sigh of relief. Nobody questions it," she says, as the light dings on the elevator.

We get in and, even though we are the only ones here, we fall silent. You can never be too cautious.

Phase Three

Keller calls me first thing Wednesday morning to say that the deed is done.

"All systems are go. Delia submitted the list for November parties to Jackie last night at six o'clock," he announces, sounding more thrilled about the prospect of Jane's downfall than you'd expect from someone who was blackmailed into participating.

"Not blackmailed," he corrects, when I whisper this observation into the receiver. "You crumbled at the first sign of a countermaneuver. I think you should stick with magazines. Clearly games of war are not your strong point."

"This isn't war."

Keller laughs. "You don't think handing that list to Jane was the first act of aggression?"

"No," I say, because that wasn't the first act. Dropping the Gilding the Lily folder on her desk was.

"Anyway," he says, "I can't help but be cheerful about it. If I was having second thoughts about my decision to help, they were banished the second I saw Delia's reaction. It's entirely possible that she minds being in my shadow a bit more than she lets on."

I think of the drawer full of files on her co-workers. "Don't take it personally. I suspect she doesn't like being in anyone's shadow."

"That's Delia—very ambitious. And she does the job better than I ever did. November's list wasn't supposed to be in for another two weeks and I would never have been able to pull it together so early. I hate talking to publicists."

"Then it's a good thing you're an architect."

"Speaking of which, I've got to get going. I'm already running late because I had to take Quik for an extralong walk this morning."

"Still no sign of Kelly?" I ask, unrepentant. Taking Quik for an extralong walk means letting him sit in the shade for another ten minutes. He can do that in the apartment.

"No. I got the name of another walker from a friend, but I don't see it working out."

"Why not?"

"The guy's name is Killer. Clearly his parents were trying to warn us of something."

"It's obviously a nickname."

"That's worse then, isn't it? He seems to be announcing his intentions."

For a reclusive ogre who growls if you get too close to his hermitage, Keller is an awfully chatty fellow. "I thought you had to get going."

"I do. I do. I just want to make sure you weren't booked for tomorrow night."

"Why's that?" I ask, thinking this is unsafe territory. Emotionally unavailable. Emotionally unavailable.

"I have a plan."

"A plan?"

"Yeah, it's nothing as lavish as yours and it won't end in the total destruction of a fellow human being but it could still be fun. What do you think?"

"It's not my plan," I say, loud enough for Allison to hear if she's listening. "I didn't come up with it."

"Huh?"

I'm tempted to explain everything. I'm tempted to tell him that Allison Harper is the evil genius behind the plan to topple Jane and that I only date men I'm not attracted to. But I don't. I hold myself back and agree to meet him at the bar at Isabella's at seven-thirty.

The Contract

Jane calls me into her office. She looks up when I enter, she tells me to take a seat, she asks after my family. Suddenly I'm anxious. This isn't just bizarre behavior, this is night-and-day, are-you-sure-you-haven't-been-lobotomized stuff.

"And your parents, are they well?" she asks.

"Yes, thank you," I say cautiously. I'm trying to keep shock out of my voice.

"Are they still in Florida?"

This is a shot in the dark. Jane doesn't know a thing about my folks. "Uh, Missouri."

"Good. Good." An awkward silence passes as Jane stares at me. She's staring at me with the sort of intensity that makes me want to fidget in my seat. If this were a doctor's office and Jane an oncologist, I'd expect her to tell me that the tumor is inoperable. "Vig, how long were you my assistant?"

I know the answer to this one and still I feel uncomfortable. "Two years."

"That's right. Two years." She gets out of her chair and takes the one next to me. We are now both on the visitor's side of the desk as if we're equals. "And in those two years we formed a bond, a bond of mutual respect and hard work."

I don't think *mutual respect* is a phrase ever before uttered in this room and the anxiety I feel grows into fear. I'm afraid Jane is going to ask something of me, something personal that you only ask a close friend, like to be your Lamaze coach. "All right," I say agreeably but I shift in my seat and move my arms behind my back. I don't want to hold hands with Jane.

I needn't have worried. Done with equality, she stands up and leans against her desk. "I think it's time for a promotion."

It's not normal for underlings to be consulted in decisions like these, but I'm not surprised. Nothing has been normal since the moment I entered this office. "Whose?"

"Yours," she says, with a tight-lipped smile. Being the bearer of good news does not come easily to her.

I'm too shocked to do anything but stare at her with wide-eyed amazement.

"How does senior editor sound?"

Senior editor sounds great. It sounds like the best thing I've ever heard. "Good."

"Good." Jane returns to her desk and her black leather swivel chair. "I'll have Jackie send out the memo. Now, the first thing I'd like you to do for me is call the publicist for Gavin Marshall."

I don't know why I'm surprised. I should have seen this coming. "Gavin Marshall?"

"Yes, the Gilding the Lily artist. Call his publicist and tell him that we want to meet with him to discuss my ideas for *Fashionista*'s covering Gilding the Lily."

"But Marguerite told me to—"

"Vig, you're a senior editor now. You don't have time to run errands for that woman. Of course if you'd rather run errands for her, I can tell Jackie not to send out that memo after all."

The threat is clear. "No, no. That's not necessary."

"I didn't think so." She smiles smugly. This is an expression that looks at home on her face. "So you'll just tell Marguerite that the whole thing didn't pan out."

"Didn't pan out?" Even though this is just a pretend game, I feel compelled to play every move.

"Yes, you called the publicist and they're not interested. End of story."

If Marguerite were really pursuing Marshall and his artwork, then "they're not interested" wouldn't be the end of anything. Lucky for Jane—or rather unlucky for her—Marguerite doesn't even know it exists. "All right."

"Good. So you'll set up the meeting then? Talk to Jackie about my schedule. I want it to be as soon as possible. We're already working on the December issue." She picks up the phone, signaling the end of the meeting. Another person would say goodbye but Jane doesn't bother.

My hand is on the door when she calls my name. "Vig, not a word about this to anyone. Not a single solitary word. Understand? I'd hate to bump you back down to associate editor."

I assure her I do and leave.

Terms of Reference, August 24: Switch Genres

Maya writes about dead bodies—in subway cars, in Roman baths, in the closets of apartments not yet rented. She scatters them about and lets unsuspecting people find them. She lets clueless bystanders stumble onto them and forces even the most indifferent amateur detective among them to go about finding the murderer. These are the books she writes, the sort where ordinary people test their mettle as they bungle their way through death. They are impossible to sell.

"They're not mysterious enough to be mysteries," she said, as we sat in the bar of the Paramount drowning the sorrow of a lost agent, "and they're too mysterious to be straight fiction. They're hybrids, neither fish nor fowl but some strange griffin mongrel that no one has a place for in their heart."

She gets maudlin when she is drunk.

Maya chose mysteries because she thought they'd be easy. She thought they'd be easy to write (built-in plots!) and easy to sell (built-in markets!). This was before she realized she couldn't actually write one. This was before she realized that the formula that so recommended them couldn't be strayed from and that she'd find the who-did-it aspect to be completely irrelevant to character development.

"I'm going to write a romance," she declares now as she opens her brown bag. She withdraws a ham and cheese sandwich, a bottle of Fresh Samantha Super Juice, a bag of Lay's potato chips and a Hostess cupcake. She has packed herself the sort of lunch your mother used to when you were in fifth grade. The only thing missing is the apple.

My lunch is less impressive. I have a peanut butter and jelly sandwich—no side dish, no refreshment, no dessert. "A romance?" I ask.

"A romance."

"Why a romance?"

"Because they're awful," she says, as if this explains everything. Her eyes are still bright red, but they're no longer puffy and drippy. The eyedrops the doctor gave her are slowly working.

But this doesn't explain anything. "They're awful?"

"Well, they're not all awful—some are actually quite decent—but a great many of them are. They simply publish too many a month for all of them to be good. It's like what happens when they expand the number of major-league baseball teams," she says, squinting into the sun. We're having lunch on a bench near the entrance to Central Park. The Plaza hotel is across the street and several unhappy horses pulling tourists go by.

This is a new development. Maya doesn't usually talk in sports metaphors. "What happens when they expand the number of major-league baseball teams?"

"It dilutes the pitching staff."

Even though this sounds vaguely familiar, like something I've read in a newspaper or a magazine, it doesn't mean anything to me. "All right."

"The demand is so great that quality can't keep up," she

clarifies. "I can dash off a hundred thousand words in a couple of months. It shouldn't be too hard."

"No," I say.

"No?"

"No."

"No what?"

"Just no."

"But what are you saying no to?"

"The entire diluted-romance-market scheme," I explain, horrified by the very idea of Maya devoting a hundred thousand words and a couple of months to something she couldn't care less about. "You're just wasting your time."

"Why am I wasting my time?"

"It won't work."

Maya grunts in annoyance or frustration and crumbs of white bread fall from her mouth. "Why won't it work?"

"Because you don't know anything about romances."

"What's to know? Two people fall in love."

"You hold the whole genre in contempt."

She shrugs. "Well-earned contempt."

"Well there!"

She's unconvinced by my logic. "Well there what?"

"Don't write a romance. Don't write another mystery. Just write a book."

"Now there's a ridiculous idea," she says, her eyes disappearing into the bag of potato chips.

"Why is it ridiculous?"

Maya doesn't answer, but this doesn't surprise me. We've had this discussion many times before, and although she always retreats behind a wall of silence, I know exactly what she's thinking. Writing genre fiction is easy: You follow a formula, do your best and in the end if you're not one-tenth as good as the people you adored growing up—E. M. Forster, Christopher Isherwood, Virginia Woolf—it doesn't really matter. No one expected anything from you anyway. Writing genre fiction is easy. It's taking yourself seriously as a writer that's hard.

"You have to stop this," I say, after a long silence.

Maya blinks innocently as she eats potato chips. "Stop what?"

"Your terms of reference. This cultivating-hustle thing, this switching-genres nonsense. It's like you're going through the five stages of grief, only with you there are five thousand. Get over it already, and start focusing on what really matters," I say, suddenly annoyed. I can only hold a hand for so long before my impatience kicks in. "I know it's hard and it's scary—it took me almost two whole days to get up the nerve to call van Kessel for an interview—but you have to do it." I don't know how I became an example of goal-oriented industriousness, but here I am—Vig Morgan, pattern card for getting it done.

Maya is silent. She crunches potato chips and stares at me with sullen eyes. Then she says, "I'm thinking of doing a historical, like England at the turn of the nineteenth century."

I sigh heavily.

Jane's File

Before giving it to me, Delia went through Jane's file and censored the things she didn't want me to see. Like a letter from your grandfather on the front in 1941, the pages are speckled with blocked-out words. Anything that might reveal where troops are stationed is crossed out with a black felt-tip Sharpie. There is nothing here that vital and I can't make sense of Delia's choices. I'm trying to establish a pattern but they are completely haphazard. She's like Yossarian declaring death to all modifiers.

Ninety percent of the file is mundane and boring, and I have to force myself to stay awake. While reading Jane's address to the Women's Editorial Society, who honored her with a coveted Helen award, for Best Magazine, I nod off and I only wake up when the telephone rings. I splash cold water on my face and try again but I have to stop. The thank-you speech is more than seven pages long and there is only so much I can take of her protestations of gratitude to the sisterhood. Jane is not a sister. She's an only child who doesn't play well with others.

The interesting part of the file is the folder filled with re-ceipts and bills of sales and vouchers that document Jane's sys-tematic stealing from the company. Every chair in her apartment, every Picasso lithograph on her walls, every stitch on her body was paid for by the Ivy Publishing Group. *Fash-ionista* foots the bill for her annual two weeks in Borneo and her lovely little weekend rental in Aspen. We pay for her hair-cuts and massages and for the skin on the heel of her foot to be rubbed off once a week. Lunch is always on the company as well as transportation and Broadway shows. The only thing Ivy Publishing does not pay for is her children's pricey Upper East Side private school educations, but that's just a matter of time. In a year or two or three she'll convince the ac-counting department that her daughter is a primary source, that her sense of style is what keeps the magazine fresh and on the cutting edge.

"That's an insane amount of information," I say to Delia, when I see her in the cafeteria. We are standing in front of the international section, a series of Sterno-heated trays that are usually filled with refried beans and ground beef with taco sauce. Today it's stocked with Southern cuisine. "Why haven't you used it?"

"I've tried. She's like the Teflon Don. Nothing sticks to her."

"You've tried?"

She spoons some grits onto her plate. "I've tried. I leaked some of those documents to Bob Carson in finance a year ago and nothing happened. He didn't even flinch when he saw that *Fashionista* paid for her face-lift."

"Her face-lift?"

"You missed that?" she asks with a smile. "She listed it on an expense report as 'massage.'"

"Massage?"

"Yes, as in massaging the truth, I believe." She gives me a curious look as she takes a piece of fried chicken. "You were her assistant. Didn't she have you doing these reports for her?"

I shrug. "I never paid the least attention to what I was doing. She could have expensed the Statue of Liberty and it wouldn't have made an impression. How'd you leak it?"

"Left it in his in-box when nobody was looking." She holds a serving spoon filled with fried okra in my direction with a questioning look. I shake my head. Although I've been following her to each station in the international section, I don't have any intention of eating. I've just had lunch with Maya and only stopped on the second floor to pick up dessert.

"Didn't flinch at all?"

"Nope. And when I leaked documents that suggested she was selling furniture the company owned and pocketing the profit—nothing. I've tried and I've tried but they don't care. She's held to a different standard of accountability. Why else do you think I'm so excited about your idea? It's about time someone else gave it a shot."

"I guess so," I say, trying to digest the fact that Delia has tried to depose Jane as often as the CIA has Castro.

She takes her tray laden down with Southern specialties to the cash registers. "I'm really excited about this. I think it could work. I think this might finally be the silver bullet that takes her down."

I watch her walk away before picking up a Rice Krispies treat and heading for the cash registers.

This Is Just a Date

Keller takes me square dancing.

"I don't two-step," I say, when we enter the large room that looks and smells like a high school cafeteria. We are in the basement of a church on the corner of Broadway and Eighty-sixth. Someone has adorned the room with purple and green streamers and they hang from the ceiling like Christmas decorations.

With a hand on the small of my back, Alex steers me to the ticket table and plunks down his ten dollars. The cashier puts it in a metal strongbox. "That's all right. Just as long as you do-si-do," he says.

I'm not sure if I do-si-do. The last time I stood in a square and danced was twenty-two years ago at a Brownie function with my father. My memory of the evening is hazy and if I didn't still have a navy-blue bandanna from the event, the experience would have erased itself completely from my mind.

"I've never been to a church social before," I say, taking in the scene. Across the room the band is setting up. A thick man with a potbelly stomach and a goatee is strumming his guitar and trying to get it in tune. "Do all the proceeds go to the orphans?"

Keller takes my hand and leads me over to the refreshment table. "I don't know if there are orphans and I don't know where the money goes. This is a first for me, too." He gestures to the list of beverages. "What can I get you?"

Although it is still early in the evening, I've already had two gin and tonics—one while waiting for him and another while we were talking. Since I've already had two strong drinks, the wise thing would be to say that he could get me a Coke. But I'm not feeling wise. I'm in the basement of a church about to square dance. I get a beer. You can't do-si-do sober.

The room is packed with a wide range of demos—MTV, AARP, PTA—and we have to snake ourselves through the crowd to find an unoccupied spot. "How did you hear about this?" I ask.

"Read about it in the *Resident*," he explains, taking a sip of beer. "I've been wanting to do this for a long time. I was a square-dancing fiend at summer camp."

"That's amazing."

"That I was a fiend?"

"No, I already knew that. I meant your reading the community paper."

He looks at me with genuine surprise. "You don't read yours?"

"Uh, no," I admit, feeling as though I'm confessing to a mortal sin. It's not up there with impure thoughts, but suddenly it seems worse. "I don't even know what it's called."

"Where do you live?"

"Cornelia, between Bleecker and West Fourth."

"The *Villager*."

"How do you know?"

"Community papers are a passion of mine."

I laugh. "No, really."

"I used to live down there."

I'm about to ask where and when but the band, the Hog-Tieds, has finished tuning and is ready to start. I finish my beer in two impressive gulps, toss out the plastic red cup and present myself, along with Alex, to a square looking for a fourth side. There is a nervous fluttering in my stomach, the unreliable sort that makes you wonder if you're going to throw up. I give my date a sidelong glance.

Alex squeezes my hand. "You'll be fine." He is trying to be reassuring and supportive, and even though he fails, I give him one of those thanks-for-playing smiles.

I check out the other people in my square, sizing them up. None of them look truly confident—the woman across from me is jiggling her partner's hand with a compulsion that seems beyond her control—and I take comfort in their obvious discomfort. By the time the band strikes up the first song and the caller tells us to promenade to the right, I'm almost relaxed.

The act of square dancing requires a certain amount of physical grace and a working knowledge of right from left. Although I have the former in short supply, I can sometimes rise to the occasion; I'm useless with the latter. In the right circumstance—laboratory, no ticking clock—there's always a chance that I'll get it correct but with a barker shouting out orders to the beat of a banjo, there is no hope. In the end I'm forced to watch my partner and follow his direction. I'm always one step behind. It's like a satellite is transmitting my image there on a two-second tape delay.

"That was fun," I say, when the band takes a break. I'm huffing because I'm out of breath and sweat is trickling down the side of my face. Square dancing does not show me to the best advantage.

"You sound surprised." He is leading me up the stairs to the street. The air in the basement is thick and hot, and in late August Broadway offers an agreeable alternative.

"Well, duh. It's square dancing."

"Ye of little faith."

"It's square dancing," I say again, trying to emphasize the unlikelihood of anyone finding it fun.

Keller shakes his head, as if I have a lot to learn. "Do you want to get ice cream? There's a place around the corner that makes excellent sundaes."

Since it's only ten o'clock and the blood is still swirling in my head, I say yes. I say yes and follow him around the corner to Time Café, where we both order chocolate-fudge sundaes with extra nuts. He's funny and sweet and likes to square-dance. I feel myself falling. Even though I'm trying my damnedest to hold fast to the edge of a cliff, I feel myself falling fast.

Enemy at the Thumbtack Wall

Allison wants my job.

"It's not fair. It was my idea and she's the one who gets a promotion and a gigantic office."

I put the last of my office supplies—stapler, paper clips, scissors—into a box with Post-its, envelopes, thumbtacks and pens and tape it closed. Even though it's only going twenty yards, I feel compelled to seal it. I only know one way to move.

"Yes, that's what I'm saying. It was my idea. We just asked her to do one small thing—one tiny thing that was practically inconsequential—and now she's taken over and stolen a senior editorship that should have been rightfully mine."

Next I turn my attention to the filing cabinet. There are three years of files here and the sensible part of me wants to go through them one by one and throw away the deadweight. Most of these files are deadweight.

"Like, cavernous. Remember my first apartment? It's bigger than that. Yes, even including the balcony."

Allison has been complaining about my promotion all

morning. Since the moment she arrived to find the memo about it on her desk, she has been on the phone. She has called every person she's ever met to rant about the injustice. Fleeting seconds of silence are accompanied by breathing or dialing.

Christine sticks her head over the thin wall and rolls her eyes in a show of solidarity. "She's awful," she says under her breath, although there's no need for discretion. Allison can only hear herself.

I throw all my manila folders into a plastic yellow crate that maintenance has supplied. I can sort through my files in my new office—in peace and quiet. "I know."

"What's she talking about?"

"Hmm?" I ask absentmindedly, looking at the pile of promotional items that have collected in my cube's corner. Do I really need a beach ball that says SPF Perfect on it?

"She keeps saying that the plan was her idea." Christine leans against the wall. "What plan?"

The more people who know about the plan, the less likely it will succeed. I hold up the beach ball as an offering and, without considering its merits, she shakes her head. I deflate it and throw it into the trash. "That's exactly what I keep wondering. What plan?"

Christine has been listening to Allison for almost as many years as I have. "I hate to say it but I think she's losing it."

"Really?" I ask, shocked by this statement. Christine rarely says a mean word about anyone, not even Jane.

"Well, she's never made sense—at least as far as I've been able to discern—but in the past week she's been nonsensical and angry." Christine leans close to my ear and whispers. "I think she might be schizophrenic."

This is not what I'm expecting her to say, but I treat the comment with respect and seriousness, although my impulse is to laugh. "Schizophrenic?"

"There's a disassociative quality to her ramblings, and she's paranoid and her conversation suggests that she might be suffering through some sort of delusional episode."

Christine makes an excellent case. Even though I know the truth, she almost convinces me. I don't know what to say.

"Do you think we should do something?" she asks.

"What?" I blurt out. It's meant to be an exclamation, but she interprets it as a question.

"Have an intervention," she says seriously.

An image flashes through my brain: Christine telling a hysterical Allison that everything will be all right as orderlies from Bellevue put her in a straitjacket. "No," I say, "I don't think we should have an intervention."

"Should we call her parents?" Her concern is real and I feel awful for nurturing it.

"No, not yet," I say, playing for time. "Charges of schizophrenia are a serious thing and we shouldn't do anything until we're absolutely sure. Let's observe her for a little bit longer."

"I've been observing her for a while now," Christine admits. "Are you sure we should wait longer?"

In a few days Allison would calm down about my promotion. The heat of anger will pass and she'll resent me silently. "Positive."

She doesn't look convinced but is willing to heed my advice, for a little while at least. When she asks if I need help packing, I assure her I've everything under control.

The Pitch

My promotion comes with a change in venue and Jane gives me Eleanor's old office. Recently turned into a storeroom out of spite, the space is filled with old issues, which maintenance has stacked neatly in the corner. March, April, May, June, July, August and September of last year form towers that stand as high as the light switch and they tremble whenever I come near. Maintenance has promised to return tomorrow or the next day to remove them, but I have little faith in that actually happening. My promotion seems as sturdy as a house of cards, and the pile in the corner is only a temporary concession. The magazines are like grains of sand and they will soon settle into every crack and crevice.

Because my office is twice the size of Marguerite's and because it should rightfully be hers, I'm feeling slightly abashed as I knock on her door.

"Vig, come in," Marguerite says welcomingly. "Congratulations on your promotion. Senior editor—*quel magnifique.* Come, sit down and tell me all about it."

Marguerite—or her factotum—has done a bit of redecorating since I was last here: The chairs now have all four legs and they don't squeak. It's a vast improvement. "There's really nothing to tell."

"Did you know something like this was in the works? How long were you at the associate level?" she asks. Her manner is pleasant, but beneath the bland smile I can see her mind working. She's trying to figure out how my advancement will lead to her downfall. Everything Jane has done in the past two weeks has been with this in mind and I can't blame her for being suspicious.

"Only a year," I say, although they were twelve very long months. "I had no idea it was even possible. You usually have to wait for someone to leave."

"Hmm, yes, that's what I thought. I guess Jane just thought you were in particular need for a reward," she says, as if reasoning aloud a mathematical equation. Jane's generosity plus Vig's promotion equals Marguerite's undoing.

Her figures are a little off but she can't know that. "I guess."

"Well, whatever the reason, I'm sure you're worthy. You strike me as a very clever girl," she says, crossing her hands on the desk and leaning forward. "Now, what can I do for you?"

"I wanted to discuss article ideas."

"Excellent. I'm all ears."

"I know we were talking about my doing more service items—"

"Yes, I have the list right here, but I haven't had a chance to look at it yet," she says, smiling apologetically.

This is not why I'm here. I can barely remember the things I'd written on that list. "Actually, I have an idea that's very different from what we talked about. It's not as useful as a service item, but it's more substantial than our usual."

Intrigued, she leans forward. "Yes?"

This is all the encouragement I need and I talk for a little while about Pieter van Kessel, explaining my idea for a series of articles that follows a young talent through all the stages of success. Marguerite is receptive and thoughtful and she takes notes, as if what I'm saying actually matters. Her enthusiastic response reinforces my decision to follow up with van Kessel. I'll follow up with him and write my article and keep my fingers crossed, but I have no illusions. A promotion means freedom and responsibility, but it gives me no control over content. *Fashionista's* content is like the Constitution of the United States: Only an act of Congress can alter it.

"Do keep me up-to-date on that," she says, when I'm done raving about van Kessel's designs. "I'd love to go to his next show."

I'm almost flushing with pleasure. I can feel the color invading my cheeks and I fight it. I can't be this susceptible to a little attention. I just can't. "I'll let you know when it is."

"Excellent. Do you have other ideas you want to talk about?" She glances at her watch. "I'm always interested in fresh, exciting ideas. Australia is a little off the beaten path but that distance gave us the freedom to do a few groundbreaking articles. Perhaps you're familiar with the series we did on young Aussie designers?"

I have never picked up a copy of Australian *Vogue* in my entire life, but I compliment her on the series anyway. It's a harmless white lie and Marguerite's smile brightens. "Excellent. Well, why don't we run through some of these fresh and interesting ideas now and the rest you can submit in outline form."

I can barely think for the deluge of thoughts that flood my head. *Fashionista* is an anomaly in the magazine world. Usually a publication is dependent on a constant influx of fresh and interesting ideas. We've managed to skirt this tricky issue by erasing fresh and interesting completely from our pages. From month to month the only thing that changes are the names, and the real challenge for our editors is finding the most current celebrities to grace our pages. The painful truth is that the guy who reads the nominees for the Academy Awards is doing my job, only he's doing it better.

"Well, I was thinking we could do an investigative piece on who the trendsetters really are," I say slowly. This is something that has been knocking about in my head, but I haven't fleshed it out yet. "We usually approach trends from the top, showing famous actresses in the latest style, but I think we should explore the flip side—the kids in the thrift stores who are the actual innovators," I say, before giving a short lecture on the theory of trends (early adopters, late adopters and mass consumption). This was not my intention and I'm sure Marguerite has heard it all before, but I can't help myself. The experience of having someone listen is too novel.

Phase Four

Gavin Marshall is like Belgium in the late teens. He's the site of other people's conflicts.

"Now you're just being ridiculous," says Jane, as she flaps her napkin in the face of the artist's publicist, Anita Smithers. "We can't have the opening party there. It's much too small a space. Where are the celebrities going to stand? Gavin, do you understand my concerns?"

"The Karpfinger is showing his work. We have to have it there, don't we, darling?" Anita says, taking the thin white hand of her client in a display of solidarity that is completely one-sided. Anita is a physically imposing woman. Her bones are large and she stands over six feet tall. If you saw her in a deserted alley after dark, you'd run the other way fast.

Gavin says nothing. He's a slight man, both in his physical appearance and the force of his presence. He seems content to stare into his gazpacho and pretend he's alone at the table. I have seen him glance around him a few times, as if planning his escape, but for the moment he's behaving admirably and staying put.

"Why can't we have it somewhere more grand, like the Guggenheim?" Jane asks, stabbing her lettuce with a fork. She's no longer trying to hide her agitation.

When we met the artist and his publicist in the bar of the Sea Grill restaurant, Jane and Anita disliked each other on sight and began snapping at each other almost instantly. I'm not surprised. They are almost the same person with their silk scarves and wraparound sunglasses.

"Because it's a gallery showing and must be shown in a gallery." She squeezes her client's hand in encouragement. "Gavin, be a dear and explain the rather simple concept to her."

Jane takes Gavin's other hand. It's his own fault. No one told him to put down the soup spoon and leave himself vulnerable. "I'm very sorry that I'm the only one at this table who thinks you deserve to be in a museum."

Gavin's work is already in several museums around the world, but Jane doesn't know that. She's like one of those seminar moderators you see at a place like the Museum of Television and Radio. The only things she knows about her guest are on the index cards her assistant wrote up.

Anita tells Gavin to list for Jane the museums that already display his work, but when he remains silent, she obligingly rattles it off for him. And there's no reason she shouldn't. Announcing his accomplishments to the world is what she's paid to do.

"We will have the opening party in the Karpfinger Gallery and that's that," Anita says, tugging Gavin by the arm. She wants him to back her up with a grandstanding gesture. She wants him to storm out of the Sea Grill in an angry huff. "If you don't like it, then there's nothing more to discuss."

Jane doesn't want to be here. She's not used to dealing with people who behave as badly as she, and she doesn't know how to handle it. If it didn't mean besting Marguerite at her own game, she'd charge out of here on a cloud of Tresor. "I'd like to indulge in the luxury of throwing a tantrum like you, but Gavin's work is too important. I must overcome my personal feelings for the sake of art. Some of us are capable of making sacrifices."

Anita's upper lip curls in disgust. She's been making sacrifices for art for more than half her life and doesn't need this philistine taking the high moral ground with her. "We're having the party at the Karpfinger."

Jane's control over her temper is slipping, and she's a hairbreadth away from walking out despite her spite.

"Jane, why don't you pick the place for the after-party," I suggest.

"The after-party?" Anita asks.

"I know just the place—Mehanata 416 B.C." Jane says, naming a run-down Bulgarian restaurant that supermodels flock to. After-parties are some of Jane's favorite things. They are usually more exclusive than the main event and you often catch celebrities on the rebound. "We'll get the back room. We'll need a DJ. Vig, sort that out." She turns to Gavin. "You'll be the guest of honor, of course. You're going to need a proper wardrobe," she says, examining his beat-up jeans and worn T-shirt. "You'll go shopping with me. I know all the right people."

I intervene before Jane can pull his arm off. She has already terrified him. He's staring at his hand in hers as if it's an alien life form. He is prepared to sacrifice the extremity to save himself. "Hey, isn't that Damien Hirst over there? And he's waving at you," I say, pointing vaguely in the direction of some potted plants in the corner.

The two women are surprised and loosen their grips. Gavin breaks free and stands up. "I must say hello. I don't want to be rude." His manner is apologetic, but there's a relieved look in his eyes.

"You'll work everything out between you?" I don't want to leave Jane and Anita alone, but I have no choice. If Gavin backs out, then the plan doesn't work.

When we're on Fifth Avenue and away from prying eyes, he turns to me. "I'm starving. Want to get something to eat?"

"All right," I say, shocked that he hasn't run away. I would. I'd flee in the opposite direction as fast I could. "What do you want?"

"Not gazpacho."

"There's a sandwich and salad place up the street."

"Sounds good. Lead the way."

"You seem surprisingly normal," I say.

"I don't know how else to handle Anita except ignore her," he explains in his posh accent. "She's really easy to take when you're catatonic."

"Why do you put up with her?"

Gavin shrugs. Now that we're away from his publicist, his features are more relaxed. His wide blue eyes no longer eat up his face. "My agent swears by her and I swear by my agent. She's good at what she does."

I consider saying the same about Jane but common sense prevails. He wouldn't believe me anyway, so I change the subject. "We're very excited about the prospect of working with you."

"You are?" he asks, his tone faintly skeptical.

Jane has done more damage than I realized. "Don't judge *Fashionista* by our editor in chief. She's more a figurehead than anything else."

We arrive at Lou's Café and I hold the door open for him. It's a tiny restaurant with only seven tables, but thanks to the lateness of the hour—somehow it's already two-thirty—we have no trouble getting a booth. The hosts sits us by the window, where sunlight is pouring in. Despite the air-conditioning, I'm warm.

"I judge *Fashionista* by *Fashionista*," he says, taking a menu from the waiter. "It's a very silly magazine."

I'm about to give a boilerplate speech about our importance in the cultural marketplace, but I can't bring myself to do it. I fall back on the truth. "Yes, I know. But we're trying to make it more substantial. That's where you come in."

"Really?"

"*Fashionista* can't suddenly be a magazine about something. Our readers would revolt. Your work provides us with the opportunity to cover something vital and important in the art world while at the same time giving readers what they want—celebrities and high-fashion designs. You'll make us look good," I explain.

He considers this for a moment. "Are you sure you won't just make me look ridiculous?"

"This is what will happen," I say, outlining the process for him with the intent of putting him at ease. "We'll send over a photographer and a journalist to your studio in London. The photographer will complain about poor lighting for ten hours while our journalist treats you to lunch and asks simple questions about your work: Where do you get your ideas from? Who are your influences? Then we'll get a few words from the designers who are used in your pieces—honored to be part of a such a fine exhibition, reminds me of myself when I was just starting out. Finally, we'll track down a few art experts who will praise and defend your controversial work—art must go forward or it must go away, the risks of eternal damnation are great, but the rewards of art are greater." I shift in my seat, trying to hide from the sun. "Nothing to fear. It'll be two thousand words that you've seen before."

"That's it?" Like someone reading a contract, he's trying to find the small print. But there is no small print.

"That's it."

"You promise?"

"I'm a senior editor. I can't promise anything to anyone," I say honestly, "but I don't see what else they can do other than work the celebrity angle. Do any famous people own your artwork?"

"Not that I know of."

"Well, then there's no reason to worry about that. There's no reason to worry about anything," I assure him. "We'll devote eight lovely pages to your work and all you have to do is have your picture taken in front of the *Fashionista* back-drop. Do you think you can handle that?"

Gavin Marshall nods and picks up a menu. He's tired of talking about business. "What do you recommend?"

"The mandarin chicken salad is delicious," I say.

When the waiter finally comes over, we both order chicken salad. We eat our salads and drink lemonade and dis-cuss his ideas behind Gilding the Lily.

Gavin's good company, and I try to relax as I listen to him explain how his work is a comment on the spiritually bereft religion of high fashion. I try to unwind, but I can't squelch a niggling feeling that his concerns are more than justified. I have spoken the truth—I don't see what else they can do—but my imagination isn't infinite. Just because I haven't thought of it doesn't mean Dot or Jane or Lydia won't. There are more things in heaven and earth than are dreamt of in my philosophy.

The Jesus Package

Lydia has a corner office. It's large and spacious and accommodates seven people comfortably. When I enter, Marguerite, Anna and Dot are sitting on the couch against the window. Dot has her feet up on the coffee table, a cup of coffee in one hand, a doughnut in the other. Two top editors whom I only speak to at the Christmas party—Soledad and Harry—walk in after me. They take Krispy Kremes from the box on Lydia's desk, claim the love seat in the corner and proceed to tell the room about their awful mornings. The atmosphere is warm and full of camaraderie and people are making eye contact as they speak. This is the sort of meeting that senior editors are invited to.

Since this is my first time at such a meeting, I'm a little nervous. It's typical first-day-at-school stuff—will anyone talk to me, what if I lose my homework—and I take a doughnut, determined to be impressive. I've spent five years preparing for this moment.

After a few minutes of small talk, Lydia turns the discussion to the matter at hand. "As some of you already know, we're going to try something a little different in December's issue. Jane has had a brainstorm."

The expressions on everyone's face is extreme interest, leading me to conclude that I'm the only one who already knows about Jane's brainstorm.

"We're going to be doing a feature article on Gavin Marshall to coincide with a party we're throwing him in November," she announces, looking discreetly in Marguerite's direction to gauge her reaction. When Marguerite doesn't react at all, Lydia hides her disappointment and continues. "As you no doubt already know, Gavin is an influential young artist from England. His work is very avant-garde and he's often criticized for his use of religious symbolism," she explains to Marguerite, just in case she didn't recognize the name.

Anna—red pants, red sweater with tiered ruffles, rhinestone choker (fiesta wear)—looks up from her notepad. "He sounds too hot for *Fashionista* to touch. Are we sure we want to do something on him?"

Although this is a legitimate question and one that Lydia would ordinarily ask herself, she breezes right by it. Her dislike of Marguerite is almost as strong as Jane's. "There is nothing too hot for *Fashionista* to handle. We are a leader in the style and fashion industries," she says, quoting our press release.

"What's the name of the exhibit?" Dot asks.

"Gilding the Lily," she says.

Marguerite almost chokes on her doughnut. "Excuse me," she says, after the choking fit has passed. "You mean the Jesus in Drag exhibit?" Marguerite is shocked. Clearly she has the sense to realize that showing Jesus in women's clothes is not the sort of thing we should be doing.

But Lydia doesn't know that. This is the reaction she has been waiting for. She can now report back to Jane in all honesty and delight that Marguerite was shocked when she learned the truth: that Jane has successfully hijacked her idea. "Yes, if you must be gauche about it, Jesus in Drag, although

Jane prefers Gilding the Lily. Gavin has collected evening gowns from some of today's best-known designers and put them on plaster-of-paris statues of Jesus," she helpfully explains to the rest of us.

Anna furrows her brow. Even though we are a leader in the style and fashion industries, she's not convinced that controversial art is our dominion. "Are you sure?"

"That the evening gowns are from some of today's best-known designers? Yes, positive," says Lydia. "I have the list right here. Tom Ford, Alexander McQueen, Michael Kors, Stella McCartney, Julien Macdonald have all donated gowns. And they're all going to be at the party, which we'll be sponsoring. It's a great opportunity for us to get our brand out there. *Fashionista* will be synonymous with avant-garde and cutting edge." Before anyone else can protest, she continues, "Jane wants us to construct the December issue around the Gilding the Lily exhibition."

"What do you mean?" I ask, suddenly very afraid.

"Let's make Gilding the Lily our centerpiece," Lydia explains, "and build out from there." Six blank faces stare back at her, but she doesn't let that discourage her. "Now, who has an idea?"

After protracted minutes of silence during which Lydia continues to look upbeat and optimistic, Soledad takes a stab at it. "I'm still not quite sure what you're thinking, but what about something like Jesus as fashion icon. How Jesus' sense of style has affected fashion for two millennia."

"Strappy sandals were very hot last summer," says Anna.

Harry raises his hand. "Everybody wears white now after Labor Day."

"We could also do a sidebar on other fashion icons," suggests Marguerite. "Audrey Hepburn, Princess Grace, Jackie O."

"Excellent idea," says Lydia before she can help herself. Audrey, Grace and Jackie always elicit cheers, no matter what the context.

"Oh, I have an idea," Anna says eagerly. She's almost bouncing in her seat. "Let's get actors who have played Jesus—Willem Dafoe, Christian Bale, Victor Garber, that guy from *Jesus Christ Superstar*—and dress them in modern interpretations."

Lydia likes the idea. She's as excited as Anna. "We could get Richard Avedon or Annie Leibovitz. *Vanity Fair,* eat your heart out."

"What about nativity scenes?" Harry asks.

We all look at him.

"What about them?" Dot asks.

"Who has what? By the end of the day I could have a list of the most popular Nativity scenes and the stars who own them." Harry used to be editor of the home decor section and even though he's a top editor now, he still clings to his old responsibilities. "A few phone calls and I'll have the info."

Lydia nods. She loves when editors volunteer to do other people's work. It saves her the troubling of assigning it. "Good, you get on that. Anything else?"

Dot: "What to Wear to Your Resurrection."

Soledad: "Crucifixes: What you can get for under $100, under $1,000, under $10,000."

Marguerite: "Great Escapes: Vacationing on the shores of Galilee."

Throughout most of this brainstorming session, I'm silent. I'm silent and sullen and consumed by awful regret. I know what the right thing to do is. I know that an honorable person would warn Gavin Marshall that his worst nightmare is about to come true, that he's about to be the main attraction at a three-ring Jesus circus. But I also know that I won't do it. I've come too far to stop the Jane-destruction train now. I will ride it to the very end—into the station or off a cliff.

"This is an extremely good start," says Lydia, winding down the meeting. They've spent thirty minutes talking about Jesus and not once did words like *Christianity* or *faith* come up. The son of God has never been so secular. "I'm going to run these ideas by Jane and let you know what she says." Lydia then holds up the remaining Krispy Kremes—two chocolates, one custard, one jelly—and asks if anyone else wants one before she throws them away.

I suggest we put them in the kitchen in case some of the other staff members are hungry, but my words are greeted with horrified looks. Lydia laughs condescendingly, tells me I'm droll and tosses the box into the trash.

While we're filing out of her office, Lydia says she is impressed by us all, but I don't think that's true. I don't think anyone is impressed by me.

Drinks at 60 Thompson

Maya is trying on deformities and distortions in an attempt to gauge which ones are the most eye-catching.

"Okay, one more time. Do you think this is better—" she blackens two teeth in the front of her mouth and smiles "—or this?" Now she puts an eye patch over her left eye.

I give the matter the consideration it deserves. "The teeth. Definitely the teeth."

She makes a check next to the answer and then looks at me through one eye. "Why?"

"It's more subtle. You only notice the teeth when you smile. Also, I think you'll be less self-conscious. And last, I don't think it'll affect job performance. You shouldn't be reading copy with only one eye," I point out practically.

Maya takes detailed notes of my explanation. She's like a market researcher, only without the two-way mirror. "Next: the pillow." Her bag of tricks is full and she reaches inside to take out another prop. She's stuffing it under her stretch-cotton T-shirt when Gavin finally appears.

We are in the bar of 60 Thompson. Gavin and his publicist are staying here during their New York sojourn and I look around just to make sure that Anita isn't close behind.

Understanding my unsubtle action clearly, he gives me a kiss on the cheek in greeting and laughs. "Don't worry. She's out schmoozing a publisher tonight." His eyes stray to Maya, who can't decide if she should take the pillow out or stuff it in completely. She's never greeted anyone midpregnancy before and doesn't know how to act.

"Gavin, this is Maya, my friend who I told you about."

"Hi, Maya," he says, holding his hand out. "It's nice to meet you."

Maya smiles. "You're just in time. I'm taking an opinion poll. Which do you prefer? The pregnant belly—" she stands up and models her misshapen bulge "—or the hunchback?" We wait while she relocates the pillow from the front to the back.

Gavin treats the question very seriously and purses his lips. "I'm going to need to see pregnant belly again."

I toss back my gin and tonic and try to control my racing heart. The guilt I feel is almost overwhelming. It makes me light-headed. I'm only seconds away from hyperventilating. In a bid for composure, I wave down the bartender and order another drink.

The light-headedness started five hours ago when Gavin called to give me the official go-ahead. "But no funny stuff. I'm holding you to that." Then he suggested a drink to toast the unholy alliance between art and commerce. "This is my last night in town."

"No," I said, panicking. I had just gotten out of the Jesus meeting and wasn't prepared to spend hours upon hours alone with him and my guilt. "I can't tonight."

"All right."

"I'd love to, of course, but it's just that I'm going to the movies with a friend of mine. I'd cancel since this is your last night in town, but she just broke up with her boyfriend and she needs my emotional support," I said, babbling freely. It's what I do when I'm nervous and consumed by guilt. I sighed heavily. "It's a shame that I can't see you."

"What time's the movie?"

I'm not a good liar and rarely are the details of my fabrications at my beck and call. "Uh, nine."

"Nine?" he asked.

He sounded suspicious so I adjusted the figure to a more believable time. "Nine-thirty."

"Well, if the movie's at nine-thirty, why don't you stop by the bar at my hotel for a drink."

"But Maya..." I began to protest.

"Bring Maya," he said. "I just finished with my girlfriend, too. We can commiserate over whiskey and sodas."

Maya doesn't drink whiskey but she loves commiseration. "All right," I said, giving in. Some things you just can't fight.

After I hung up with him, I called Maya and related my distraught tale. Since she didn't have plans for the evening and was very amused by my predicament ("Tell me again about the Nativity scenes and the stars who love them"), she readily agreed to swap war stories with a famous artist from England.

"This is good," she said. "I'm working on an article idea and need to bounce some things off you."

"I don't know the ten best ways to get him to love you," I warned her.

She laughed and assured me it was nothing like that.

"What do you do?" Gavin asks, after he decides he prefers the hunchback's hump to the pregnant belly. I concur with his pick and the pillow goes back into a pink plastic bag.

"I work with strangers," she says, scribbling wildly on her pad.

Although he's expecting her to say a more common career like costume designer or interior decorator, he accepts this answer with a nod. "Is that a full-time gig?"

"It's as much time as I want it to be." She has another bag on her lap now and is digging through it.

"Maya's a writer," I explain.

She raises her head and gives me an angry, pointed look. "I'm a copy editor."

This is basic terms-of-reference stuff from day one: Don't call yourself a writer until you've sold a piece of writing.

Smart enough to stay clear of the tension, Gavin says, "Copy editor?"

"Your people call us subeditors," she says, very close to sneering, "as if we're not quite human."

Gavin coughs and looks down, obviously uncomfortable. He's used to defending the empire and colonialism and Marmite sandwiches, not magazine terminology. "And you write?"

"Some."

Maya's petulance crushes my guilt and for the first time in five hours I inhale easily. "She's working on a piece right now. Maya," I say, sounding like a talk-show host, "tell us about your current project."

She doesn't like having the stage cleared for her act but she complies anyway. She's too enthusiastic about her article idea not to. "I work with strangers," she says.

I roll my eyes impatiently. There are only so many times you can say that in an evening. Gavin just waits.

"My co-workers rarely look me in the eye and most of them don't know my name," she explains. "Two weeks ago I had a virulent case of pinkeye and not one person noticed."

"Maybe they were being polite," Gavin suggests.

Maya shakes her head. "They're not polite people. I wear a cute sweater, no one comments. I sneeze, no one gesundheits. I've never once been asked how I am. A surfeit of good manners is not the problem. Anyway, the pinkeye gave me a great idea." She pauses for effect. "I'm going to go into work with increasingly bizarre and prominent conditions and see how long it takes for someone to comment."

"In that case I change my vote," says Gavin. "I'm going with the pregnant belly."

She marks that down in her book. "Why?"

"Because while I think a hump that materializes on your back one day is extremely bizarre, there could conceivably be a medical explanation for it, say, a car accident or a family history of suddenly materializing humps. But an overnight third-trimester pregnancy?" he says, relishing the idea. Suddenly I see twenty Jesuses in maternity clothes. "That's brilliant stuff. It'll make them wonder if they've been overlooking something for nine months."

"He makes a good argument. I change my vote, too."

"Overwhelming majority for pregnant belly duly noted. Now, onto the next event." She holds up a plastic mask, the sort children wear on Halloween. "Frankenstein or the Wolf Man?"

Gavin nixes both without a moment's thought. "Neither. Way too obvious. You want to provoke a reaction, not force it with the jaws of life. How about copying those notchy things that Frankenstein wears on the sides of his neck?"

Maya claps. "Excellent! This is the kind of feedback I need."

"So who do you plan on marketing your idea to?" Gavin asks. "What magazines do you have in mind?"

She shrugs and her excitement dims. "The only connections I have are in women's magazines and this is not the type of thing they're interested in."

I nod in enthusiastic agreement. "*Cosmo:* My Boyfriend Works with Strangers—and Eight Other Things You Need To Know Before You Commit."

"What about general interest? Doesn't the Sunday paper have a magazine? They must run true experience pieces. All the papers do," he observes.

"The *New York Times* has a section in the back called *Lives* but it's not right," I explain. "Everything is from the baby boomer angle: My Daughter Works with Strangers."

"All right, all right," he says, spirits still high. He's not going to be bested by the publishing world, not when he already has the art world in a choke hold. "What about an up-town rag like the *New Yorker?* Something like this would be perfect for them."

Maya laughs. "Yeah, perfect. Like I could get their attention. They're just so fond of upstart copy editors who drop manuscripts over the transom."

He tries again. "*Salon?* They did a piece on my work a few months ago."

Maya doesn't know a thing about *Salon,* so she looks at me.

I shrug my shoulders. "It's worth looking into, I suppose. What's their demo?"

Since nobody has the answer, we all agree that it's a viable option. Maya thanks Gavin for this enthusiasm and his help and offers to buy him a drink.

"No," he says, "I insist on treating. I invited you to join me for a drink."

They argue over the accuracy of this statement for five minutes before reaching a compromise. Maya agrees to let Gavin pay for her drink as long as he concedes that it was his intention to invite me, not her, out in the first place.

"I'm extra," she says, after accord has been reached. "I'm like the rice that comes with your sweet-and-sour chicken."

"You are the sweet-and-sour chicken," he insists.

If Maya is both the chicken and the rice, I'm loath to contemplate what that makes me (perhaps a packet of soy sauce). But neither is thinking of me. Gavin and Maya have hit it off. They're getting along so well that no mention is made of the nine-thirty movie. Ten, eleven and twelve o'clock all pass without comment.

At twelve-thirty I give in to my exhaustion and make my goodbyes. They hardly notice. After several cosmopolitans Maya has relaxed enough to talk about her writing—her real writing. She tells Gavin all about her mysteries that aren't very mysterious and her lost agent. The way she relates it, it sounds like Marcia is in Africa somewhere with Dr. Livingston. Telling stories about his own agent travails, Gavin is upbeat and optimistic, and although Maya explains term of reference, August 15, she's too drunk to enforce it.

When I leave they're discussing the comic potential of poisoning an anorexic. Maya has a new idea for a book and I'm relieved to report it's not a romance.

The Fine Print

Jane blames the Botox injections.

"In the old days you always knew exactly what Marge was up to. You'd see those tiny spidery lines between her overgrown brows and you knew she was hatching something. God, she was easy to read. Knit eyebrows meant she was thinking up petty revenge for some imagined wrong and deeply furrowed brows meant she was plotting your ruin. Now, thanks to modern science, it's impossible to know for sure," Jane says scornfully, as if science doesn't erase her laugh lines every six months. "But that's where you come in."

"Me?" I ask cautiously, wondering if I should try making a break for the door while there's still time. Something is up. Something very unpleasant is in the works. I can tell because her eyes are shining brightly with anticipation and her lips are turned upward at the corners. Jane only looks happy when she's planning someone's demise.

"You'll be my eyes and my ears," she says, her fingers tapping gently on the shiny wood veneer of her desk. "I want you to stick close to her—but not too close. We don't want it to be obvious. Linger outside her office when she's on the telephone. Poke around her desk. Rifle through her computer files. Get her Outlook password. Tail her when she goes out to lunch."

I listen politely and take notes, but I have no intention of following through. Despite what Jane thinks, I'm not her man in Havana.

"Give George a call," she says. "He'll hook you up with equipment."

George is our tech writer. He lives in a cabin in Montana and writes a monthly column on expensive toys. "George?" I ask. I can't imagine what he has to do with Jane's spy games.

She nods. "George is doing an article on the sophisticated surveillance equipment of the stars. He should have some names and numbers of local outfitters. Put whatever you buy on your credit card and expense it."

"All right," I say agreeably, as if buying illegal bugging devices has just jumped to the top of my to-do list for the day. It hasn't. I'll give George a call in case Jane checks up on me, but I won't spend my lunch hour scouring New York for complicated cameras and tiny microphones that can pass through the eye of a needle. I'll keep a low profile for a couple of days and then report back from my fact-finding mission with the details of a small invented intrigue to pacify Jane.

"I want regular reports," she says, continuing her list of demands. I've been in her office for almost twenty-three minutes now and she's done nothing but issue orders—call the caterer, set up an appointment with Anita, send a fax to the Karpfinger Gallery, write promotional copy for the Gilding the Lily press release. In recent weeks I've become Jane's aide-de-camp. Despite my senior editor title, I've been relegated to the position of assistant. It's no great mystery how it happened—this is how Jane treats people whose soul she thinks she owns. "I want to know what she's up to every minute of every day. Knowledge is power. Now that she knows I've improved upon her idea, she'll be seething with anger," Jane says, so pleased with this notion of Marguerite as an irate bull with steam pouring out of her ears that she shivers. "All right—shoo. I have more important things to do and you're in my way."

I leave her office and brush by Jackie, who is pretending to be engrossed in reading a memo, but she's really calculating the minutes I've been behind closed doors with her boss. Jackie, resentful of the time that I've been spending with Jane, is convinced I'm after her job. The idea of anyone wanting to do a second tour of duty with Jane is so ludicrous it makes me smile. But Jackie thinks I'm gloating and glares bitterly at my departing back.

This Is Just Another Date

Alex wants to know why I'm still at *Fashionista*.

For forty-five minutes he listens patiently as I vent about Jane's vindictiveness and Dot's vapidness and the general celebrity whoring that my life has been slowly reduced to in the past five years. Then he tilts his head to the side, examines me quietly and asks the obvious question: Why? Why do I put up with it? Why haven't I moved on already? Why are the seeds of my discontent watered and nurtured and loved?

"I think *love* is a bit strong," I say, feeling defensive.

"You know my reason for hanging around. What's yours?"

There are several answers to this question and I consider them all carefully as I wait for our food to arrive. The most truthful answer is that I'm an inert creature. The next truth is that I don't know what I want to do with the rest of my life so I might as well stay where I am. The truth after that is that I'm afraid of change—I'm terrified of going from the frying pan into the fire. But I don't want to give any of these answers. Alex is still new to me. His scent, his laugh, the way his lips feel on my cheek—these things are still gleaming silver candlesticks and I don't want to tarnish them too soon. I don't want to reveal my inert, passive, fearful self. Even though he's emotionally unavailable and we have no future, I'm still trying to make a good first impression.

"Have you heard of Pieter van Kessel?" I ask, launching into a detailed explanation of his work and my idea for a series of articles. It seems like I'm changing the subject, but I'm not. Van Kessel is at the heart of why I stay. It's not enough anymore that I work in a kinder, gentler office. It's not enough anymore that we're freed from Jane's petty despotism. The scales have fallen from my eyes—thanks, in part, to Maya's twenty zillion stages of grief—and I'm left with a desire to give the world more than a list of ten really good shampoos. I don't want to settle for the black-and-white practicality of consumer advice. That's where Marguerite comes in. She's a hope to hang your hat on.

"Sounds good," Alex says, after I finish selling him the job-interview version of myself—proactive, resourceful and creative. "And that's definitely not something Jane would be interested in. When I first took over as events editor six years ago, I tried pitching parties that were a little bit outside our well-trod path—important events that weren't supported by A-list stars—and she shot me down immediately. Actually, 'shot me down' is overstating the case. It implies that she paid attention to me."

The waiter brings two platters of cheeseburgers to our table and makes room for a separate plate of steaming French fries. We're at a greasy-spoon hole-in-the-wall deep in the East Village that serves the best burger in all of Manhattan. This is the first time I've taken Alex to one of my haunts—all our other dates have been planned and executed by him. I don't know why, but I woke up this morning determined to share something I enjoy with him. "Is that why you decided to go back to school?" I ask. He wouldn't be the first person Jane sent scurrying for bluer skies, though he is, as far as I know, the only one to keep his foot in the door.

"Nah, I didn't mind being ignored by Jane. As you know, I've worked that to my advantage."

"So when did the help-Alex-become-an-architect scheme first occur to you?"

He holds the ketchup bottle over his plate and waits for it to drip out. Then he puts it down. "I don't know. It wasn't a decision I can recall making. I started taking one class a semester just because tuition reimbursement was one of the job's perks and it seemed stupid not to take advantage of it. Somehow I ended up in a drawing class with an excellent instructor who suggested I try architecture." He shrugs. "Before I knew it, I was taking almost a full course load at Cooper Union and fielding telephone calls from writers between classes. Howard helped, but it was a mad, mad time until Delia came onboard and took over. What about you?"

Since I'm wasting the tuition-reimbursement job perk and I don't have a Delia to make my time a little less mad, I stare at him, unsure of what the best-foot-forward answer to this question is. "Me?"

"How'd you wind up here? Did you always know you wanted to be a muckraker?"

I laugh at the very idea of my being a muckraker. I deal with bullshit twenty-four hours a day, but that doesn't mean I'm bringing scandalous behavior to light. "I didn't know what I wanted to be when I moved here from Bierlyville, Missouri, with my fabulous clips from the *Bierlyville Times* and my two suitcases. I only knew I wanted to work somewhere glamorous. *Fashionista* fit the bill."

"Be careful what you wish for..." he says, trailing off.

I smile wisely to show I've learned my lesson, but I keep the embarrassing part to myself. I don't let on that I used to believe that glamour could rub off, like fairy dust, if you stood shoulder to shoulder with it.

"Bierlyville, huh?" Alex asks, digging for information

about my upbringing. There aren't many details to uncover, but I ramble for a few minutes anyway about Bierlyville, population 1,244—half of which are descendants of the Bierly corn barons who founded the town in 1873. Although Alex and I have seen a lot of each other in the last few weeks, this is the first time we've talked about our pasts. We usually stick to the here and now. This is how it works with emotionally unavailable men—if you don't have a past, then you can't have a future.

"There was only one traffic light, in the middle of town, and the only time you stopped at it was during your road test. The rest of the time it was decoration, like the blinking martini glass in front of the West Hollow Saloon," I say.

When I'm done telling him about my short ignoble stint at the Dairy Queen ("Smaller scoops of ice cream, Ms. Morgan!"), Alex reciprocates. He regales me with stories from his childhood in suburban New Jersey. He's funny and charming, and when it's time to leave, he picks up the check. He pays the bill despite my protests and walks me home with my hand in his.

When we get to my door, I pause, gripping the keys tightly. My instinct is to invite him in. My instinct is to unlock the door and throw myself at him, but I've stood on this threshold too many times and for once I want to be wise.

Alex lowers his head and kisses me. His lips are soft and lush, and I lean my body into his. I wrap my arms around his neck. I run my fingers through his hair. I know I should pull away, but the cautious chant in my head (emotionally unavailable, emotionally unavailable) is muffled by his kiss. It's silenced by his soft, lush lips, and I forget to be wise.

The Majordomo Counterstrike

Jane doesn't hire a butler, although she does engage a man to oversee her affairs and call her mum. Stickly is imported from England and has a pedigree as thick as a dictionary. When Jane introduces him to the staff at a special meeting convened for this very purpose, she runs down the list of nobles he and his ancestors have served faithfully, an endeavor that quickly dwindles into an exercise in counting (George I, George II, George III, George IV, Harold I, Harold II, Elizabeth I). It seems that a Stickly was there at every significant English moment—Hastings, Culloden, the signing of the Magna Carta—to wipe a brow and offer a spot of tea. They have all the serendipity of a Forrest Gump, only without the philosophy and spread over generations.

Jane refers to him as a majordomo, which has more of a Gilbert and Sullivan ring to it than butler and appeals to her sense of drama. Stickly is a physically imposing man—he's built like a quarterback, with large hands stuffed into white gloves like sausage casings—and has the air of someone who's accustomed to running palaces. Our small offices on the twenty-second floor do little to sharpen his skills—making a reservation at the Judson Grill is nothing like arranging a luncheon for the Duchess of Greater North Chesterborough—and he is forced to suffer the curse of most detail-oriented self-starters: too much downtime. Jane has given him a large corner office uncluttered with back issues and trade publications, but you often see him gossiping with Mrs. Beverly in her furnished corridor.

They are sitting together in a corner now as Lydia runs the weekly meeting. "Allison," she says, "do you have that article on the plunging neckline we talked about?"

"Vig offered to do that for me," she says, her eyes wide and innocent, as if she's telling the truth. "She knows how swamped I am."

Although this is the first I'm hearing of my generosity, I nod like I'm expecting this question. "I'm almost done. I just need to tweak it. What's the final word count?"

Lydia consults her notes. It takes her a moment to locate the information. "It looks like it's down to only three hundred words. Let's have the copy in by the end of the day. Remember, the focus is on celebrities," she says, as if I need such a reminder. The focus is never on anything else.

I add this article to the list of things I need to do before leaving for the day and begin to feel like Cinderella. There's now so much on my plate that it'll take a team of fairy godmothers to finish it all.

The weekly meeting, once a source of complete apathy, now elicits feelings of dread and apprehension. The first time Allison pawned her work off on me, I fought back. I demurred with a carefully worded reminder that I had been too busy to help out when she asked. Jane, who is always looking for ways to be a leader, made an example of my lack of responsibility. She did it loudly and emphatically and in front of the entire staff. This is the sort of thing she used to do to me every day when I was her assistant—humiliation is not a private matter—and the memories it brought back were overwhelming. I spent the rest of the day fighting flashbacks and shivers.

"Marguerite, how are we doing on those bridesmaid dresses?" Lydia asks.

"Mrs. Beverly is going to pick up the last one today." Marguerite looks at her factotum. "When will you get to it?"

"Actually, Stickly volunteered to go for me," Mrs. Beverly says with a fond look at her friend. "He's so very helpful."

"Thank you, Stickly," says Marguerite.

Stickly bows slightly. "Not at all, mum."

Jane, who has been sitting at the conference table looking bored out of her mind, perks up. She doesn't like her majordomo bowing at Marguerite and calling her mum and picking up her bridesmaid dresses. "Stickly doesn't have time for running errands today."

"I don't, mum?"

"No, I need you to reorganize my files," she says.

"I've already done that, mum."

"My files in accounting," she improvises quickly, before turning to Marguerite with a smug look. She doesn't even know how to feign contrition. "I'm sorry but it's an all-day task."

"That's all right," says Mrs. Beverly. "I can pick up the dress myself. And, Elton, if you need help with those files, you just let me know."

This spirit of bipartisan teamwork is not what *Fashionista* is about and both Jane and Marguerite try to squelch it in its infancy. There is a short, snappish discussion on the matter of just who exactly will be reorganizing the files in accounting and I wait for Allison to volunteer me for the job.

Although Stickly and Mrs. Beverly observe all this with identical expressions of placidity, I can't help but feel that underneath their polite indifference they are horrified. They are horrified by Jane's screeching and Marguerite's snide counterblows and the way we watch as though spectators in the Colosseum. The two of them together are like an episode of *Upstairs, Downstairs* and sometimes you feel like a chambermaid from the lower quarters.

More Plotting

Kate summons me to the bathroom. She sends me an e-mail with a winking emoticon and tells me to show up at three-thirty sharp. It's been several weeks since we've had our last conference, and things have changed. Now Allison hates me. Now she fumes in my presence and makes snide comments behind my back. She's not a comfortable person to be around and I don't relish the idea of being trapped in a small space with her, no matter how beneficial the meeting will be for both of us in the long run.

Sarah and Kate are waiting for me when I arrive. Sarah is sitting on the couch and she instantly moves over to make room for me. Kate is standing by the sink. She's holding a clipboard and a red pen and is flipping through the many sheets of paper and sporadically shaking her head. She's having a silent conversation with herself and Sarah and I respect her privacy, talking about the Beverly-Stickly affair while she sorts herself out. "All right," she says after a few minutes, in an authoritarian voice I've never heard her use before. Kate seems different—and it's not just the clipboard and the commanding tone. Her back is straight and her head is up. Despite her Stuart Weitzman flats, she is taller. "We have a few weeks before the big event and there are several things we need to go over."

I look around, surprised that we're starting the meeting without a key member of our fashion infantry.

"She's not coming," Kate says, reading me correctly.

"She's not coming?"

"She's not coming," Sarah confirms. "We've taken her out of the loop."

"Taken her out of the loop?" I find the notion shocking. I've never taken someone out of the loop and am oddly uncomfortable with the concept.

Kate nods emphatically. "Yes, she's completely out of the loop."

Since I've spent the last several weeks dodging Allison bullets, I'm glad she's not here. I'm relieved she's not here to frown in my face and hurl accusations at me and embarrass me with her anger. She has a mean streak as wide as Jane's and she's learned much during her tenure. Still, I feel a need to protest. "But it's her plan."

Sarah is examining the fringe on her western-style skirt and avoiding eye contact. She's not entirely comfortable with Allison's loop removal.

Kate picks up the thread. "We know it was her plan," she says, clearly annoyed by the reminder. "But she seems unnaturally fixated on the idea of your being promoted and the plan needs our total attention. Allison couldn't focus, so we took her out of the loop." She pauses for a moment and looks at Sarah. "She was hurting the cause."

Sarah nods begrudgingly. "I know. It's really like she took herself out of the loop."

"All right," I say. I'm not convinced that Sarah believes her own words, but it's not my concern. I'm just happy to be in an Allison-free zone. "What do you want to go over?"

Kate flips back to the first page and looks at me. "One: party plans. How are they going?"

"Smoothly," I say, wondering about the truth of the statement. This afternoon Jane had lunch with Anita to iron out a few remaining party details and I'm still waiting for a damage estimate. "I've hired the caterer and the band and photographers."

But this isn't what Kate meant. The minutiae of my job doesn't interest her and she cuts to the glamour. "What's the celebrity count? What kind of press coverage are we getting? Are any national networks interested?"

"The celebrity response has been good. His people are promising to deliver a stable of young British celebrities. As for press, we haven't sent out releases yet."

Kate raises an eyebrow. "No releases yet?"

I think of the pile of work on my desk, a pile that this meeting isn't helping me get through. "No releases yet."

"Hmm," she says, in a disproving way before jotting something down. "When can we expect releases then?"

I assure her they'll be done by the end of the week, but I don't really know. I'm just telling lies now to avoid more red marks against me.

Kate sighs and makes a quick note. "Very well. But remember when you finally do get around to writing the press release, that the most important thing is to play up Jane's participation. I want her fingerprints all over this. And on the night of the party, make sure she's in every photo op. There shouldn't be one single picture of Jesus in a dress that doesn't have Jane's smiling mug somewhere in the background." Kate turns her interrogation eyebrows on Sarah. "Where are we with alerting the religious groups?"

"As you know, I've finished my press release calling for action," Sarah says, with a slightly smug look in my direction. Darn teacher's pet. "It's from the CFCD. I just have to go to Kinko's, make photocopies and distribute them to Christian organizations."

"The CFCD?" I ask.

"Christians for Christian Decency," Kate explains. "I made it up. I thought it captured the all-purpose decency of Christians. Now, which Kinko's?"

This isn't something Sarah has thought about, but we're in midtown and there's a Kinko's on every corner. "The one down the block?"

"Nope. Go to Astor Place. Pay cash and don't forget to wear a disguise."

Sarah isn't prepared for this, either. So much for doing all her homework. "A disguise?"

"A disguise."

"Like a wig?"

"Hats, sunglasses, shoes, jewelry," Kate says impatiently. Accessories are her life—she spends most days cataloging and inventorying the accessories closet: one gold necklace, one braided leather belt with silver buckle, one pavé diamond watch—and she takes Sarah's neglect of them personally.

"Of course," Sarah says, once again playing with the fringe on her skirt. "I've rented a voice mailbox."

Kate's sense of organization overcomes her indignation and she nods slowly. "Be sure to leave a message from the CFCD that's inflammatory and God-fearing. Which brings us to point number three: writing a letter from the CFCD warning all of *Fashionista*'s advertisers that our members will start boycotting their products if they continue to support this tool-of-Satan magazine. I'm currently working on the fifth draft and should have a final version for your review by the end of business day tomorrow. Watch your in-boxes. I'm also working on CFCD's letterhead. I'm thinking something simple with one large cross down the center and maybe a few smaller crosses in the margin. Sarah, consult with me before you photocopy your letters. All CFCD communications should come on the same letterhead." Kate takes a breath and flips through her clipboard. "That seems to be it. Right, next meeting. One week from today, same time. Put it on your calendars. On the agenda will be timing questions—when to alert the advertisers, when to alert the religious groups. Vig, I expect to see the final draft of the press release by then and I'd like a list of celebs who'll be at the party. Any questions?" she asks with the same chop-chop efficiency with which she's run the meeting. Kate has only been lead fashionista for twenty minutes, but she's taken to it like a duck to water. Her cheeks are flushed and her eyes are glowing happily. She likes telling people what to do. She likes giving orders and watching people jump in response. Her talents are wasted in the dark depths of the accessories closet.

Marguerite's File

With her arms wrapped around a thick manila folder, Delia enters my office, sweeps her eyes quickly over the room and closes the door. Then she sits down in my one visitor's chair and pulls it forward, knocking over a stack of last January's issue that was piled precariously on an angle like the leaning tower of Pisa. Delia apologizes profusely and insists on dropping to her knees to clean up the mess, even though I tell her not to bother. You can't move in my office without toppling something. Despite their lavish claims, maintenance never returned to remove the magazines, and staff members—at, I suspect, Allison's urging—continue to use my office as a storage closet.

When the magazines are neatly stacked, Delia tries again, this time moving the chair gingerly. "I've discovered something," she says softly.

Delia is clutching the folder tightly in her arms. She has a hunted-fox look about her and seems skittish. I keep my voice low so I won't frighten her. "All right."

She nods, takes a deep breath and just says it: "Jane had Marguerite deported."

I stare at her for several seconds, not quite sure that I heard her correctly. Jane had Marguerite deported? How could Jane have anyone deported? Her power is limited to making editorial assistants cry and tearing up layouts seconds before they're supposed to go to the printer. "What?"

"Jane had Marguerite deported." She relaxes her arms, puts the file on the table and pushes it toward me. "Eight years ago."

I open the folder and flip through it slowly. There are photos of Marguerite when she was young and articles she wrote for *Parvenu* and Australian *Vogue*. There are photocopies of newspaper clippings and scribbled notes of telephone conversations Delia had with former co-workers and family members. This file is uncensored. There are no black marks or whited-out words. Either Delia is beginning to trust me or she was in too much of a rush to waste the time.

"She was born Marge Miller in a Perth suburb," Delia says.

For a moment I'm incapable of speech and my lips move without sound coming out of them. "Perth?"

"It's in Australia," she explains.

"I know where it is. I'm just not sure I understand."

"What's not to understand? Marguerite's Australian."

"She's Australian?"

Delia nods. "Born and bred."

"She's not French?"

"Nope, she didn't become French until—" Delia checks her files before committing to any details "—her twenty-third year."

"Huh," I say, trying to digest the strange fact that the in-house Audrey impersonator isn't even from Europe.

"She moved to Sydney when she was fifteen. Worked there for a few years at a series of trashy magazines. Then she disappeared for a year, only to reemerge in London at the age of twenty-one as Marguerite Tourneau. She got an editorial assistant job at *Hello!* magazine. After two years, she moved to New York and got an assistant editor job at *Parvenu,* where she met Jane and adopted a French ex-pat persona," Delia says, running quickly through the file's highlights. "The details of her stint there are still murky. I have calls out to former colleagues, who should be getting back to me soon. But we know some general facts: Marguerite got the senior editor position and Jane left a few months later. They stayed out of each other's way for the next few years until they came up for the *Face* editor in chief gig. According to the publisher's assistant at the time, they were neck and neck until Marguerite got deported. Then the job was all Jane's."

"No," I say.

Delia smiles. This is why she keeps files on all of us—because sometimes she uncovers something juicy. "Yes."

"But people don't behave like that."

She shrugs. Her sense of moral outrage isn't as keen as mine.

"How?" I ask.

Delia reaches over and sorts through the papers in front of me. Then she hands me a photocopied document. "Read the name of the INS officer who was in charge of the case."

David Whiting—it means nothing to me.

She sighs impatiently at my confused look. I'm an unworthy co-conspirator. "Didn't you look at the file I gave you at all? Whiting is Jane's maiden name. David Whiting is her brother."

I look at the document again, expecting it to somehow sprout horns and a tail. "But that's so immoral and unscrupulous and just plain mean."

Delia shrugs again. "That's Jane. Or maybe the whole Whiting clan. Her brother doesn't seem to be a very decent sort, either. It seems he made a habit of kicking people out of the country. In exchange for a small fee, he'd trump up charges against anyone. He was busted a few years ago but the whole thing was hushed up—friends in high places and all that. He's working in the State Department now."

I look at her sharply, suddenly terrified of being called before Congress on some dubious treason charge. A Whiting
in the State Department can do a lot of mischief.

"Don't worry," she says, laughing at my concern. "He's a
glorified lackey with low-level security clearance. He's mostly
just marking time until he can collect his pension."

I'm too anxious to be comforted by her assurances. I'm
too disconcerted by the new truth about Jane—that she isn't
just an unruly child who throws tantrums and tears the heads
off her dolls—to be placated by logic. "Still, it wouldn't hurt
us to tread more carefully from now on."

"Speaking of which, how is everything going?"

I run through the highlights of this week's bathroom meeting. I gloss over Allison's loopectomy and focus on the things
that are right on track—press releases, A-list celebrities, letters to advertisers. While I run through the details, I'm forced
to admit that the plan is coming together smoothly. I'm
forced to concede that my initial reservations were wide off
the mark. Overthrowing Jane Carolyn-Ann McNeill isn't a
long shot—it's an inevitability. And, in light of recent disclo-
sures, it's no longer a matter of enlightened self-interest. No,
now it's more like vigilante justice.

Senior Editor: Day 31

Soledad is trying to defend the word *urbania*.

"It's like *suburbia* but it applies to cities," she says, her voice distant and echoey as she does three other things in addition to arguing with me. Soledad has one of those lives that doesn't work without speakerphone. "It's cute and fun. What objection can you possibly have?"

I wait a moment for the background noises to die down. Although she's on the phone with me, Soledad is running a departmental meeting. Fashionistas are sitting around her desk pitching article ideas during the lulls. "*Urbania* is not a word. Webster's doesn't have it," I say, bringing the dictionary into the conversation for the fourth time. Soledad and I have been talking in circles for the past ten minutes and it doesn't help that she has her entire department there to back her up. This has just added to her sense of righteousness.

"But it sounds like what it is—the city," Soledad insists. The fashion department concurs in a series of background murmurs.

I don't agree. As far as I'm concerned, *urbania* sounds nothing like the city. Rather, it sounds like someplace in Eastern

Europe where suave, polished people live. It's a country populated by the urbane tribe.

"All right," I say, conceding the field. I don't want to go another round. I don't want to listen to her dismiss that niggling little book called a dictionary for a fifth time.

When I called Soledad up to talk about the new headline, I didn't expect an argument or the peanut gallery. I thought she would shrug her shoulders and move on with her life. But I misread the situation, which I've been doing a lot lately. Negotiating power struggles is now part of my job, but I'm no good at it. I never know when to step lightly around a fragile ego or when to stand my ground, and I can no longer rely on people like Dot to run interference for me.

"Can we just take my name off it completely?" I ask. I know this question is unwise, but I'm too tired of this conversation to consider my words carefully. And I hate being on speakerphone. I hate the one-second delay that makes it sound as though she's somewhere far away in East Africa like Mozambique and not down the hall.

There's a two-second pause—one for the speakerphone, one for Soledad's petulance. My request reveals too much passion. It shows that I don't just object to *urbania,* I find it repellent. "If that's the way you want it," she says in frosty tones as the spectators speak softly among themselves.

For a swift, brief moment, I contemplate backtracking to save my career. I consider telling her that that isn't the way I really want it, but I hold myself back. The damage has already been done and I might as well stand by this thin conviction if none others. A headline like "Urbania's Unlikely Undergrads" is not the sort of thing I ever thought I'd go to the mat for, but life is full of surprises. "Thank you."

"Was there something else?" She is testy and abrupt, and despite the crowd congregated in her office, has every intention of going straight to Lydia's office to complain about me. With very little effort and in very little time, I've earned the description of *difficult.*

"No, that was all." I put down the phone, take a deep breath and tell myself again to surrender. Surrender to the cutesy headlines and the silly puns and the nonsensical captions filled with belabored wordplays. Although I can't quite locate where my soul is in the agreement, I know there's something Faustian here and I resist. The senior editor deal already has all the elements of a cautionary tale: Be careful what you wish for, kids, because it might come true.

There are things I like about being a senior editor. I like choosing what I want to write about and assigning the really boring stuff to someone else. I enjoy talking to writers and deciding what direction a piece should take. My editing style is still in the developing stage, but I have a good ear for an author's voice and I try to preserve it despite the changes I make. I'm not like the other editors here. My instinct isn't to make everything sound as if I just typed it up myself.

The celebrity undergrad package was my first significant assignment as a senior editor and I think I handled it well. The story had several parts—lush photo spreads of actresses' dorm rooms, fashion layouts of the most stylish clothes to study in, comfort-food recipes from some of the best chefs in New York, a yoga routine to ward off the freshman fifteen, a superficial if well-intentioned examination of what it's like to be the most recognizable face in Bio 101—which I was able to pull together into a cohesive whole. The section was good. At least it had been good before Soledad started tweaking and tinkering and making up words like *urbania*.

Despite the inevitable frustrations, I'm happier in my storage-closet office than in the shantytown cubicle around the corner. There's a freedom here and a sort of nose-to-the-grindstone glamour I hadn't expected. *Fashionista* is just a comic book. It's just a Batman cartoon with "pow," "bam" and "kaplooey" under the pictures, but it's so much more satisfying to draw the lines instead of coloring them in.

The Spring Collection

The theme for Pieter van Kessel's show is urban renewal.

"Urban renewal?" says Marguerite as she pulls her wrap tighter around her shoulders. It's not that she's cold—the room is hot with heaters and people—it's that she doesn't want to get dirty. "This feels more like urban decay."

Van Kessel is holding his fall show on the construction site for a new Lower East Side library. The contractor has barely broken ground, but I'm still surprised that he let van Kessel pitch a tent and invite the press. This seems like the sort of thing that leads to disaster. "It's not so bad," I say, when we finally find our seats. It took us ages because we're in the front row. I'm not used to being so close to the runway and naturally I had to work myself forward. During this process, Marguerite trailed behind me, examining the crowd.

She wipes a thin layer of dust off her seat with a handkerchief and sits down. "This is an impressive showing."

The turnout is better than anyone could have expected. Word of mouth spread like wildfire, making van Kessel's show the hottest ticket of Fashion Week. Marguerite recognizes buyers from Barneys and Neiman Marcus and says hello. I'm excited. I'm excited because van Kessel deserves the attention, because my instincts were right, because there is a second article here.

Marguerite is not unknown in the fashion world and she holds court with an assortment of admirers who want to be seen in the front row, if only for a minute or two. While Marguerite talks about van Kessel's classic Old World style (she's been reading my notes) I sit quietly in my chair, staring at my hands folded in my lap. I don't know anyone here. This is only my second fashion show and I'm not sure yet how to comport myself. Minding my own business seems the most safe, though least enterprising, way to behave.

"Vicious, spiteful cat," a woman whispers in my ear.

Clearly my pose is not as innocuous as I assume. I turn to her, my eyes wide and defensive. The woman is old and glamorous, with white chin-length hair in a wavy bob, vintage silk pajamas and diamonds. There's something vaguely familiar about her, like she's one of the bodies I sweep past every day on the subway. "Excuse me?" I ask, my voice almost shrill.

The woman is surprised by my attentions. Either she hadn't been addressing me or she suffers from a Tourette's-like syndrome that she's unaware of. "I'm sorry, dear. I was just mumbling to myself. Please pay me no mind."

"Excuse me," I say again, my inflection dramatically altered.

"Don't be silly, dear. You were perfectly within the bounds of proper behavior." She laughs and runs a hand over her hair, smoothing it. "I should know better. I've certainly been to enough of these."

"It's all right," I say, smiling awkwardly for a moment before turning my eyes back to the runway. The woman next to me is clearly a veteran of the fashion wars and I don't want to intrude.

"I haven't seen you before," she says conversationally. "Is this your first time at one of these things?"

"Almost. The only other one I've been to was van Kessel's first show in June."

She raises a drawn-in eyebrow, impressed. Only opinion makers and me had been at that show. "I wish I'd gone but I'd never even heard of van Kessel until I read a review in the *Times*. I pride myself on staying current but it's more work than it used to be."

"Oh, I only went to the show because a friend of mine's mother, who used to work with van Kessel's assistant, had an extra ticket," I say, feeling compelled to explain. I don't want her to think I'm a fashion genius. I'm not a genius; it's just that sometimes I get lucky. "It was a very exciting collection. It was so good that I dashed over to his shop and spent half a day with him and his team."

"Clever girl," she says approvingly.

I blush more from the approbation than from the compliment. It's nice to have one's instincts validated. "Thank you. I thought it would be interesting to follow the career of a hot new talent. I envisioned a series of articles charting van Kessel's rise."

She nods. This, too, is a good idea. "When will it run?"

"It probably won't."

Her expression is puzzled.

"I work for *Fashionista*."

This is explanation enough. "Ah."

"Yes," I say sadly. "I tried pitching it, but it's really not the sort of thing we run."

She pats my hand kindly. "That's a shame."

I shrug. There have been many shameful things during my tenure and it wouldn't do to linger over one of them now. "It's all right. As you said before, I should know better."

"I'm Ellis Masters, by the way," she says, offering me her hand. "I don't know where my manners have gone. I should have introduced myself long before."

Ellis Masters is a legendary fashion maven, the sort who makes careers and breaks careers and doesn't think of the fallout. She is always spoken of with the type of reverence usually reserved for the dead and dying, but she is still vitally alive. She's vibrant and friendly and muttering to herself in the front row of fashion shows.

"It's an honor to meet you," I say, resisting the urge to bow my head, which wouldn't be appropriate. She's fashion royalty, not the queen. "I'm Vig Morgan."

"I'm pleased to meet you, Vig." She surveys the crowd and then glances at her jeweled watch. "I do wish they'd get started. I have three other shows to get to tonight."

"I'm sure you're too busy," I say, at this reminder of how jam-packed her schedule is, "but if you have a moment free Thursday night, *Fashionista* is hosting a party for Gavin Marshall and I'd love for you to come. He's a British artist who—"

"I know Gavin," she says. "I was very surprised that *Fashionista* was involved at all. Controversial art is really not the sort of thing they run, I believe is how you'd term it."

Suddenly I'm overwhelmed with the desire to confess everything, but I resist the urge. "We expect it to be high-profile."

"Yes, I can see that. Well, I'll keep it in mind," she says, but she's only being polite. Ellis Masters is too mannerly to refuse an invitation outright.

Marguerite's admirers disperse and she notices for the first time whom I'm sitting next to. "Ellis darling," she drawls, jumping out of her seat to hug the grand dame of fashion. "How lovely to see you again."

Ellis doesn't share the sentiment. It's obvious in the way she suffers the embrace with impatience. She frees herself as quickly as possible. "Marge," she says in a voice that's no longer warm and welcoming.

Marguerite doesn't notice the difference and chatters away about the old days and Paris and friends they've lost touch with. Ellis Masters looks trapped for a second, but before I can intervene with my look-isn't-that-Damien-Hirst-wav-

ing-to-you trick, she smoothly extricates herself from the
conversation and starts talking to the man on the other side
of her. He's an easily recognizable actor, and although he has
no idea whom he's talking to, he recognizes a woman of importance.

"She's such a darling and I haven't seen her in ages," Marguerite says, returning to her seat. "I'm sorry I didn't introduce you, Vig. Sometimes she's a temperamental old thing
and there's nothing you can say to it."

"How do you know her?" I ask, wondering at her chilly
reception.

"I worked at her magazine, *Parvenu*. It was a hundred
years ago when I was starting out. God, I was just an associate editor. I made no money and had to wear designer suits
with the tags still on. I'd return them afterward."

Marguerite is about to reminisce more but she doesn't get
a chance. Music starts playing, and although she makes several attempts to shout over it, the drums are too loud. They're
deafening and they drown her out completely. I sit back in
my seat and wait for the show to start, but my mind is elsewhere. It's on Ellis Masters and Marge and the words *vicious,
spiteful cat*.

This Is Not a Relationship

Alex's parents are in town for the night.

"It's only a stopover on their way to London," he said on the phone earlier, explaining why he couldn't meet me for dinner after the van Kessel show. "They have an early flight tomorrow, so they should be back in their hotel room by ten. I could drop by your apartment afterward."

Although I was disappointed that he hadn't invited me to join them, I agreed to this plan and told him I'll see him later. But I'm not surprised that he doesn't want me to meet his parents. Our relationship isn't the say-hi-to-in-laws sort. We see each other regularly and have fun, but we don't talk about things. I don't ask about the breathy blonde who lives next door and he doesn't ask if I'm seeing anyone else.

The answer is no, of course. The answer is that I'm so thoroughly besotted by this charming ogre that sometimes I can't think of anything else. But I've dated enough men to know when to keep my distance. I've been out here in singleland long enough to know when to play it safe.

At ten-seventeen he shows up on my doorstep with vanilla

Häagen Dazs and chocolate syrup and, while he makes sundaes, he asks me about the show. He questions me about Pieter van Kessel and my story ideas, and when I ramble excitedly for a half hour, he doesn't interrupt. He just nods encouragingly, offering the sort of support you've always wanted from a boyfriend.

After he washes the bowls and spoons, he tells me he has to go home and walk Quik. He says he can't stay but he does and when I climb out of bed at three in the morning, I have to crawl over his legs because a narrow set of drawers is in my way. When I come back, I stare at him. In the red glow from the alarm clock, I can see a beauty mark on his back. It's just beneath his shoulder blade and I run my hand over it gently. I glide my fingers over his warm skin for a moment, but before I can move away he's pulling me toward him. He's pulling me toward him and wrapping my body against his. I'm held fast in a prison of warm skin.

I lie there awake for a long time, my arm encased in his, and I try very hard to remind myself of the truth. Despite what it feels like, this is not a relationship.

Urban Renewal

After his tremendously successful show in a Lower East Side parking lot, Pieter van Kessel went into seclusion. He made polite and ecstatic conversation with everyone who came backstage to congratulate him on a brilliant collection and then disappeared into the night. No one has seen neither hide nor hair of him since except his assistant, Hans, and he's not talking.

"It would be a huge coup for us," the woman says, after she introduced herself as Leila Chisholm from the *Times*. "We've been trying to get something out of his people for hours, but everything seems to be in disarray over there. They don't even have a publicity department."

I think of the ramshackle basement I visited months ago during the height of summer. No, I'm not surprised they don't have a publicity department. "Who told you about the interview?" I ask. I'm still trying to grasp the fact that the *New York Times* wants to buy a piece from me.

"Ellis Masters mentioned it to my editor," she explains.

"She said you were proposing to do a series of articles charting the success of a hot young property."

"It's an idea I've been toying with," I say, understating the case and playing it cool and collected as though my heart weren't flying.

"We love it."

"Excuse me?" It's not that I didn't hear the words the first time. It's just that I want to hear them again.

"We love it," she obligingly repeats. "We want you to do the series for us."

"All right," I say. Although I've signed documents giving Ivy Publishing ownership to any ideas I think of while working for them, I'm not worried. Jane isn't going to suddenly be interested in Pieter van Kessel. He might be a sensation in the fashion world, but *Fashionista* isn't about fashion.

"Good. We'd like to run the interview in Friday's paper," she announces matter-of-factly. "We'll say three thousand words. When do you think we can have it?"

I do some rapid calculations. I have a dozen pages of notes to read through and organize and two hours of tapes to transcribe. "How is tomorrow?"

"In the morning?" she asks.

I was thinking in the afternoon, but I readily agree. The pile of work on my desk is boring and inconsequential and nothing compared with this. I have no intention of touching any of it until my piece on Pieter van Kessel is perfect. "By eleven?"

"Eleven's a little later than I'd like, but it'll do," she concedes. "If you give me your fax number, I'll send over the contract right away."

I've had so few things faxed to me that I don't know the number, and I spend several anxious moments rifling through my drawers for a piece of paper with this sort of information on it. After I hang up the phone, I stand at my desk, trying to decide what I should do next. Call my parents or hover by the fax machine? A paranoid sense that nothing good ever happens to me washes over me and I run to the fax machine to wait. I don't want any fingers but mine to touch that document. It takes fifteen minutes and the ink is faint but it's beautiful to my smitten eyes.

Before calling my parents or doing a triumphant jig, I duck my head in Marguerite's office and casually ask if she thinks *Fashionista* will ever be interested in my van Kessel article idea.

She shakes her head sadly. "Not the way things are right now. Maybe if I were editor in chief...." She lets the sentence trail off seductively, but I'm in no condition to indulge her. She has said exactly the words I want to hear.

I can no longer control my exuberance and I give her my brightest, happiest smile.

"Thank you," I say, demure and breathless at the same time. Then I return to my office, close the door and dance around happily. Three thousand words in the *New York Times!* I can scarcely believe it. This is the sort of thing you dream about. This is the reason you went into journalism in the first place.

I take deep calming breaths and decide it's time to get to work. However, before I find my Dictaphone and microcassettes, I write a thank-you note. I dash off a gracious letter to Ms. Ellis Masters and drop it into the mail slot, but it's only a gesture and an inadequate one at that. The truth is I can't ever thank her enough.

Jane Carolyn-Ann Whiting McNeill

Fifty-two hours before the party, Jane adds her maiden name to her already inflated appellation. Stickly distributes the memo, which Jane deems too time-sensitive to go through regular channels. It could take up to four hours for it to wind its way through the system, and she doesn't want us to lose crucial Whiting-memorization minutes. The addition of her middle name has not gone as smoothly as she'd like, and she's had to call a few unfortunate individuals into her office for inopportune dropping of "Jane McNeill." One publicist has already been fired because of a slip in the *Observer*.

The memo is printed on elaborate monarch-size letter-head, and Stickly wears a stoic mask of indifference as he drops it on my desk. He's trying to be brave. He's trying to keep a stiff upper lip but he's practically radiating despair. This isn't what Sticklys do. They deliver peasants to monarchs, not monarchs to peasants.

"Ms. McNeill will see you at one-thirty," he says in that imperial voice that could fill amphitheaters.

I shake my head. I have no intention of leaving my office

right now. I will not budge a tiny fraction of an inch until I know what Leila Chisholm thinks of my article. I'm expecting the worst. I'm expecting her to hate it. I'm expecting her to scream loudly in my ear that it's the worst tripe she's ever read in her entire life. I will suffer her abuse unflinchingly. I will endure it without a whimper; then I'll hang up the phone and weep.

The article is on my desk, but I can't bring myself to look at it again. I've read it too many times already and still cannot decide if it's good or not. I'm exhausted from lack of sleep and suspicious of my own judgment and terrified that the sort of genius that strikes at three in the morning is just nonsense in sheep's clothing.

"One-thirty's no good for me," I say, taking my eyes off the phone. A watched pot never rings.

"It's very important."

I raise an eyebrow. There are many important things to be done, but Anita Smithers's assistant is devoted and thorough and is taking care of all of them. There is nothing important that Jane has to do. "Is it?"

He nods. "Ms. McNeill wants to discuss whether she should stand in front of the blue *Fashionista* banner or the red *Fashionista* banner."

Jane doesn't have discussions; she takes polls, gives quizzes and lectures. "What did you say?"

"The blue."

"The blue?"

"Yes, mum is wearing a red dress and would run the risk of clashing." Stickly is still using his imposing voice and holding himself with dignity, even though neither one befits the subject matter.

I compliment this excellent reasoning and exhort him to tell Jane that I too say the blue background. Stickly wants to argue further with me—my intractability offends him—but he has to move on. He has to hand out the memos in less time than it would take the in-house mail service to do it.

Stickly leaves and I return to my previous activity of phone staring. When Leila Chisholm finally calls three hours later, I'm fast asleep at my desk. My head is at an uncomfortable angle and there are paper clip indentations in my cheek. The ringing telephone is jarring, like a splash of cold water on my face, but I'm still groggy when I answer it. My thoughts are muddled, and it takes me a full minute to realize that she doesn't hate it.

"It needs tweaking, of course," she says, before rattling off a list of changes that I'm too slow-witted to understand. I'm not used to the fast-paced world of daily newspapers. "Don't worry if you didn't catch all that. I'm going to fax over my notes right now. Same fax number?"

After picking up the fax, I head to the kitchen to get a fresh cup of coffee. Leila's notes are dense and copious and require an alertness that I'm not capable of right now without artificial stimulants. Flipping through her comments, I realize that the word *tweaking* is an understatement but I'm not worried. I'm exhilarated and thrilled and on fire to start the second draft.

Tweaking aside, the future is bright. The editor from the *New York Times* said she was sure I'd have a better feel for their style next time.

Drinks at the W

Maya loves hotel lounges and bars. She loves their glamour and evanescence and the way they make her feel as though she's almost far away from home. Here people are immersed in their lives; elsewhere they are running away.

"I never loved Roger," she says after the waiter brings her a capirinha. She's never had one before but she's looking for a new drink—cosmopolitans are for mourning Roger, whom she never loved—and she fancies the idea of alcohol made out of sugar cane.

I take a sip of my mojito—a new drink in the spirit of new beginnings—and wait for her to elaborate on her topic sentence. I have revelations of my own to share, but they must take a back seat. Relationship conversations always trump.

"It's not like I ever thought I did," she continues, after the capirinha passes muster. "That ring was like Kryptonite, it made me weak. When I found it in that drawer, I felt something overwhelming and assumed it was love. I think now that it was just nostalgia for something—the Cleavers at the dinner table—that doesn't exist," she confesses with a hint of

embarrassment. It's hard to realize that you are just as susceptible as your friends from the suburbs who want to stay
in the suburbs.

"The smell of other people's barbecues," I say.

"Hmm?" she asks, her eyes on the entrance, as if she's
waiting for someone. We are in the bar at the W hotel in
Union Square. We are surrounded by sleek counters and
large velvet couches and beautiful people in tight skirts, but
don't let the W fool you. It's still your parents' Westin.

"The smell of other people's barbecues when I'm sitting
on my fire escape. It's the same thing," I say, explaining.

She nods understandingly. "And some songs."

"It's a universal," I say, as if our three examples are proof
of basic human experience.

She turns to me and smiles brightly. "Which means this
thing with Gavin isn't completely doomed. I can't be re-
bounding if there's nothing to rebound from."

I'm in the act of swallowing rum and lime juice when she
makes her statement, and the randomness of it causes me to
cough and sputter. I'm aware of no things with Gavin.
"What?"

"Gavin and I have been in touch," she says, looking away.
She is somewhat abashed.

"Why haven't you said anything?"

"What am I going to say? 'Hey, Vig, Gavin and I talk every
night and have really great conversations. I think I'm falling
in love,'" she says, mockingly. "It's embarrassing. I can't even
say the words *really great conversation* without cringing."

I sweep by her hyper self-consciousness and zoom in on
the significant piece of information. "You're in love?"

She shrugs, trying to appear indifferent. She didn't mean
to reveal so much and is now trying to backtrack.

"You like him a lot?" I ask, trying to temper the immen-
sity of the admission.

Her eyes shift again to the entrance, which she expects
Gavin to walk through at any minute, I realize now. He ar-

rived in town late last night and went directly to the gallery first thing this morning to oversee the final stages of setup.

I've come up against the Maya brick wall enough times to know when I'm about to bash my head against it. "I sold an article to the *Times.*"

She flings her head around and she grabs my hand with such tremendous force that my drink spills. "You what?"

"I sold my interview with Pieter van Kessel to the *New York Times.* And not just the interview," I say, drying my arm with a cocktail napkin. "They liked my idea for a series. They want the whole thing."

Maya is speechless for a few seconds; then she starts hitting her hand on the bar. "My good man," she calls, when she finally has the bartender's attention, "we'd like a bottle of your worst champagne."

"That's not necessary. I—"

"What? We can't have a celebration without champagne. What are you going to toast with?"

I'm about to say that we can toast with mojitos and capirinhas, but the bartender is already opening a bottle of Moët.

"Besides," she adds, handing me a flute, "I've got something I want to toast to as well."

"What?"

"No, no, you first." She raises her glass. "To my dear friend Hedwig Morgan, journalist."

It sounds weird and lovely, and I swallow six ounces of champagne in a single gulp. "All right, now your news."

"I started a new book—"

"That's excellent. What's it about?"

"Trying to poison an anorexic, but it's not a mystery because nobody dies."

I refill our glasses and raise mine for a toast. I gesture for her to do the same, but she does not comply. "To literature!"

"I don't think—"

"Uh-uh. If I must suffer your toasts, then you must suffer mine."

Maya knows better than to go up against a slightly in-
ebriated Vig. "All right. To literature."

She doesn't say it with any sort of feeling, but I let the lack
of conviction slide. At least she said it.

"Anyway, the point is that I gave the first few chapters to
an agent in New York who is friends with Gavin's agent in
London. She read it as a favor to Gavin, but she thinks it's promising. She wants to see the whole thing as soon as I'm done."

In rigorous compliance with term of reference, August 15,
the word *agent* has not passed my lips in almost three months.
I'm happy and relieved to discover that others haven't been
so circumspect. "That's excellent."

"It doesn't really mean anything. It could be that she's just
being polite and there's always a very good chance that she
won't like the rest of the book," she says discouragingly. "It's
a long way from being something."

Her knee-jerk pessimism is an uninvited guest at the party
and I brush it aside. "To promising."

This toast has a melancholy mix of hopeful and hopeless
(the possibility of succeeding, the inevitable falling short) that
appeals to Maya and she raises her glass with enthusiasm.

By the time Gavin shows up, we are invincible. We are invincible and giddy and convinced that anything is possible.
We are like Godzilla, and all those tiny obstacles in our way
are just the rooftops of small Japanese villages.

Maya throws her arms around Gavin and gives him a
sloppy, enthusiastic kiss, which he receives with a shy smile.
He makes eye contact with me over her shoulder and waves.
Because their only dates have been really great telephone
conversations, I leave them alone for a few minutes. I go to
the bathroom and admire the fixtures and feel a little sorry
for myself that Alex isn't here. When I called earlier to tell
him the good news, I'd intended to invite him. I'd intended
to ask him out for a drink, but something stopped me. Cel-
ebrating huge lifetime milestones seems too much like a relationship thing.

When I return, Maya is signing the credit card receipt. With our debt settled, we bundle into a cab and go to Maya's favorite restaurant for dinner, where we gorge on mushroom crepes and olive crostini and crème brûlée. Someone orders a bottle of wine, and I eagerly accept a glass, even though I know I'm about to be ambushed by exhaustion. Because he missed out on the earlier round of ecstatic toasting, Gavin makes a series of toasts that are hilarious and sweet and bring tears to drunken Maya's eyes.

The evening concludes happily with the customary scuffle over who gets to foot the bill, which I win because my reflexes are the least impaired by alcohol. Outside the air is chilly and fresh and before I grab a cab home, I insist on walking them back to Maya's apartment. The Future is just around the corner.

Omens

For Christine the bathroom is the last unexplored storage frontier, and she's covered the tile walls of her shower with white plastic baskets, the sort that suction-cup on. This is where she keeps her Lysol and her Soft Scrub and her Fantastic.

"They all fell," she says, entering my office and shutting the door. "I've had those baskets up for two years and they never once budged and now all six have fallen, even the little one in the corner that holds my loofah."

Although I've cleared the guest chair for her, Christine prefers to stand. She'd rather pace and dodge scattered stacks of magazines that litter the floor than take a seat.

"Then this morning when I opened my door, my doormat was gone." She looks at me, her eyes wide and blue, and waits for my response.

"Gone?"

"Gone."

"Someone stole your doormat?" I ask, oddly disturbed. Nobody steals doormats. It's a violation of the social contract.

"But that's not all. Get this—when I woke up this morning there was a squirrel in my bed. He was on my comforter staring at me with his beady red eyes," she says, recalling the experience with a shudder.

I don't know what to say. These morning mishaps seem unimportant and inconsequential to me, but an inexplicable vehemence has crept into Christine's voice, making me realize that she thinks she's listing disasters. To fill the expectant silence, I mutter something about always remembering to close your windows before going to sleep.

"You don't see," she says, her voice flat. It's only 10:23 in the morning but I've already disappointed her. "These are all signs."

"Signs?"

"Signs."

"The squirrel in your bed is a sign?"

She rolls her eyes. "Like a red cow in Israel. It's a sign that something terrible is going to happen. What do you need," she asks, her voice scornful of my lack of faith, "a plague of locusts?"

The answer to this question is yes. Yes, I need a plague of locusts. "Nothing bad is going to happen." I'm trying to treat the matter with the solemnity that Christine feels it deserves, but I'm having a hard time keeping a smile off my lips.

"You can't dress Jesus up in a bias-cut halter-top silk dress by Givenchy," she says, "and not expect something biblical to happen. You must be *humble* in the presence of the Lord."

I know little about the Bible and humility and being in the presence of the Lord, but I recognize panic when it's striding around my office. "Nothing bad is going to happen," I say in soothing tones as the door opens.

Sarah enters. She has a huge smile on her face, and although momentarily distracted by seeing Christine in my office, she recovers quickly. "They're picketing."

"What?" I ask.

"They're picketing the building," she says, barely able to

contain her excitement. This is the first indication that our plan is working. "We're completely surrounded by irate Christians holding signs that quote scripture. The police are down there right now trying to break it up because the demonstrators don't have a permit." She laughs. "Police—can you believe it? This is better than anything I expected."

Christine gives Sarah a cross look. She sees nothing here to be exultant about. "You should call it off now before the locusts arrive."

Sarah raises an eyebrow. "What locusts?"

"Go talk to Jane about it," I say. "It's her party."

But Christine doesn't want to talk to Jane. She's frightened of her. "Couldn't you do it?"

The idea is so ridiculous, I almost laugh. "Me?"

"Jane listens to you," she insists, her hands jumping agitatedly in front of her.

There it is again—this odd assumption that Jane respects me. "I'm not asking Jane to cancel the party. There's no reason to."

"But I told you about the squirrel and everything. These are all omens." She pauses for a moment, as if considering her next move. "And then there's Allison."

I stiffen at the mention of the one person who could bring our plan tumbling down. "Allison?"

Christine looks around the room and then leans in. "I think she's talking in tongues," she says softly.

Sarah starts giggling. I'm also amused but contain my laughter. Christine is one hundred percent serious. "Speaking in tongues?" I ask.

"She's excited, almost fevered, and she's muttering incessantly under her breath. I've tried to make sense of it but I can't. It's not English."

Although I'm pretty sure that Allison isn't speaking in tongues, I realize there's no way to convince Christine of that. So I placate her with promises. "Tell you what—if Allison is still excited and muttering at four o'clock, I'll see what I can do."

Four o'clock is too late to call off the party, but Christine doesn't notice that. She lets out a relieved sigh. "Thank you, Vig."

I shrug, as if it's nothing, which it actually is. Even if I wanted to talk to Jane today, I couldn't get in touch with her. She's gone deep into the belly of the beauty beast and isn't scheduled to emerge until she's been plucked, exfoliated and coiffed.

Christine leaves and Sarah and I press our heads against the window to watch police officers interact with the picketing crowd. This is how Delia finds us.

"Pretty cool, huh?" she says, looking over our shoulders.

Sarah squeals happily. "I have to get closer than this. Care to come?"

Delia and I both decline and we watch her skip out of the office and down the hall. "Well," I say, "it looks like things are going according to plan."

She nods and sits down. "They are, only there's one small thing."

Despite my atheism, my heart catches and for a split second I fear that she's going to tell me about a horde of locusts coming up Fifth Avenue. "One small thing?"

"Remember Australia?"

"Australia?"

"You know, the continent that Jane had Marguerite deported to?"

"Yes, of course. Australia."

"Well, it turns out that was an act of reprisal," Delia says, pushing a legal-size yellow notebook across the desk.

I pick it up and try to read it but I can't. Delia's handwriting is a series of tight wide swirls. None of it is legible. "What's this?"

"My shorthand notes. I just got off the phone with *Parvenu*'s editor in chief's old assistant, Lucy Binders. A very friendly woman. She works in car insurance now."

Although a large part of me wants to know how she found

Ellis Masters's assistant twelve years later, I control my curiosity. Delia's investigative skills are not the point. "What'd
Lucy Binders say?"

"That Marguerite is a manipulative scheming bitch and
that after her promotion to senior editor, which she got by
sleeping with the managing editor, she made all the junior
staff's life hell, particularly Jane's. She gave her crap assignments, changed deadlines on her so that all her articles were
in late and rewrote her copy to make her look inept and in-
coherent. Five months later Jane was fired." She flips the
page and starts reading from her notes. "I've been in touch
with a few editors over at Australian *Vogue* but nobody's
talking. Marguerite's rise through the ranks there was mete-
oric. She went from senior editor to editor in chief within
sixteen months. You'd think *someone* over there would have
an opinion but they're all hush-hush. However, on the bright
side, she seems to have no issues with age," Delia says, breaking down the staff of Australian *Vogue* by age and education.

My instinct is to break into a Christine-size panic. My instinct is to call the whole thing off and run away, but this is
now beyond my control. Religious groups are picketing the
building and nothing I say will make them go home. "All
right. Keep digging. Maybe we can find something on Marguerite that we can use later on if she becomes a problem,"
I say, more than a little disturbed by my own expediency.
Plotting against Jane was supposed to be a onetime deal, not
a new way of life.

"That's exactly what I was thinking, chief," she says, a
bright approving smile on her face. Delia's happy with my
newfound ruthlessness. She thinks it means that I'm inching
closer to the dark side. She thinks it means that any minute
now I'll start keeping files on my co-workers.

I don't really know what it means, but I sincerely hope
she's wrong.

Judas

W hen I arrive at the gallery, Gavin is dismantling the Gilding the Lily exhibit. He's packing up his Jesus statues as if they're marbles he can stick in his pocket and take home.

"What's up?" I ask when I spot him in the corner pulling sheer panty hose off a Jesus in a classic Chanel suit. Everything else is going smoothly—the caterers are setting up the bar, the sound engineer is double-checking the microphones, the protesters are assembling their podium and booing at fashionistas who walk by. Only Gavin is working against the common goal.

I know Gavin heard me—it's obvious from the way his shoulders stiffen—but he doesn't look up or answer. He simply balls up the stockings and tosses them into a brown cardboard box. Then he starts unbuttoning the jacket.

The silence and the Jesus-stripping are two very bad signs, but I don't panic. I hold on to my cool and walk over to Gavin for further investigation. "Hey, is something wrong?"

Gavin turns to face me. His eyes are hot and angry and his lips are pulled together in a tight, straight line. This isn't the easygoing, familiar Gavin who made drunken toasts and ate greasy crepes and kissed me on the forehead at three o'clock in the morning. This is frightening stony-faced Gavin.

I put a hand on his arm as a gesture of comfort; he tries to shrug it off. I hold fast, suddenly scared that something truly awful has happened. "Tell me what's going on."

He takes a deep breath and says, with more scorn than I've ever heard in my life, "Jesus' New Birthday Suit."

"Oh," I say, dropping my hand and taking a step back. I've known for more than three months that this moment was inevitable, but somewhere in the *New York Times*-Van Kessel champagne haze, it slipped my mind. I should have warned him about *Fashionista*'s December issue last night. I should have confessed everything while he was giddy from wine and giggling at awful knock-knock jokes.

Gavin sneers. He actually lifts and curls his top lip like a rabid dog and sneers at me. "Oh?"

His anger is completely justified and I don't know what to say. For several long moments we stand there facing each other—he with a curled lip, me with uncertainty—listening to the speakers squeak and the engineer say, "Testing one-two-three." "I wanted to tell you—I *meant* to tell you—but I didn't know how."

He glares at me and his contempt becomes something almost palpable—it's another half-dressed statue in the room. "Christ: Trendsetter or Savior?"

I flinch as if struck. The lines on the cover of the December issue were always in bad taste and vaguely embarrassing, but they never seemed this awful. Somehow they're ten times worse coming from the wronged artist himself. "I'm so sorry this happened. I'm still not even sure *how* it happened," I say, my eyes making contact with the offending magazine, which is lying half open on the floor. There are footprints on the belly of the bikini-clad cover model. "One minute we're doing a tasteful spread on your artwork and the next we're brainstorming article ideas related to Jesus." I'm trying to sound calm, but I'm seconds away from dropping to my knees and begging. And not just because I want to overthrow Jane. There's more than one evil editor in chief on the line now. *Fashionista* promised the New York art scene and the national media a party. We can't renege now, not without a lot of humiliation and rolling heads. Mine, certainly. Suddenly Christine's stolen doormat doesn't seem so innocuous.

Gavin is about to rattle off another December bon mot when Maya arrives. She's wearing a floor-length black dress and a glittering tiara.

"Hello, darling," she says, greeting Gavin with a heartfelt kiss on the lips before looking around at the dozens of gleaming Jesus statues. She's momentarily taken aback by the unexpected beauty of the sight. I can hardly blame her. Gilding the Lily isn't what I expected, either. It's not shoddy, overdressed plaster-of-paris mannequins grabbing fifteen minutes of attention, but lovely sculptures with exquisite details. She points to one statue in particular—Jesus in Givenchy. "I don't want to sound catty, but doesn't that dress make Jesus look fat?" she asks, glowing happily.

Gavin doesn't respond in kind to her jest. His disappointment in Maya is keen and he stares at her with puppy-dog eyes and a quivering mouth. Maya doesn't get stony-faced Gavin. She gets sad-faced, on-the-brink-of-tears Gavin. "Loincloth Lust: Resurrect an Ancient Fashion Staple," he says.

Maya isn't familiar with *Fashionista's* December issue, and she stares at him blankly. Although she doesn't know what he's talking about, she has an inkling that something is wrong. The caterers and the sound-check guy and the protesters on the doorstep might think everything is okay, but Maya knows better. The air is tense and prickly and she looks to me for an explanation.

"He's angry about the Jesus articles that the magazine did in honor of this exhibit," I say.

Maya blinks. "Oh."

"You're not going to deny it?" Gavin asks, yanking the

jacket off the statue. It's a haute couture garment with delicate seams, but he tugs at it as if it's an old painter's smock.

"Deny it?" Maya echoes. It's obvious from her blank look
that she has no idea what she's supposed to be denying. The
Jesus package isn't a living, breathing thing to her. It's not a
page she bookmarked or number she jotted down in her
Filofax. It's just a Post-it note buried under piles of newspaper in her mind.

But Gavin doesn't understand this. He crumples the jacket
and tosses it into the cardboard box. "You knew they were
going to humiliate me and you didn't say a thing. Even last
night when we were—" He breaks off here, as if memories
of last night are too painful to be remembered now. "You still
didn't say one damn thing about it."

While he's busy glaring at Maya, I walk behind him, pull
the jacket out of the box and shake out the wrinkles gently.
Even if the show doesn't go on, I can't leave the jacket in an
indifferent ball. I've been at *Fashionista* for too many years to
stand idly by while a Chanel is abused.

"It's not Maya's fault," I say, impatient with his unfair behavior. "Stop taking it out on her. Blame me. Be angry at me."

He laughs mockingly. "Oh, I am angry at you. Don't get
me started."

But I want to get him started. Now that he's talking to me
in full sentences and not cryptic magazine headlines, I very
much want to get him started. His rage needs a place to go.
I'm the best target. I'm the *right* target. "Look, I'm very, *very*
sorry this happened and I'm very, *very* sorry that I didn't have
the power to stop it, but we don't have time for this. Not now.
As soon as the evening is over I'll do whatever you want to
make it up to you. I swear—whatever you want. But we must
have the party." I glance quickly at my watch. It's already 7:12.
In forty-eight minutes glittering debutantes and sarcastic
wits will be walking through that door and Chanel Jesus is
only half-dressed. "Please, *please* don't do this," I say, panic
edging its way into my voice. Hysteria is only seconds away.

Gavin dismisses my entreaties with an indifferent shrug. He picks up the discarded issue, rolls it up and waves it under my nose. There is now a blue vein popping out of his forehead. "You've made me a laughingstock with this...this—" he sputters for a moment as he searches for the right word "—prurient nonsense. You've trivialized everything I've done. You've turned Gilding the Lily into an elaborate punch line." He throws the magazine against the wall, where it flutters and falls to the floor. "Do you have any idea how hard I've worked to gain respect? Do you have any sort of clue how tough it is for a bloke with a royal crest and a Tudor castle to be taken seriously as an artist? For God's sake, I even have a bloody Victorian plunge pool in my backyard. Critics love to skewer poor little rich boys who dabble in art. *Dabble*. Well, I don't fucking dabble. I'm not Prince bloody Charles with his watercolor stamps. This is important to me. This is what I do. It's not a goddamn three-ring circus for your magazine to shit on."

I look at Gavin. His blue vein is throbbing and his breathing is coming in short, ragged bursts. His anger is solid and real, but I'm not sure about his intentions. Calling off the party is a magnificent, grandstanding gesture—it punishes me, it shows the editors of *Fashionista* that they can't treat his work like an elaborate punch line, it assuages his ego—but it might be an empty one. Still, I can't take the chance. You don't call the bluff of irate artists who hold your future in the cardboard box next to them. "You can do this," I say quietly, deciding to give in to the inevitable debasement. I won't win this battle with logic or threats. "You can slam the door in the faces of eager party-goers and go merrily on your way. Your career will survive, perhaps even flourish because of it—being an enfant terrible has never been terrible for business—but you'll be ruining me."

He runs a hand over his eyes and is silent for a long time. Maya watches with her fingers clenched at her side. She wants to help, but there's nothing she can do to make this

better. *Fashionista* isn't her fight. She's only an innocent by-
stander, a tiara-wearing sedan at a stop sign, which had the
bad luck to be sideswiped by drag-racing sports cars. "Damn
it, Vig," Gavin says. He sounds tired.

"I know it's not fair," I say, pressing my advantage. I recognize pity when it stands in front of me with weary eyes.
"I know you're not here to do me any favors, but think about
it. *Fashionista* can't hurt you. It's just a silly magazine with lots
of beautiful photographs that people love to flip through.
That's all. We're something to occupy your hands while you
wait for a haircut or for the train to pull into Grand Central.
We're not permanent. We won't be around in two hundred
years when your statues are gracing the entrance to the Vat-
ican. But you *can* hurt us. You *can* punish us. Please don't."

Gavin gives in. Maybe if he hadn't drunk to my success
last night or kissed me on the forehead fifteen hours before,
he would've been able to withstand my pathetic pleading.
But he had. And he doesn't. "All right."

Maya cheers and throws herself into his arms. "Thank
God that's settled. Now, will someone please comment on
my tiara? I wore it to work as part of my article and not one
person commented. I'm half convinced it's invisible."

Gavin laughs and rushes to assure her that she—and the
tiara—are perfect. Then he extracts from her the promise to
warn him the next time her best friend intends to make a
fool of him. I'm somewhat offended by the wording—it
wasn't my intention so much as Jane's—but I appreciate the
sentiment and remain quiet.

With one disaster narrowly averted, I do a quick inspec-
tion of the gallery to make sure *Fashionista* hasn't inadver-
tently offended some other crucial party. I even stick my head
outside to check on the protest, which is coming together
nicely. The three-foot podium is standing solidly and the
demonstrators are practicing their chants. God bless them.

I drop by the bar to get a drink. I know I shouldn't start
consuming alcohol until the party is officially under way, but

I can't resist. Recent events demand something stronger than tonic water. They require vermouth and two generous ounces of gin and a stuffed green olive.

After thanking the bartender, I wander over to Gavin to see if he needs help dressing Chanel Jesus.

"No, I've got it under control," he says confidently as he wraps a scarf around Jesus' head. He ties it under the chin and slides on a pair of large wraparound sunglasses. Suddenly Jesus Christ looks just like Jane McNeill on a lunch date.

Since there's nothing for me to do, I walk over to the stage, which is set up for the four-piece band, and sit down on the edge. The room is festive, with white-cloth-covered tables and shimmering votive candles, and alive with expectation. Something is about to happen here. The smell of hors d'oeuvres—baby quiches and tiny crab cakes—wafting in from the kitchen confirms it. We're having a party.

I sigh deeply, take another sip of my martini and wait for the next disaster.

Calgary

Krystal Karpfinger wants to open an outdoor shopping mall in New Jersey.

"In one of those places redolent of suburban New Jersey like King of Prussia. We'll put down cobblestones and re-create the layout of Soho exactly. Prince Street south: Face Stockholm, Mimi Ferzt Gallery, Olives, Reinstein/Ross, Harriet Love, Pleats Please, etc. Prince Street north: Replay, the Met shop, Club Monaco, Myoptics, Camper, etc. With the right streetlights and some well-placed scaffolding, shoppers won't even notice the difference. They'll save on sales tax for items more than $110—and, really, what in Soho costs less than $110—and they won't have to deal with Holland Tunnel traffic. It's win-win," she says conversationally. But this isn't a conversation; it's the first act of her one-woman show. "And we'll call it Faux-Ho." Pause here for laughter.

I don't laugh, but I smile politely and glance around for someone to save me from the gallery owner's wife. Maya is standing less than three inches away talking to a hipster in black, but right now she's useless. She's too engrossed in the woman's story to care if I live or die of boredom and ignores my pointed looks as though I were a complete stranger with a twitching-eye problem.

Gavin, who is also a few feet away from me, isn't in the mood to throw me a lifeline either. He's here and he's playing affable host but he's quite happy to watch me dangle over hot coals. Krystal Karpfinger at the Jesus party is almost worse than no Jesus party at all.

The gallery owner's wife launches into act two—how to spot a suburbanite at a hundred paces—and I grab the arm of a passing waitress. The woman is startled by my attention and tries to brush me off like I'm an unwanted fly, but I hold tight.

"I'm sorry, did you just say that the band refuses to play unless someone removes all the green M&M's from the candy dish?" Before the waitress can voice her denial or call me insane, I turn to Krystal. "I have to go. Band emergency. You know how it is with temperamental artists. One minute they're like self-sufficient human beings, the next they're helpless babies in diapers. You do understand, don't you?"

It's clear from her expression that she doesn't understand anything—three cards have been shuffled quickly under her nose but it all happened so fast. While she's trying to find the dollar, I make a beeline for the other side of the room. I get a club soda and a puff pastry filled with lobster and stand quietly in a corner next to Jesus in a blue Badgely Mishka. I'm watching the crowd mingle when Jane taps me on the shoulder. The room is thick with people, but Jane finds me easily, as though there's some sort of computer-chip homing device in my right top molar. "Vig, you're supposed to be controlling the press," she says angrily over the conversational din. A woman slinks behind Jane, causing her to spill white wine all over my silk dress. Jane doesn't apologize. She is too annoyed with me to care about my dry-cleaning bill. I shouldn't be standing by while Rome is burning. But the only thing burning here is her rage: The photographers are taking pictures of Gavin against the Karpfinger banner. This is unacceptable.

Jane darts off, clearing a path through the crowd with her shoulders, and I make my way to the press area slowly. The room is packed, and you have to slither between socialites and art-world critics to cross it. The huge crowd—glittering and unexpected—are here in support of freedom of speech. They are defending the First Amendment and having their pictures taken as they push through the angry mob that lines the streets. This is not turn-of-the-last-century China and the protesters are not Boxers, but it feels as though the gallery is a mission under siege. Outside the demonstrators chant and hurl insults and we try our best to ignore them like picnickers on the edge of a storm.

Gavin is standing in the middle of the gallery's banner, so that from whatever angle you take the picture you see either *K-A-R* or *I-N-G-E-R*. Our more media savvy backdrop— the word *fashionista* repeats in forty-four-point type from one corner to the other—is on the adjacent wall being neglected. Gavin is supposed to stand between the two, but he's feeling rebellious and not at all willing to comply. When he looks at me, the corners of his lips turn into a smile. Smug bastard.

Jane is behind me, with a hand on the small of my back. "Go on. Fix it," she says, as if this were an easily solved problem like a loose lightbulb or an uneven hem. "Go on."

I look around, wishing Kate or Sarah or even Allison were here. This was their plan; things like this should be their problem. But it's my problem now, and as I consider my options, I realize there's only one thing to be done: I must make a fool of myself. Taking a deep breath, I walk behind Gavin, lose my balance and clutch on to the banner for support. We both tumble to the floor—the banner with more grace and enthusiasm than I—and Anita Smithers rushes in and adjusts Gavin's position. She doesn't want her client being upstaged by an editor with two left feet.

Once justice is served, Jane rushes to Gavin's side and grabs the attention for herself. She is not just a sponge, she is a leech, and every moment she sucks belongs to someone else. Her smiles are bright as she flirts with reporters and cameras, but her knowledge of art is appalling—she cites Rodin as the greatest living painter—and I stand there watching Gavin flinch.

Jane's thirst for the spotlight is ardent and brazen and is the sort of compulsion that doesn't acknowledge boundaries. She will stand there on that makeshift stage until the prop guys carry her off and the stage manager locks the doors. I'm not one of the prop guys and I don't think I can lift Jane, but I approach her anyway with resolve. We have taken enough from Gavin and I'm determined to leave him this.

"...and if I had to compare him to only one artist of the twentieth century, I'd have to say Seurat. They both have the same cleanness of line," Jane explains, falling back on a common *Fashionista* cliché, even though *Sunday in the Park* is not a modern sofa or a sleek Calvin Klein dress.

Although she is annoyed at me for blocking her light, I lean over to Jane and whisper into her ear that the demonstrators outside are waiting for her statement. Such a statement was never part of the game plan, but the idea appeals to her. There are five times as many people outside, and she is suddenly envisioning sixties protest rallies that she never attended and Martin Luther King, Jr. on the steps of the Lincoln Memorial. She has a dream.

After fielding a what-took-you-so-long glare from Gavin, I follow Jane through the crowd. The protest outside is loud but orderly, with hundreds of people gathered behind blue police barricades. A short, neat man wearing an unobtrusive brown suit leads the rally, and the street lamps of Mercer shine off his bald head, giving him an odd sort of halo as he stands on a platform with a megaphone in his hand. "No Jesus, no justice, no joke," he shouts, in sync with his audience. "Respect our icon, respect our beliefs, respect us."

The man pauses to inhale and Jane takes this as her cue. She climbs the five steps to the top of the podium, seizes the megaphone from the shocked man's hand and greets the crowd. "Hello," she says, her voice booming down the cobblestone street. "My name is Jane Carolyn-Ann Whiting Mc-Neill." She expects instant name recognition from them—it's what she expects from everybody—and when they cheer wildly she assumes she got it. "My name is Jane Carolyn-Ann Whiting McNeill," she announces again, because she likes the way it echoes off the tenements, "and I'm a Christian."

The crowds roars with approval. They have mistaken her for one of their own. They think she has been moved to speak by the spirit, like a follower at a tented revival meeting. "I want to talk about art, *real* art," she says, reciting the speech she used earlier to introduce Gavin Marshall. "Art that makes us cry. Art that makes us laugh. Art that makes us reflect. Art that makes our hearts bleed. Art that makes us believe in a being greater and better than ourselves." The applause and yells grow louder, and Jane soaks up the approbation for a moment before gesturing for silence. Jane is good with crowds—only ninety percent of her success is just showing up—and she knows how to play them. "Real art is godly. Real art is pure. Real art isn't about shock value and offending the most number of people in the least amount of time. Real art doesn't use gimmicks. Gimmicks are for people who don't know what real art is. I'm Jane Carolyn-Ann Whiting McNeill and I'm a Christian," she says, pausing because she knows from recent experience that a pause works well here.

The cheers are almost deafening and Jane takes a deep breath in order to conclude on a high note, but before she can finish her speech—And this is Christian art; it's devout and honest and God-fearing and insightful and instinctive and a reminder to all of us not to rush to judgment; Gilding the Lily is art, *real* art—she is embraced by the crowd. They lift her off the podium. They take her onto their shoulders.

They parade her around like she's a beloved trophy, hollering and yelling and hooraying with joy. Jane takes it in stride, with a calm smile and a gracious wave. She's always known that one day she would be treated like this, like Cleopatra or Elizabeth Taylor.

I watch the proceedings with a sense of awe and helplessness, and the last I see of Jane, she is being carried off by a sea of fellow Christians down the narrow valley of Mercer toward the gleaming lights of Canal Street.

Resurrection

Jane's a hit. She's a media superstar, the go-after get, the name on everybody's lips. Her image is endlessly replicated and reproduced, and when you turn on the television at eight o'clock the next morning, there are Jane clones staring back at you from the sets of *Good Morning America*, *The Today Show* and *CBS This Morning*.

Sometime during the past twelve hours, she has become an avatar of free expression, a foot soldier on the front lines of liberty. Flipping compulsively back and forth between three stations, I listen to her tell how she won over the demonstrators, opened their minds, raised their consciousness. There's nothing to support her lavish claims of success, but she makes them anyway. She's like Napoleon writing reports of victory from Alexandria.

I switch the channel to get away from her but you can't get away from Jane. She's everywhere—NY1, CNN, MSNBC, Fox News Channel. Although her outfits change with each demo (black silk for NY1, double-breasted navy-blue suit for Fox) her rhetoric remains the same and she talks incessantly about moderating the great art debate. Her answers are well organized and articulate her point clearly, and when she embarks on a semiotic interpretation ("*Fashionista* and Gilding the Lily explore the possibilities of gender roles: What is a dress? What does it mean to wear a dress?"), I become suspicious. I become wary and skeptical and examine her closely. Although I can't see the strings, I know there's someone behind the scenes tugging on them.

I don't know it yet, but issues of *Fashionista* are flying off the shelves. By eight-thirty, you can't find a copy in any of the seven Hudson Newsstands in Penn Station. Grand Central is in similar straits, although the newsstand on the lower level that everyone forgets about has three remaining copies hidden behind a misplaced *Glamour*.

Advertisers are calling to pledge their continued support. Even after Jane's assured performance this morning, they still have concerns, but their customer services departments haven't gotten angry telephone calls yet from irate Christians and sticking up for the Constitution in this indirect way won't hurt their brand identification.

The CEO of Ivy Publishing is delighted by the media blitzkrieg. He can't remember the last time one of his magazines dominated the national consciousness. As a thank-you, he's taking Jane to dinner this evening (providing she's not taping *Crossfire* or appearing on *Hardball with Chris Matthews*) and having her to his ski chalet in Vermont next weekend. He will add a sizable amount to her Christmas bonus and insists that she call in any designer she wants to redecorate her office.

Jane's position is secured. She's been elevated to status of media goddess, and although it will only last for a little while, the hangover will never go away. Jane Carolyn-Ann Whiting McNeill is now a *Fashionista* fixture. It's the site of her greatest triumph and she would no sooner leave it than Kurtz would the Belgian Congo.

My Last Day of Work

When I get to the office, Allison is waiting for me. She's standing by my door with her shoulders against the wall. She's patiently reading the *Times* and lifts her head with almost careless indifference as I breeze by. I take out my key and open the door. Although I don't say anything, she follows me in.

"You are so fired," she announces without preamble and with a huge smile.

I put my shoulder bag down and pick up my phone to check messages.

"Didn't you hear me?" she asks, leaning forward on the desk.

"I'm so fired," I repeat. There are ten new voice mail messages and I reach for a pen to jot them down, but before they start playing, Allison lays her hand on the phone and cuts the connection.

She's annoyed with me now. She hoped to get a response and can't do anything with this sort of languid apathy. "Don't you care?"

"You don't have the power to fire me," I say, dialing voice

mail again. I don't often have ten messages and I'm reason-ably sure that they all have some fantastic statistic to report about Jane.

"No, but Human Resources does." She throws the news-paper onto my desk with a flick of her wrist. It's opened to my article on Pieter van Kessel. I give her a blank look. "You wrote and investigated that on *Fashionista* time. *Fashionista* owns that article. You are in direct violation of Code 43, sub-section B of your contract," she says triumphantly. "You might want to start packing up your stuff now. Human Re-sources takes these violations very seriously and I've got an appointment with Stacy Shoemaucher in three minutes. You should be out of here by noon."

I sandwich the receiver between my ear and shoulder and glance at her with faint interest. "Is that all?"

"Don't you want to know why I'm doing this?" she asks, almost plaintively. Allison wants a show with fireworks and dancing bears, something with pizzazz to tell her audience on the other side of the line.

I have no intention of giving it to her. I shrug.

Grabbing the phone out of my hand, she yells, "You stole my promotion! Marguerite said that I would be senior edi-tor as soon as she was in charge, but that's not going to hap-pen now, is it? Nothing went according to the plan. Jane's a fucking hero and they'll never fire her and it's all your fault, you stupid bitch. Marguerite said I would be senior editor, not you. She came to *me* with her plan. Me, the hardest working editor at *Fashionista*. I deserve it. Not you. Not fucking you."

She runs out of my office ranting about Marguerite and promotions and things that should have been hers. I'm still piecing together the truth when Delia knocks on my door.

"Hey there," she says, coming into my office, "we're all a little stunned about Jane landing so steadily on her feet, but you can't spend the whole day in shell-shocked mode."

I smile at her. "No, it's not that, although I am reeling from

that strange plot twist. It's Allison actually. I just figured something out. Remember her plan?"

Delia makes herself comfortable in my guest chair and
nods. "Her brilliant plan, which has ended in the exaltation
of Jane Carolyn-Ann Whiting McNeill. Yes, I have some
vague recollection of it."

"It was Marguerite's."

She tilts her head, not quite following. "Marguerite's?"

"Marguerite's. She's behind everything. If Allison's mad
ravings are to be believed—and I think they are—Marguerite
promised her a senior editorship as soon as she became editor in chief in exchange for her help. It explains a lot," I say,
recalling how amazed I had been by the soundness of the
plan. I should have known something was up from the very
beginning. That someone like Allison, who never lifts her
head up from her own life to look around, had heard of obscure British artist Gavin Marshall should have sent up red
flares immediately.

"I like it," Delia says, after a moment of thought. Respect
lightens her tone. "Take it to the people. Make the plot seem
homegrown—what an evil thing to do. I'll have to remember that."

The thought of Delia pairing her investigative skills with
Marguerite's knack for manipulation terrifies me and I'm
about to woo her back to the side of the angels when the
phone rings. I glance at the display. Although I don't recognize the extension, I know before I pick it up that it's Human
Resources. Allison works quickly.

"I've got to go be fired now," I say to Delia, undisturbed
by the notion. In the past twenty-four hours, life has taken
on an odd quality of unrealness or surrealness, and things that
should matter no longer do. I don't mind giving up my senior editor position at *Fashionista* in exchange for a single
three-thousand-word profile in the *New York Times.* It's a fair
trade.

My meeting with Stacy Shoemaucher is abrupt and professional, and we only discuss business matters like Cobra payments and the confidentiality clause in my contract and how long I'll need to pack up my things. Then she hands me a brown cardboard box and tells me to shave thirty minutes off my estimated time.

With Jane's superstar status, Stickly's situation has improved greatly and he sits outside Jane's office, stiff and proud, like a guard outside the gates of Buckingham Palace. Having no patience for untrained campaigners, he has cashiered Jackie and commandeered Mrs. Beverly, who is running around fielding telephone calls and taking messages for Jane.

"Hi, can I see Jane?" I ask. I've come straight from Human Resources—the cardboard box is still in my grip—but I'm not sure why. "It'll only take a minute."

Stickly looks down his patrician nose at me and recalls past grievances, such as the meeting with Jane he arranged yesterday that I was too busy to attend. "Mum isn't accepting visitors at the moment. Please leave your card and I will arrange something as soon as she's available. Shall we say early next week?" Stickly's manner is supercilious and haughty and there's no longer a defeated air about him. He is serving monarchs again.

I say early next week is fine and turn around to leave, knocking the pencil holder onto the floor with my cardboard box. While Stickly is chasing pens, I enter Jane's office. She's sitting with a notepad on her lap watching herself on three different television sets.

She glances at me and pauses one of the Jane clones. "Here, Vig, look at that. See how I'm holding my head at a sixty-degree angle as I consider my answer? Stickly says it should never be more than forty-five degrees." She makes a note. "I must work on that. Stickly says that how you hold your head is very important in how people perceive you."

"I just wanted to let you know I'm leaving," I say.

She freezes with the remote control in her hand. "Where are you going?" she asks sharply.

"Nowhere. I've been fired."

Jane is relieved. My finding greener pastures elsewhere is unacceptable, but my getting kicked off the farm is a matter of complete indifference. "That's all right then," she says before turning away and hitting Play.

This is an archetypal Jane moment and yet still I'm surprised. I've come here expecting something in exchange for five years of service. Not outrage on my behalf or exhortations to stay but something small and heartfelt and sincere like thank you or good luck.

But Jane is a shell. She is a shell with only air inside and sometimes she manages to hold her head at the correct angle.

I'm walking out of her office when Marguerite pushes Stickly forcefully to the side and brushes past me. Anger is radiating from every pore in her body as she marches up to Jane and slaps her across the face. Jane is stunned for a moment but she quickly shakes it off and springs into action, attacking Marguerite with a snarl and dragging her to the ground. Amid hair pulling and screeching, I close the door. I close the door and leave them fighting like cats, under the benevolent gazes of a thousand empty stars.

Epilogue

As though this were a relationship, I invite Alex to the bar at the Paramount hotel to have drinks with Maya, Gavin and me. And he comes. As if he were a boyfriend, he comes, even though he has class, a work assignment to finish and an upcoming test on urban planning to study for.

"Okay, I've got one," says Gavin, laughing so hard he's in danger of falling off his stool. "New Soles: The Best Shoes for Carrying Your Cross."

"Excellent," says Maya, raising her glass. "To new soles!"

We've been drinking to Jesus article ideas all morning and fielding curious glances from other patrons. Only one person has figured it out—a matronly British tourist who shyly asked Gavin for his autograph. He good-naturedly signed his name under the Jesus' New Birthday Suit coverline. His anger has been somewhat tempered by the misplaced optimism of our plan and the success of his show. He sold every one of his pieces last night.

Maya puts down her drink and reaches across the bar for the menu. It's time for lunch.

"Let's get the cheese plate," I say, leaning back in my chair. Although alcohol has loosened my joints, it's not the only reason I'm feeling limber. Being unemployed has had an unexpected effect on my muscles and for the first time in ages I'm relaxed. This is what happens when your future suddenly settles itself. This is what happens when your next few moves—drink to Jesus article ideas, go home to visit your parents and return to New York revitalized and refreshed—don't involve Jane. When I come back from a week in Bierlyville, I'll get another job—a better job, a less glamorous job, a job that doesn't involve celebrities or their plungers.

"Vig, you've got to come back," says Delia, who is suddenly and inexplicably at my side.

"How'd you know I was here?" I ask suspiciously. I don't want Delia adding details to my file. We're not co-workers anymore.

"Alex left me a message."

I look at Alex, who shrugs. "Habit," he says.

"I don't want to go back," I say, finishing my gin and tonic in one gulp. Maya and Gavin cheer my independent attitude and instantly order me another drink.

"You have to come back," she says again. "Holden was on the floor looking for you."

"What?" I'm immobilized by shock.

Alex is equally surprised. "He was actually on the floor?"

"He was asking people where you were."

"Who's Holden?" Gavin asks. He has heard the whole fashionista saga from beginning to end but never the name Holden.

"The reclusive genius behind *Fashionista* and several other high-profile magazines," I explain. "Getting a meeting with him is like getting one with the pope, only the pontiff is more accessible. I wonder why he wants to see me."

"Yeah, that's what's killing me," says Delia. "You have to come back or we'll never know."

Her logic is sound and I slide off my bar stool to take a

meeting with Jack Holden, even though three gin and tonics are swimming through my veins and head. Delia escorts me to his office and waits while the tight-lipped secretary informs him I'm here. She doesn't think I belong in her reception room and she can't hide her shock when Holden tells her to bring me right in.

Jack Holden's office is bright and messy and he has none of the shiny toys that high-level executives usually have. The only fun thing on his desk is a stapler and from the way its guts are strewn across the desk, I can only assume that it's broken.

"Ah, Ms. Morgan," he says, standing up to shake my hand, "you're a very tough woman to track down. You should stay closer to your desk."

"I was fired," I say by way of explanation, but Holden isn't listening. He has already moved beyond pleasantries.

"We are starting a new publication," he announces, "a style glossy like *Fashionista* but without the aggressive celebrity angle. I want you to be on the team, maybe even head it up."

I am flabbergasted. I'm flabbergasted and stunned and can only stare at him as if he were an escaped patient from an asylum.

"I read that piece you did for the *Times* on van Kessel. Excellent work. That's just the sort of thing I want to see in our new book."

"Thank you," I say, trying not to break out into a fit of giggles. Three gin and tonics are swimming through my veins and head. "Excuse me, sir. Did you say *head up* the new magazine?"

He barely glances at me. My incredulity has made no impression. "Yes. Here are some notes I've been reading over. Mrs. Carson out front can give you the rest of the file."

I accept the sheets with listless fingers. "Why me?"

"Our original candidate had to be escorted from the building today after an unpleasant episode. You were the next logical choice. Your article in the *Times* was excellent and is exactly what I'm looking for. What do you say?"

I take a look at the notes to get a sense of what this new magazine will be like and pause over a list of article ideas. At first these ideas just seem familiar, but then the truth penetrates my alcohol-soaked brain: These ideas are mine. They are ones I had given Marguerite for *Fashionista*. No wonder my profile of van Kessel is exactly what he's looking for.

I digest this information quickly, but I'm too shocked and drunk to feel anger. My mind can only focus on the question at hand: What do I say?

I don't know what I say. I'm not an editor in chief. I'm only an associate editor who has been dressed up in senior editor's clothing for expedience. I know nothing about running a magazine. I know nothing about four-color separation and telling people what to do and positioning a product.

But these things are just the rooftops of small Japanese villages. They are the rooftops of small Japanese villages and I'm Godzilla.

★ ★ ★ ★ ★

From Lynn Messina's upcoming novel
Mim Warner's Lost Her Cool,
available from Red Dress Ink in March 2005.

Prologue

Mim holds up the pink baby tee with the word *Slut* emblazoned on the front in twirly, frilly sky-blue letters and declares it the perfect gift for third graders trying to establish a distinctive sense of style. Her upbeat tone is relaxed and familiar despite the television crew that's following her around. The director zooms in on her smiling face as she unselfconsciously hands the tee to the salesclerk of the small NoLita boutique. The image is grainy and stylized and every so often it jumps to a wide shot before lurching back to a close-up, but Mim is unaffected by the frenzied camerawork. Wearing her usual uniform—Sigerson Morrison flats, Chanel slacks and a crisp white shirt from Ungaro or Prada—and sporting her customary loose French twist, she seems like typical Mim, archetypal Mim, the Mim you hold up in front of the class as a prime example of standard-issue Mimness. But something is wrong: You don't give *Slut*-emblazoned T-shirts to girls in elementary school.

While the saleswoman wraps the present in vibrant yellow paper, Mim explains that the slut trend is going to be huge in the coming year. The hip-hop beat that has played with quiet menace throughout the entire segment stops with a comical screech, but Mim, unaware of what will happen in postproduction, chats blithely on with her host.

"Lunch boxes, notebooks, pencil cases, stickers, backpacks," she says as she puts the present, now topped with a pretty pink bow, in her Kate Spade tote. "This is going to be the year that slut merchandising finally breaks through."

The camera jumps to the next scene, which is equally disastrous—Mim in the Metropolitan Museum of Art gift shop picking out a reproduction twelfth-century samurai sword for ten-year-old Timmy. The sword, sharp enough to slice effortlessly through a sheath of silk as Mim proudly demonstrates with her own Hermès scarf, will no doubt make Timmy a superhero in the schoolyard.

"It's fun, but educational," Mim says to a nodding, confused Harmony Cortez. "It's never too early for men to learn about honor. The samurai lived by a strict chivalric code called Bushido—that's *B-u-s-h-i-d-o* for those taking notes at home—which valued honor above life. It's a worthy goal for everyone."

Harmony Cortez is a well-known clothing designer. She has a weekly cable television show on which she does fun, offbeat things with her celebrity guests. This year for her holiday special she gathered several of New York's shopping elite—the editor in chief of *Lucky*, the creative direction of Barneys—and gave them each a portion of her Christmas list. Mim got the nieces and nephews. When she'd been invited onto the show two weeks before, her shopping assignment had seemed like a solid idea. Mim had her own pair of young nieces who could always depend on getting something chic from Bergdorf's Juniors department. But now the adventure seemed like a disaster.

Mim Warner is known for two things: her unquestionable good taste and the eerie way she can predict the future. As one of the most successful coolhunters in the business—

some would say *the* most successful—people rely on her for a clear picture of what's coming next.

Calling trends is Mim's thing, and she's never gotten one wrong: the great Hush Puppy revival of '96, the celebrated tattooing craze of the early zeros, the illustrious terry-cloth fad of '03. She sees what's coming next so clearly that it sometimes seems as if she lives sixteen months in the future and beams back her image to the present in holographic form. Run your hand over her arm and you're almost surprised that your fingers don't pass right through her.

For almost fifteen years, Mim Warner has been at the top of her game—ever since she broke through with the Potter high-top. She'd been hired by the ailing sneaker company to answer phones for the marketing director but within a year she'd reinvented the brand. It wasn't intentional. Mim only took the job to make enough money to return to Asia, where she'd been bouncing around since college. Her life savings finally ran out in the middle of the Gobi Desert—somewhere near Gurvansaikhan National Park in Mongolia—forcing her to wire her parents for the airfare home. The plan was simple: Work hard, live cheaply, hop a plane to Bangkok as soon as she had enough cash to cover the flight and several months' worth of pad thai. But then she noticed that the kids at the pizza parlor where she picked up dinner every night were wearing bulky sneakers with thick rubber soles. Potter had a similar model—the Kong—which it was in the process of phasing out. Mim, in a flash of intuition that's become her trademark, realized this was a terrible mistake. Wrestling shoes had been huge for more than a year, but their run was almost over. Teens, tired of the exaggerated sleekness, were looking for something a little unwieldy. That's what she saw coming—the backlash against the odd compact daintiness of the wrestling shoe.

Her plans to travel deferred indefinitely, Mim stayed another year at Potter. She struck gold a second time with its square-toed tennis sneaker but decided against heading up the development department. Instead, she hooked up with a friend who had start-up cash and an MBA and opened Pravda, a youth-focused research service that predicts what consumers will be buying in a few months.

Under Mim's watchful stewardship, Pravda has flourished. The steady and inexorable rise of youth culture—the way lust for the teenage dollar dictates most of our consumer choices—has created a thirst for the kind of information Mim provides. She makes it look effortless, but it's not. Knowing what to watch for and understanding what you're seeing—it's actually pretty tricky. Sometimes there's only a hairbreadth between one person's idiosyncratic taste and the next revolution in embryonic stage. This is the void that Mim stares into every day without flinching.

Or so we all thought.